W9-ASY-334

THE
HAPPY
RETURN

THE
HAPPY
RETURN

C. S. FORESTER

This edition published in 2020 by Arcturus Publishing Limited
26/27 Bickels Yard, 151–153 Bermondsey Street,
London SE1 3HA

Copyright © Arcturus Holdings Limited

All rights reserved. No part of this publication may be reproduced,
stored in a retrieval system, or transmitted, in any form or by any means,
electronic, mechanical, photocopying, recording or otherwise, without
prior written permission in accordance with the provisions of the
Copyright Act 1956 (as amended). Any person or persons who do any
unauthorised act in relation to this publication may be liable to criminal
prosecution and civil claims for damages.

Typesetting by Palimpsest Book Production Limited

Cover design: Peter Ridley
Cover illustration: Peter Gray
Design: Steve Flight

AD008129UK

Printed in the UK

CONTENTS

INTRODUCTION

Cecil Louis Troughton Smith was born in Cairo in 1899, the youngest child of a broken marriage. He was three when his parents separated, and his mother took him to London. A voracious reader, his favourite writers by the time he was ten were Jane Austen, Henry James and H. G. Wells.

After leaving school, he tried to enlist in the army but failed the medical. He then studied medicine at Guy's Hospital but dropped out. His ambition was to write, and taking the pen name C. S. Forester, he published his first novel in 1924. Two years later came considerable success with *Payment Deferred*, a novel that would inspire first a play and then a film.

In 1935, he published *The African Queen*. Its inspiration was the Battle for Lake Tanganyika, and its success contributed to Forester's growing reputation. The book was adapted by John Huston for the big screen in 1951 and starred two of America's best-known actors – Humphrey Bogart and Katharine Hepburn.

The Happy Return (1937) was the first novel to feature his most famous creation: Horatio Hornblower, a Royal Navy officer during the Napoleonic Wars. Honest, brave and merciful, the character was inspired by some of the leading figures of the era – none more prominent than Admiral Horatio Nelson. *The Happy Return* was quickly followed by two more novels in the series, *A Ship of the Line* and *Flying Colours*, which earned Forester the James Tait Black Memorial Prize in 1938. These three books were made into the 1951 film *Captain Horatio Hornblower R.N.* The character earned praise from his fellow writers, including Ernest Hemingway, who said: 'I recommend Hornblower to everyone literate I know.' In total, Forester wrote 11 novels in the Hornblower saga, as well as a number of short stories.

During the 1930s, he served as a correspondent for the *Daily Telegraph* and *The Times*. While working for these newspapers, Forester reported on the Spanish Civil War and the Nazi occupation of Czechoslovakia. During World War II, he worked for the British Ministry of Information in America and met the young Roald Dahl. Asking Dahl for a few notes about his experience as a pilot to turn into a story, Forester was so impressed that he published them as they were. 'Did you know you were a writer?' he said to Dahl.

Forester published his last novel, *The Good Shepherd*, in 1955. Using the skills he had developed writing his Hornblower stories, Forester turned his attention to a new setting: the Battle of the Atlantic in World War II. On publication it was widely acclaimed as one of his greatest books.

Forester was known for his honesty and self-deprecation. Despite both critical and commercial success, he suspected that his death might merit 'a paragraph or two in the newspapers', but afterwards his reputation would quickly fade. Once, he even confessed that his success made him feel 'such a fraud'. As was ever the case, he had greatly underestimated himself. He died of a stroke in 1966, but his popularity has never waned.

CHAPTER I

It was not long after dawn that Captain Hornblower came up on the quarterdeck of the *Lydia*. Bush, the first lieutenant, was officer of the watch, and touched his hat but did not speak to him; in a voyage which had by now lasted seven months without touching land he had learned something of his captain's likes and dislikes. During this first hour of the day the captain was not to be spoken to, nor his train of thought interrupted.

In accordance with standing orders – hallowed by now with the tradition which is likely to accumulate during a voyage of such incredible length – Brown, the captain's coxswain, had seen to it that the weather side of the quarterdeck had been holystoned and sanded at the first peep of daylight. Bush and the midshipman with him withdrew to the lee side at Hornblower's first appearance, and Hornblower immediately began his daily hour's walk up and down, up and down the twenty-one feet of deck which had been sanded for him. On one hand his walk was limited by the slides of the quarterdeck carronades; on the other by the row of ringbolts in the deck for the attachment of the carronade train tackles; the space of deck on which Captain Hornblower was accustomed to exercise himself for an hour each morning was thus five feet wide and twenty-one feet long.

Up and down, up and down, paced Captain Hornblower. Although he was entirely lost in thought, his subordinates knew by experience that his sailor's instinct was quite alert; subconsciously his mind took note of the shadow of the main rigging across the deck, and of the feel of the breeze on his cheek, so that the slightest inattention on the part of the quartermaster at the wheel called forth a bitter rebuke from the captain – the more bitter in that he had been disturbed in this, the most important hour of his day. In the same way he was aware, without having

taken special note, of all the salient facts of the prevailing conditions. On his awakening in his cot, he had seen (without willing
it) from the telltale compass in the deck over his head that the
course was north east, as it had been for the last three days. At
the moment of his arrival on deck he had subconsciously noted
that the wind was from the west, and just strong enough to give
the ship steerage way, with all sail set to the royals, that the sky
was of its perennial blue, and that the sea was almost flat calm,
with a long peaceful swell over which the Lydia seared and
swooped with profound regularity.

The first thing Captain Hornblower was aware of thinking was
that the Pacific in the morning, deep blue overside and changing
to silver towards the horizon, was like some heraldic blazon of
argent and azure – and then he almost smiled to himself because
that simile had come up in his mind every morning for the last
fortnight. With the thought and the smile his mind was instantly
working smoothly and rapidly. He looked down the gangways at
the men at work holystoning; down on the main deck, as he came
forward, he could see another party engaged on the same task.
They were talking in ordinary tones. Twice he heard a laugh.
That was well. Men who could talk and laugh in that fashion
were not likely to be plotting mutiny – and Captain Hornblower
had that possibility much in mind lately. Seven months at sea
had almost consumed the ship's stores. A week ago he had cut
the daily ration of water to three pints a day, and three pints a
day was hardly sufficient for men living on salt meat and biscuit
in ten degrees north latitude, especially as water seven months
in cask was half solid with green living things.

A week ago, too, the very last of the lemon juice had been
served out, and there would be scurvy to reckon with within
a month and no surgeon on board. Hankey the surgeon had
died of all the complications of drink and syphilis off the Horn.
For a month now tobacco had been doled out in half ounces
weekly – Hornblower congratulated himself now on having
taken the tobacco under his sole charge. If he had not done so

the thoughtless fools would have used up their whole store, and men deprived of tobacco were men who could not be relied upon. He knew that the men were more concerned about the shortage of tobacco than about the shortage of fuel for the galley which caused them each day to be given their salt pork only just brought to the boil in seawater.

The shortage of tobacco, of water and of wood was nothing nearly as important, however, as the imminent shortage of grog. He had not dared to cut that daily issue, and there was only rum for ten more days in the ship. Not the finest crew in the world could be relied on if deprived of their ration of rum. Here they were in the South Sea, with no other King's ship within two thousand miles of them. Somewhere to the westward were islands of romance, with beautiful women, and food to be got without labour. A life of happy idleness was within their reach. Some knave among the crew, better informed than the rest, would give the hint. It would not be attended to at present, but in the future, with no blessed interval of grog at noon, the men would be ready to listen. Ever since the crew of the *Bounty* had mutinied, seduced by the charms of the Pacific, the captain of every ship of His Britannic Majesty whose duty took him there was haunted by this fear.

Hornblower, pacing the deck, looked sharply once more at the crew. Seven months at sea without once touching land had given an admirable opportunity for training the gang of gaolbirds and pressed men into seamen, but it was too long without distraction. The sooner now that he could reach the coast of Nicaragua, the better. A run ashore would distract the men, and there would be water and fresh food and tobacco and spirits to be got. Hornblower's mind began to run back through his recent calculations of the ship's position. He was certain about his latitude, and last night's lunar observations had seemed to confirm the chronometer's indication of the longitude – even though it seemed incredible that chronometers could be relied upon at all after a seven months' voyage. Probably less than one hundred miles ahead, at most three hundred, lay the Pacific coast of Central America. Crystal, the master, had shaken his head in doubt at Hornblower's positiveness, but Crystal was an old fool, and of no use as a navigator. Anyway, two or three more days would see who was right.

At once Hornblower's mind shifted to the problem of how to spend the next two or three days. The men must be kept busy. There was nothing like long idle days to breed mutiny – Hornblower never feared mutiny during the wild ten weeks of beating round the Horn. In the forenoon watch he would clear for action and practise the men at the guns, five rounds from each. The concussion might kill the wind for a space, but that could not be helped. It would be the last opportunity, perhaps, before the guns would be in action in earnest.

Another calculation came up in Hornblower's mind. Five rounds from the guns would consume over a ton weight of powder and shot. The *Lydia* was riding light already with her stores nearly all consumed. Hornblower called up before his mental eye a picture of the frigate's hold and the positions of the store rooms. It was time that he paid attention to the trim of the ship again. After the men had had their dinner he would put off in the quarter boat and pull round the ship. She would be by the stern a little now, he expected. That could be put right tomorrow by shifting the two No. 1 carronades on the forecastle forward to their original positions. And as the ship would have to shorten sail while he was in the quarter boat, he might as well do the job properly and give Bush a free hand in exercising the crew aloft. Bush had a passion for that kind of seamanship, as a first lieutenant quite rightly should. Today, the crew might beat their previous record of eleven minutes fifty-one seconds for sending up topmasts, and of twenty-four minutes seven seconds for setting all sail starting with topmast housed. Neither of those times, Hornblower agreed with Bush, was nearly as good as they might be; plenty of ships had set up better figures – at least so their captains had said.

Hornblower became aware that the wind had increased a tiny amount, sufficiently to call forth a faint whispering from the rigging. From the feel of it upon his neck and cheek he deduced it must have shifted aft a point or perhaps two, as well, and even as his mind registered these observations, and began to wonder how soon Bush would take notice of it, he heard the call for the watch. Clay, the midshipman on the quarterdeck, was bellowing like a bull for the afterguard. That boy's voice had broken since they left England; he was learning to use it properly now, instead of alternately squeaking and croaking. Still without taking visual notice of what was going on, Hornblower, as he continued pacing the quarterdeck, listened to the familiar sequence of sounds as the watch came tumbling aft to the braces. A crack and a yelp told him that Harrison, the boatswain, had landed with his cane on the stern of some laggardly or unlucky sailor. Harrison was a fine seaman, but with a weakness for using his cane on well-rounded sterns. Any man who filled his trousers out tight was likely to get a welt across the seat of them solely for that reason, especially if he was unluckily engaged as Harrison came by in some occupation which necessitated bending forward.

Hornblower's meditations regarding Harrison's weakness had occupied nearly all the time necessary for the trimming of the sails; as they came to an end Harrison roared 'Belay!' and the watch trooped back to their previous duties. Ting-ting, ting-ting, ting-ting, ting went the bell. Seven bells in the morning watch. Hornblower had been walking for well over his covenanted hour, and he was aware of a gratifying trickle of sweat under his shirt. He walked over to where Bush was standing by the wheel.

'Good morning, Mr Bush,' said Captain Hornblower.

'Good morning, sir,' said Bush, exactly as if Captain Hornblower had not been walking up and down within four yards of him for the last hour and a quarter.

Hornblower looked at the slate which bore the rough log of the last twenty-four hours; there was nothing of special note – the hourly casting of the log had given speeds of three knots, four and a half knots, four knots, and so on, while the traverse board showed that the ship had contrived to hold to her north easterly course throughout the day. The captain was aware of a keen scrutiny from his first lieutenant, and he knew that internally the lieutenant seethed with questions. There was only one man on board who knew whither the *Lydia* was bound, and that was the captain. He had sailed with sealed orders, and when he had opened and read them, in accordance with his instructions, in 30° N 20° W, he had not seen fit to tell even his second in command what they contained. For seven months Lieutenant Bush had contrived to refrain from asking questions, but the strain was visibly telling on him.

'Ha – h'm,' said Hornblower, clearing his throat non-committally. Without a word, he hung up the slate and went down the companion and entered his sleeping-cabin.

It was unlucky for Bush that he should be kept in the dark in this fashion, but Hornblower had refrained from discussing his orders with him not through any fear of Bush's garrulity, but through fear of his own. When he had first sailed as captain five years ago, he had allowed his natural talkativeness full play, and his first lieutenant of that time had come to presume upon the licence allowed him until Hornblower had been unable to give an order without having it discussed. Last commission he had tried to limit discussion with his first lieutenant within the ordinary bounds of politeness, and had found that he had been unable to keep himself within those limits – he was always opening his mouth and letting fall one word too many to his subsequent regret. This voyage, he had started with the firm resolve (like a drinker who cannot trust himself to drink only in moderation) to say nothing whatever to his officers except what was necessitated by routine, and his resolution had been hardened by the stress which his orders laid upon the need for extreme secrecy. For seven months he had held to it, growing more and more silent every day as the unnatural state of affairs took a firmer grip upon him. In the Atlantic he had sometimes discussed the weather with Mr Bush. Round in the Pacific he only condescended to clear his throat.

His sleeping-cabin was a tiny morsel of space bulkheaded off from his main cabin. Half the room was occupied by an eighteen pounder; the remainder was almost filled by his cot, his desk, and his chest. His steward, Polwheal, was putting out his razor and lather bowl on a bracket under a strip of mirror on the bulkhead – there was just room for the two of them to stand. Polwheal squeezed himself against the desk to allow his captain to enter; he said nothing, for Polwheal was a man of gratifyingly few words – Hornblower had picked him for that reason, because he had to guard against his besetting sin of garrulity even with servants.

Hornblower stripped off his wet shirt and trousers and shaved standing naked before the mirror. The face he regarded in the glass was neither handsome nor ugly, neither old nor young. There was a pair of melancholy brown eyes, a forehead sufficiently high, a nose sufficiently straight; a good mouth set with all the firmness acquired during twenty years at sea. The tousled curly brown hair was just beginning to recede and leave the forehead a little higher still, which was a source of irritation to Captain Hornblower, because he hated the thought of going bald. Noticing it, he was reminded of his other trouble and glanced down his naked body. He was slender and well muscled; quite a prepossessing figure, in fact, when he drew himself to his full six feet. But down there where his ribs ended there was no denying the presence of a rounded belly, just beginning to protrude beyond the line of his ribs and of his iliac bones. Hornblower hated the thought of growing fat with an intensity rare in his generation; he hated to think of his slender smooth-skinned body being disfigured by an unsightly bulge in the middle, which was the reason why he, a naturally indolent individual who hated routine, forced himself to take that regular morning walk on the quarterdeck.

When he had finished shaving, he put down razor and brush for Polwheal to wash and put away, and stood while Polwheal hung a ragged serge dressing gown over his shoulders.

Polwheal followed him along the deck to the head-pump, removed the dressing gown, and then pumped up seawater from overside while his captain solemnly rotated under the stream. When the bath was finished, Polwheal hung the dressing gown again over his dripping shoulders and followed him back to the cabin. A clean linen shirt – worn, but neatly mended – and white trousers were laid out on the cot. Hornblower dressed himself, and Polwheal helped him into the worn blue coat with its faded lace, and handed him his hat. All this was without a word being spoken, so well by now had Hornblower trained himself into his self-imposed system of silence. And he who hated routine had by now so fully called in routine to save himself from speech that exactly as he stepped out again on the quarterdeck eight bells rang, just as happened every single morning.

'Hands to punishment, sir?' asked Bush, touching his hat.

Hornblower nodded. The pipes of the boatswain's mates began to twitter.

'All hands to witness punishment,' roared Harrison on the main deck, and from all parts of the ship men began to pour up and toe their lines in their allotted positions.

Hornblower stood rigid by the quarterdeck rail, setting his face like stone. He was ashamed of the fact that he looked upon punishment as a beastly business, that he hated ordering it and dreaded witnessing it. The two or three thousand floggings he had witnessed in the last twenty years had not succeeded in hardening him – in fact he was much softer now (as he was painfully aware) than as a seventeen-year-old midshipman. But there had been no avoiding the punishment of this morning's victim. He was a Welshman called Owen who could somehow never refrain from spitting on the decks. Bush, without referring to his captain, had sworn that he would have him flogged for every offence, and Hornblower had necessarily to endorse the decision and back up his officer in the name of discipline, although Hornblower had the gravest doubts as to whether a man who was fool enough not to be deterred from spitting on the decks by the fear of a flogging would benefit by receiving it.

Happily the business was got over quickly. The boatswain's mates triced Owen, naked to the waist, up to the main rigging, and laid into him as the drum rolled. Owen, unlike the usual run of seamen, howled with pain as the cat-o'-nine-tails bit into his shoulders, and danced grotesquely, his bare feet flapping on the deck until at the end of his two dozen he hung from his bound wrists motionless and silent. Someone soused him with water and he was hustled below.

'Hands to breakfast, Mr Bush,' snapped Hornblower; he hoped that the tan of the tropics saved him from looking as white as he felt. Flogging a halfwitted man was not to his taste as a before-breakfast diversion and he was sick with disgust at himself at neither being strong enough to stop it nor ingenious enough to devise a way out of the dilemma Bush's decision had forced him into.

The row of officers on the quarterdeck broke up as each turned away. Gerard, the second lieutenant, took over the deck from Bush. The ship was like a magic tessellated pavement. It presented a geometrical pattern; someone shook it up into confusion, and at once it settled itself into a new and orderly fashion.

Hornblower went below to where Polwheal had his breakfast awaiting him.

'Coffee, sir,' said Polwheal. 'Burgoo.'

Hornblower sat down at table; in the seven months' voyage every luxury had long since been consumed. The coffee was a black extract of burnt bread, and all that could be said in its favour was that it was sweet and hot. The burgoo was a savoury mess of unspeakable appearance compounded of mashed biscuit crumbs and minced salt beef. Hornblower ate absentmindedly. With his left hand he tapped a biscuit on the table so that the weevils would all be induced to have left it by the time he had finished his burgoo.

There were ship-noises all round him as he ate. Every time the *Lydia* rolled and pitched a trifle as she reached the crest of the swell which was lifting her, the woodwork all creaked gently in unison. Overhead came the sound of Gerard's shod feet as he paced the quarterdeck, and sometimes the pattering of horny bare feet as some member of the crew trotted by. From forward came a monotonous steady clanking as the pumps were put to the daily task of pumping out the ship's bilges. But these noises were all transient and interrupted; there was one sound which went on all the time so steadily that the ear grew accustomed to it and only noticed it when the attention was specially directed to it – the sound of the breeze in the innumerable ropes of the rigging. It was just the faintest singing, a harmony of a thousand high-pitched tones and overtones, but it could be heard in every part of the ship, transmitted from the chains through the timbers along with the slow, periodic creaking.

Hornblower finished his burgoo, and was turning his attention to the biscuit he had been rapping on the table. He contemplated it with calm disfavour; it was poor food for a man, and in the absence of butter – the last cask had gone rancid a month back – he would have to wash down the dry mouthfuls with sips of burnt-bread coffee. But before he could take his first bite, a wild cry from above caused him to sit still with the biscuit halfway to his mouth.

'Land ho!' he heard. 'Deck there! Land two points on the larboard bow, sir.'

That was the lookout in the foretop hailing the deck. Hornblower, as he sat with his biscuit in mid-air, heard the rush and bustle on deck; everyone would be wildly excited at the sight of land, the first for three months, on this voyage to an unknown destination. He was excited himself. There was not merely the imminent thrill of discovering whether he had made a good landfall; there was also the thought that perhaps within twenty-four hours he would be in the thick of the dangerous and difficult mission upon which my lords of the Admiralty had despatched him. He was conscious of a more rapid beating of his heart in his breast. He wanted passionately to rush out on deck as his first instincts dictated, but he restrained himself. He wanted still more to appear in the eyes of his officers and crew to be a man of complete self-confidence and imperturbability – and this was only partially to gratify himself. The more respect in which a captain was held, the better for his ship. He forced himself into an attitude of complete composure, crossing his knees and sipping his coffee in entire unconcern as Mr Midshipman Savage knocked at the cabin door and came bouncing in.

'Mr Gerard sent me to tell you land's in sight on the larboard bow, sir,' said Savage, hardly able to stand still in the prevailing infection of excitement. Hornblower made himself take another sip of coffee before he spoke, and he made his words come slowly and calmly.

'Tell Mr Gerard I shall come on deck in a few minutes when I have finished my breakfast,' he said.

'Aye aye, sir.'

Savage bolted out of the cabin; his large clumsy feet clattered on the companion.

'Mr Savage! Mr Savage!' yelled Hornblower. Savage's large moonlike face reappeared in the doorway.

'You forgot to close the door,' said Hornblower, coldly. 'And please don't make so much noise on the companionway.'

'Aye aye, sir,' said the crestfallen Savage.

Hornblower was pleased with himself for that. He pulled at his chin in self-congratulation. He sipped again at his coffee, but found himself quite unable to eat his biscuit. He drummed with his fingers on the table in an effort to make the time pass more rapidly.

He heard young Clay bellowing from the masthead, where presumably Gerard had sent him with a glass.

'Looks like a burning mountain, sir. Two burning mountains. Volcanoes, sir.'

Instantly Hornblower began to call up before his mind's eye his memory of the chart which he had so often studied in the privacy of this cabin. There were volcanoes all along this coast;

the presence of two on the larboard bow was no sure indication
of the ship's position. And yet – and yet – the entrance of the
Gulf of Fonseca would undoubtedly be marked by two volcanoes
to larboard. It was quite possible that he had made a perfect
landfall, after eleven weeks out of sight of land. Hornblower
could sit still no longer. He got up from the table, and, remembering just in time to go slowly and with an air of complete
unconcern, he walked up on deck.

CHAPTER II

The quarterdeck was thronged with officers, all the four lieutenants, Crystal the master, Simmonds of the marines, Wood the purser, the midshipmen of the watch. The rigging swarmed with petty officers and ratings, and every glass in the ship appeared to be in use. Hornblower realised that a stern cold-blooded disciplinarian would take exception to this perfectly natural behaviour, and so he did the same.

'What's all this?' he snapped. 'Has no one in this ship anything to do? Mr Wood, I'll trouble you to send for the cooper and arrange with him for the filling of the water casks. Get the royals and stun'sails off her, Mr Gerard.'

The ship burst into activity again with the twittering of the pipes and Harrison's bellowing of 'All hands shorten sail' and the orders which Gerard called from the quarterdeck. Under plain sail the *Lydia* rolled smoothly over the quartering swell.

'I think I can see the smoke from the deck, sir, now,' said Gerard, apologetically raising the subject of land again to his captain. He proffered his glass and pointed forward. Low on the horizon, greyish under a wisp of white cloud, Hornblower could see something through the telescope which might be smoke.

'Ha-h'm,' said Hornblower, as he had trained himself to say instead of something more conversational. He went forward and began to climb the weather foremast shrouds. He was nothing of an athlete, and he felt a faint dislike for this task, but it had to be done – and he was uncomfortably aware that every idle eye on board was turned on him. Because of this he was morally compelled, although he was hampered by the telescope, to refrain from going through the lubbers' hole and instead to make the difficult outward climb up the futtock shrouds. Nor could he pause for breath – not when there were midshipmen under his command who in their follow-my-leader games thought nothing of running without a stop from the hold to the main royal truck.

The climb, hand over hand, up the fore topgallant shrouds tried him severely; breathing heavily, he reached the fore topgallant masthead, and settled himself to point the telescope as steadily as his heaving chest and sudden nervousness would allow. Clay was sitting nonchalantly astride the yardarm fifteen feet away, but Hornblower ignored him. The slight corkscrew roll of the ship was sweeping him in a vast circle, up, forward, sideways, and down; at first he could only fix the distant mountains in snatches, but after a time he was able to keep them under fairly continuous observation. It was a strange landscape which the telescope revealed to him. There were the sharp peaks of several volcanoes; two very tall ones to larboard, a host of smaller ones both to starboard and to port. As he looked, he saw a puff of grey steam emerge from one peak – not from the summit, but from a vent in the side – and ascend lazily to join the strip of white cloud which hung over it. Besides these cones there was a long mountain range of which the peaks appeared to be spurs, but the range itself seemed to be made up of a chain of old volcanoes, truncated and weathered down by the passage of centuries; that strip of coast must have been a hell's kitchen when they were all in eruption together. The upper parts of the peaks and of the mountains were a warm grey – grey with a hint of pink – and lower he could see what looked like green cataracts which must be vegetation stretching up along gullies in the mountainsides. Hornblower noted the relative heights and positions of the volcanoes, and from these data he drew a map in his mind and compared it with the section of the chart which he also carried in his mind's eye. There was no doubting their similarity.

'I thought I saw breakers just then, sir,' said Clay. Hornblower's gaze changed direction from the tops of the peaks to their feet.

Here there was a solid belt of green, unbroken save where lesser volcanoes jutted out from it. Hornblower swept his glass along it, along the very edge of the horizon, and then back again.

He thought he saw a tiny flash of white, sought for the place again, experienced a moment of doubt, and then saw it again – a speck of white which appeared and disappeared as he watched.

'Quite right. Those are breakers sure enough,' he said, and instantly regretted it. There had been no need to make any reply to Clay at all. By that much his reputation for immobility diminished.

The *Lydia* held her course steadily towards the coast. Looking down, Hornblower could see the curiously foreshortened figures of the men on the forecastle a hundred and forty feet below, and round the bows a hint of a bow wave which told him the ship must be making four knots or very nearly. They would be up with the shore long before nightfall, especially as the breeze would freshen as the day went on. He eased himself out of his cramped position and stared again at the shore. As time went on he could see more breakers stretching on each side of where he had originally seen them. That must be a place where the incoming swell broke straight against a vertical wall of rock and flung its white foam upwards into sight. His belief that he had made a perfect landfall was growing stronger. On each side of the breakers was a stretch of clear water on the horizon, and beyond that again, on each side, was a medium-sized volcano. A wide bay, an island in the middle of the entrance, and two flanking volcanoes. That was exactly how the Gulf of Fonseca appeared in the chart, but Hornblower was painfully aware that no very great error in his navigation would have brought them anything up to two hundred miles from where he thought he was, and he realised that on a coast like this, littered with volcanoes, one section would appear very like another. Even the appearance of a bay and an island might be simulated by some other formation of the coast. Besides, he could not rely on his charts. They had been drawn from those Anson had captured in these very waters sixty years ago, and every one knew about Dago charts – and Dago charts submitted to the revision of useless Admiralty draughtsmen might be completely unreliable.

But as he watched his doubts were gradually set at rest. The bay opening before him was enormous – there could be no other of that size on that coast which could have escaped even Dago cartographers. Hornblower's eyes estimated the width of the entrance at something over ten miles including the islands. Farther up the bay was a big island of a shape typical of the landscape – a steep circular cone rising sheer from the water. He could not see the far end of the bay, not even now when the ship was ten miles nearer than when he first saw the entrance.

'Mr Clay,' he said, not condescending to take his eye from the telescope. 'You can go down now. Give Mr Gerard my compliments and ask him please to send all hands to dinner.'

'Aye aye, sir,' said Clay.

The ship would know now that something unusual was imminent, with dinner advanced by half an hour. In British ships the officers were always careful to see that the men had full bellies before being called upon to exert themselves more than usual.

Hornblower resumed his watch from the masthead. There could be no possible doubt now that the *Lydia* was heading into the Gulf of Fonseca. He had performed a most notable feat of navigation, of which anyone might be justifiably proud, in bringing the ship straight here after eleven weeks without sighting land. But he felt no elation about it. It was Hornblower's nature to find no pleasure in achieving things he could do; his ambition was always yearning after the impossible, to appear a strong, silent, capable man, unmoved by emotion.

At present there was no sign of life in the gulf, no boats, no smoke. It might be an uninhabited shore that he was approaching, a second Columbus. He could count on at least one hour more without further action being called for. He shut his telescope, descended to the deck, and walked with self-conscious slowness aft to the quarterdeck.

Crystal and Gerard were talking animatedly beside the rail. Obviously they had moved out of earshot of the man at the wheel and had sent the midshipman as far away as possible; obviously also, as indicated by the way they looked towards Hornblower as he approached, they were talking about him. And it was only natural that they should be excited, because the *Lydia* was the first British ship of war to penetrate into the Pacific coast of Spanish America since Anson's time. They were in waters furrowed by the famous Acapulco galleon which carried a million sterling in treasure on each of her annual trips; along this coast crept the coasting ships bearing the silver of Potosi to Panama. It seemed as if the fortune of every man on board might be assured if only those unknown orders of the captain permitted it. What the captain intended to do next was of intense importance to them all.

'Send a reliable man with a good glass to the fore t'gallant masthead, Mr Gerard,' was all Hornblower said as he went below.

CHAPTER III

Polwheal was waiting with his dinner in the cabin. Hornblower meditated for a moment upon the desirability of a dinner of fat salt pork at noontide in the tropics. He was not in the least hungry, but the desire to appear a hero in the eyes of his steward overrode his excited lack of appetite. He sat down and ate rapidly for ten minutes, forcing himself to gulp down the distasteful mouthfuls. Polwheal, too, was watching every movement he made with desperate interest. Under his avid gaze, he rose and walked through, stooping his head under the low deck, to his sleeping cabin and unlocked his desk.

'Polwheal!' he called.

'Sir!' said Polwheal instantly appearing at the door.

'Get out my best coat and put the new epaulettes on it. Clean white trousers – no, the breeches and the best white silk stockings. The buckled shoes, and see that the buckles shine. And the sword with the gold hilt.'

'Aye aye, sir,' said Polwheal.

Back in the main cabin, Hornblower stretched himself on the locker below the stern window and once more unfolded his secret Admiralty orders. He had read them so often that he almost knew them by heart, but it was prudent to make certain that he understood every word of them. They were comprehensive enough, in all conscience. Some Admiralty clerk had given his imagination loose rein in the wording of them. The first ten paragraphs covered the voyage up to the present; firstly the need for acting with the utmost possible secrecy so that no hint could reach Spain of the approach of a British frigate to the Pacific shores of her possessions. 'You are therefore requested and required—' to sight land as little as possible on the voyage, and 'you are hereby entirely prohibited—' from coming within sight of land at all in the Pacific until the moment of his arrival at the mouth of the Gulf of Fonseca. He had obeyed these orders to the letter, although there were few enough captains in the service who could have done and who would have done. He had brought his ship here all the way from England without seeing any land save for a glimpse of Cape Horn, and if he had allowed Crystal to have his way regarding the course to be set a week ago, the ship would have gone sailing into the Gulf of Panama, completely forfeiting all possibility of secrecy.

Hornblower wrenched his mind away from the argument regarding the amount of compass-variation to be allowed for in these waters and forced himself to concentrate on a further study of his orders. 'You are hereby requested and required—' to form an alliance as soon as he reached the Gulf of Fonseca with Don Julian Alvarado, who was a large landowner with estates along the western shore of the bay. Don Julian intended, with the help of the British, to rise in rebellion against the Spanish monarchy. Hornblower was to hand over to him the five hundred muskets and bayonets, the five hundred pouch-belts, and the million rounds of small-arm ammunition which were to be provided at Portsmouth, and he was to do everything which his discretion dictated to ensure the success of the rebellion. If he were to think it necessary, he could present to the rebels one or more of the guns of his ship, but the fifty thousand guineas in gold which were entrusted to him as well were only to be disbursed if the rebellion would fail without them, on pain of his being brought to a courtmartial. He was to succour the rebels to the utmost of his power, even to the extent of recognising Don Julian Alvarado's sovereignty over any territory that he might conquer, provided that in return Don Julian would enter into commercial treaties with His Britannic Majesty.

This mention of commercial treaties apparently had acted as an inspiration to the Admiralty clerk, for the next ten paragraphs dealt in highflown detail with the pressing necessity for opening Spanish possessions to British commerce. Peruvian balsam and logwood,

cochineal and gold, were awaiting exchange for British manufac-
tures. The clerk's quill had fairly dipped with excitement as it penned
these details in a fair round hand. Furthermore, there was an arm
of the bay of Fonseca, called, it was believed, the Estero Real,
which approached closely to the inland lake of Managua, which
was thought to communicate with the lake of Nicaragua, which
drained to the Caribbean by the river San Juan. Captain Hornblower
was requested and required to do his utmost to open up this route
across the isthmus to British commerce, and he was to guide Don
Julian's efforts in this direction.

It was only after Don Julian's rebellion should be successful
and all this accomplished that the orders went on to give Captain
Hornblower permission to attack the treasure ships to be found
in the Pacific, and moreover no shipping was to be interfered with
if doing so should give offence to those inhabitants who might
otherwise be favourable to the rebellion. For Captain Hornblower's
information it was noted that the Spaniards were believed to
maintain in these waters a two-decked ship of fifty guns, by the
name the *Natividad*, for the enforcement of the royal authority.
Captain Hornblower was therefore requested and required to 'take,
sink, burn or destroy' this ship at the first opportunity.

Lastly, Captain Hornblower was ordered to open communications as soon as might be convenient with the Rear Admiral
commanding the Leeward Islands station for the purpose of
receiving further orders.

Captain Hornblower folded up the crackling paper again and
fell into contemplation. Those orders were the usual combination
of the barely possible and the quite Quixotic, which a captain on
detached service might expect to receive. Only a landsman would
have given those opening orders to sail to the Gulf of Fonseca
without sighting other land in the Pacific – only a succession of
miracles (Hornblower gave himself no credit for sound judgement
and good seamanship) had permitted of their being carried out.

Starting a rebellion in the Spanish American colonies had long
been a dream of the British government – a dream which had

been a nightmare to the British officers ordered to make it a reality. Admiral Popham and Admiral Stirling, General Beresford and General Whitelocke had, during the last three years, all lost in honour and reputation in repeated efforts to raise rebellion on the River Plate.

Opening up a channel to British trade across the Isthmus of Darien had long been a similar dream cherished by Admiralty clerks with small-scale maps before them and no practical experience. Thirty years ago, Nelson himself, as a young captain, had nearly lost his life in command of an expedition up that very river, San Juan, which Hornblower was ordered to clear from its source.

And to crown it all was the casual mention of the presence of a fifty-gun ship of the enemy. It was typical of Whitehall to send a thirty-six-gun frigate so lightly to attack an enemy of nearly double that force. The British navy had been so successful in single-ship duels during these wars that by now victory was expected of its ships against any odds. If, by any chance, the *Natividad* should overwhelm the *Lydia*, no excuse would be accepted. Hornblower's career would be wrecked. Even if the inevitable courtmartial did not break him, he would be left to languish on half pay for the rest of his life. Failure to capture the *Natividad*, failure to start a successful rebellion, failure to open the isthmus to trade – any one of these quite probable failures would mean a loss of reputation, of employment, of having to face his wife on his return condemned as a man inferior to his fellows.

Having contemplated all these gloomy possibilities, Hornblower thrust them aside with determined optimism. First and foremost he must make contact with this Don Julian Alvarado, which seemed to be a duty involving some little interest and only small difficulty. Later, there would be treasure-ships to capture and prize money to be won. He would not allow himself to worry about the rest of the future. He heaved himself off the locker and strode back to his sleeping-cabin.

Ten minutes later he stepped up on the quarterdeck; he noted with sardonic amusement how his officers tried without success to appear not to notice his splendid best coat with the epaulettes, his silk stockings, his shoes with the cut-steel buckles, his cocked hat and his gold-hilted sword. Hornblower cast a glance at the fast-nearing shore.

'Beat to quarters, Mr Bush,' he said. 'Clear for action.'

The roll of the drum set the ship into a wild fury as the watch below came tumbling up. Urged on by the cries and blows of the petty officers, the crew flung themselves into the business of getting the ship ready for action. The decks were soused with water and strewn with sand; the bulkheads were knocked away; the fire parties took their places at the pumps; the boys ran breathless with cartridges for the guns; down below the purser's steward who had been appointed acting surgeon was dragging together the midshipmen's chests in the cockpit to make an operating table.

'We'll have the guns loaded and run out, if you please, Mr Bush,' said Hornblower.

That was only a sensible precaution to take, seeing that the ship was about to sail before the wind straight into Spanish territory. The guns' crews cast off the frappings of the breeches, tugged desperately at the train tackles to draw the guns inboard, rammed home the powder and the shot, depressed the gun muzzles, strained madly at the gun tackles, and ran the guns out through the opened ports.

'Ship cleared for action. Ten minutes, twenty-one seconds, sir,' said Bush as the last rumble died away. For the life of him he still could not tell whether this was an exercise or in earnest, and it gratified Hornblower's vanity to leave him in doubt.

'Very good, Mr Bush. Send a good man with the lead into the main chains, and make ready to anchor.'

The breeze off the sea was strengthening every minute now, and the *Lydia*'s speed was steadily increasing. With his glass from the quarterdeck Hornblower could see every detail of the entrance to the bay, and the broad westerly channel between Conchaquita Island and the westerly mainland which the chart assured him afforded twenty fathoms for five miles inland. But there was no trusting these Spanish charts.

'What have you in the chains, there?' called Hornblower.

'No ground with this line, sir.'

'How many fathom have you out? Pass along the deep sea line.'

'Aye aye, sir.'

A dead hush descended on the ship, save for the eternal harping of the rigging and the chatter of the water under the stern.

'No ground, sir, within a hundred fathom.'

The shore must be very steep-to, then, because they were within two miles of land now. But there was no purpose in risking running aground under full sail.

'Get the courses in,' said Hornblower. 'Keep that lead going in the chains, there.'

Under topsails alone, the *Lydia* crept in towards land. Soon a cry from the chains announced that bottom had been reached in a hundred fathoms, and the depth diminished steadily at every cast. Hornblower would have been glad to know what was the state of the tide – if he was going aground at all it would be far better to do so on the flow than on the ebb – but there was no possible means of calculating that. He went halfway up the mizzen rigging to get a better view; everyone else in the ship save for the man in the chains was standing rigid in the blinding heat. They were almost in the entrance channel now. Hornblower sighted some driftwood afloat on the the near side, and, training his glass on it, he saw that it was floating in up the bay. The tide was making, then; better and better.

'By the deep nine,' chanted the leadsman.

So much for the Dago chart which indicated ten fathoms.

'And a half eight.'

The channel was shoaling fast. They would have to anchor soon in this case.

'And a half eight.'

Plenty of water still for the present. Hornblower called down to the helmsman, and the *Lydia* swung to starboard round the slight bend.

'And a half eight.'

Well enough still. The *Lydia* steadied on her new course.

'By the mark seven.'

Hornblower's eyes searched the channel in an attempt to determine the line of deepest water.

'By the mark seven.'

An order from Hornblower edged the *Lydia* towards the further side. Bush quietly sent the men to the braces to trim the yards on the new course.

'And a half eight.'

That was better.

'By the deep nine.'

Better still. The *Lydia* was well up the bay now, and Hornblower could see that the tide was still making. They crept on over the glassy water, with the leadsman chanting monotonously, and the steep conical mountain in the middle of the bay drawing nearer.

'Quarter less eight,' called the leadsman.

'Are the anchors clear?' asked Hornblower.

'All clear, sir.'

'By the mark seven.'

No useful object could be served in going in farther.

'Let go the anchor.'

The cable roared through the hawsehole while the watch sprang to furl the topsails, and the *Lydia* swung round to wind and tide while Hornblower descended to the quarterdeck.

Bush blinked at him as at a miracle worker. Seven weeks after sighting the Horn, Hornblower had brought the *Lydia* straight in to her destination; he had arrived in the afternoon with the sea breeze and a flowing tide to bring him in, and if there were danger for them here nightfall would soon bring them the ebb tide and the land breeze to take them out again. How much was fluke and how much was calculation Bush could not guess, but as his opinion of Hornblower's professional merit was far higher than Hornblower himself cherished he was inclined to give him more credit than was really his due.

'Keep the watch at quarters, Mr Bush,' said Hornblower. 'Dismiss the watch below.'

With the ship a mile from any possible danger and cleared for action there was no need to keep every man at his station. The ship broke into a cheerful buzz as the watch below lined the rails to stare out at this land of green jungle and grey rock, but Hornblower was puzzled for a moment, wondering what to do next. The excitement of bringing the ship into an unknown harbour had prohibited his usual careful planning of his next step. His mind was made up for him by a hail from the lookout.

'Deck there! Boat putting out from shore. Two points abaft the starboard beam.'

A double speck of white was creeping out towards them; Hornblower's glass resolved it into an open boat under two tiny lateen sails, and as she drew nearer he could see that she was manned by half a dozen swarthy men wearing wide straw hats. She hove-to fifty yards away, and someone stood up in the stern sheets and shouted across the water with hands cupped round his mouth. It was Spanish that he spoke.

'Is that an English ship?' he asked.

'Yes. Come on board,' replied Hornblower. Two years as a prisoner of Spain had given him the opportunity of learning the language – he had long before decided that it was merely on account of this accomplishment that he had been selected for this special service.

The boat ran alongside and the man who had hailed scrambled lightly up the ladder to the deck. He stopped at the side and looked round him with a certain curiosity at the spotless decks and the rigid order which prevailed on every hand. He wore a sleeveless black waistcoat aflame with gold embroidery; beneath it a dirty white shirt, and on his legs dirty white trousers terminating raggedly just below the knees. His feet were bare, and in a red sash round his waist he carried two pistols and a short heavy sword. He spoke Spanish as his native tongue, but he did not look like a Spaniard; the black hair which hung over his ears was long, lustreless and lank; there was a tinge of red in his brown complexion and a tinge of yellow in the whites of his eyes. A long thin moustache drooped from his upper lip. His eyes at once picked out the captain, gorgeous in his best coat and cocked hat, and he advanced towards him. It was in anticipation of just such a meeting that Hornblower had donned his best, and he was pleased with his foresight now.

'You are the captain, sir?' asked the visitor.

'Yes. Captain Horatio Hornblower of His Britannic Majesty's frigate *Lydia*, at your service. And whom have I the pleasure of welcoming?'

'Manuel Hernandez, lieutenant general of el Supremo.'

'El Supremo?' asked Hornblower, puzzled. The name was a little difficult to render into English. Perhaps 'The Almighty' might be the nearest translation.

'Yes, of el Supremo. You were expected here four months, six months back.'

Hornblower thought quickly. He dared not disclose the reason of his coming to any unauthorised person, but the fact that this man knew he was expected seemed to indicate that he was a member of Alvarado's conspiracy.

'It is not to el Supremo that I am ordered to address myself,' he temporised. Hernandez made a gesture of impatience.

'Our lord el Supremo was known to men until lately as His Excellency Don Julian Maria de Jesus de Alvarado y Moctezuma,' he said.

'Ah!' said Hornblower. 'It is Don Julian that I want to see.'

Hernandez was clearly annoyed by this casual mention of Don Julian.

'El Supremo,' he said, laying grave accent on the name, 'has sent me to bring you into his presence.'

'And where is he?'

'He is in his house.'

'And which is his house?'

'Surely it is enough, Captain, that you should know that el Supremo requires your attendance.'

'Do you think so? I would have you know, señor, that a captain of one of His Britannic Majesty's ships is not accustomed to being at anyone's beck and call. You can go, if you like, and tell Don Julian so.'

Hornblower's attitude indicated that the interview was at an end. Hernandez went through an internal struggle, but the prospect of returning to face el Supremo without bringing the captain with him was not alluring.

'The house is there,' he said sullenly, at last, pointing across the bay. 'On the side of the mountain. We must go through the town which is hidden behind the point to get there.'

'Then I shall come. Pardon me for a moment, General.'

Hornblower turned to Bush, who was standing by with the half-puzzled, half-admiring expression on his face so frequently to be seen when a man is listening to a fellow countryman talking fluently in an unknown language.

'Mr Bush,' he said, 'I am going ashore, and I hope I shall return soon. If I do not, if I am not back nor have written to you by midnight, you must take steps to ensure the safety of the ship. Here is the key of my desk. You have my orders that at midnight you are to read the government's secret orders to me, and to act on them as you think proper.'

'Aye aye, sir,' said Bush. There was anxiety in his face, and Hornblower realised with a thrill of pleasure that Bush was actually worried about his captain's wellbeing. 'Do you think – is it safe for you on shore alone, sir?'

'I don't know,' said Hornblower, with honest indifference. 'I must go, that is all.'

'We'll bring you off, sir, safe and sound, if there is any hanky-panky.'

'You'll see after the safety of the ship first,' snapped
Hornblower, visualising a mental picture of Bush with a valuable
landing party blundering about in the fever-haunted jungles of
Central America. Then he turned to Hernandez. 'I am at your
service, señor.'

CHAPTER IV

The boat ran softly aground on a beach of golden sand round the point, and her swarthy crew sprang out and hauled the boat up so that Hornblower and Hernandez could step ashore dry shod. Hornblower looked keenly about him. The town came down to the edge of the sand; it was a collection of a few hundred houses of palmetto leaves, only a few of them roofed with tiles. Hernandez led the way up towards it.

'Agua, agua,' croaked a voice as they approached. 'Water, for the love of God, water.'

A man was bound upright to a six foot stake beside the path; his hands were free and his arms thrashed about frantically. His eyes were protruding from his head and it seemed as if his tongue were too big for his mouth, like an idiot's. A circle of vultures crouched and fluttered round him.

'Who is that?' asked Hornblower, shocked.

'A man whom el Supremo has ordered to die for want of water,' said Hernandez. 'He is one of the unenlightened.'

'He is being tortured to death?'

'This is his second day. He will die when the noontide sun shines on him tomorrow,' said Hernandez casually. 'They always do.'

'But what is his crime?'

'He is one of the unenlightened, as I said, Captain.'

Hornblower resisted the temptation to ask what constituted enlightenment; from the fact that Alvarado had adopted the name of el Supremo he could fairly well guess. And he was weak enough to allow Hernandez to guide him past the unhappy wretch without a protest – he surmised that no expostulation on his part would override the orders given by el Supremo, and an unavailing protest would only be bad for his prestige. He would postpone action until he was face to face with the leader.

Little miry lanes, filthy and stinking, wound between the palmetto huts. Vultures perched on the roof ridges and squabbled with the mongrel dogs in the lanes. The Indian population were going about their usual avocations without regard for the man dying of thirst within fifty yards of them. They were all brown with a tinge of red, like Hernandez himself; the children ran naked, the women were dressed either in black or in dirty white; the few men to be seen wore only short white trousers to the knees and were naked from the waist up. Half the houses appeared to be shops – open on one side; where were displayed for sale a few handfuls of fruits, or three or four eggs. At one place a black-robed woman was bargaining to make a purchase.

Tethered in the little square in the centre of the town some diminutive horses warred with the flies. Hernandez' escort made haste to untether two of them and stood at their heads for them to mount. It was a difficult moment for Hornblower; he was not a good horseman, as he knew, and he was wearing his best silk stockings, and he felt he would not cut a dignified figure on horseback with his cocked hat and his sword. There was no help for it, however. He was so clearly expected to mount and ride that he could not draw back. He got his foot into his stirrup and swung up into the saddle, and was relieved to find that the tiny horse was submissive and quiet. He trotted alongside Hernandez, bumping awkwardly. The sweat ran down his face, and every few seconds he had to reach up hurriedly and adjust his cocked hat. A path wound steeply up the hillside out of the town, only wide enough for one horseman at a time, so that Hernandez, with a courteous gesture, preceded him. The escort clattered along fifty yards behind them.

The narrow path was stifling hot, hemmed by trees and bush on either hand. Insects buzzed round them, biting viciously. Half a mile up the path some lounging sentries came awkwardly to attention, and beyond this point there were other men to be seen – men like the first one Hornblower had encountered, bound to stakes and dying of thirst. There were dead men, too – mere stinking masses of corruption with a cloud of flies which buzzed more wildly as the horses brushed by them. The stench was horrible; gorged vultures, hideous with their naked necks, flopped along the path ahead of the horses, unable to fly, seeking escape into the forest.

Hornblower was about to say 'More of the unenlightened, General?' when he realised the uselessness of comment. It was better to say nothing than to say anything ineffectual. He rode silently through the stink and the flies, and tried to estimate the mentality of a man who would allow rotting corpses to remain, so to speak, on his doorstep.

The path rose over a shoulder of the mountain, and for a moment Hornblower had a glimpse of the bay below, blue and silver and gold under the evening sun, with the *Lydia* riding to her anchor in the midst of it. Then suddenly the forest at each side changed as if by magic into cultivated land. Orange groves, and trees laden with fruit, bordered the path, and through the trees Hornblower could gain a glimpse of fields bearing crops. The sun, sinking fast to the horizon, illuminated the golden fruit, and then, as they turned a corner, shone full on a vast white building, stretching low and wide on either hand, before them.

'The house of el Supremo,' said Hernandez.

On the patio, servants came and took their horses, while Hornblower stiffly dismounted and contemplated the ruin which riding had caused to his best silk stockings. The superior servants who conducted them into the house were dressed in clothes similar in their blend of rags and finery to those Hernandez wore – scarlet and gold above, bare feet and rags below. The most gorgeous of all, whose features seemed to indicate a strong dash of negro blood in his ancestry along with the Indian and the slight trace of European, came up with a worried look on his face.

'El Supremo has been kept waiting,' he said. 'Please come this way as quickly as you can.'

He almost ran before them down a corridor to a door studded with brass. On this he knocked loudly, waited a moment, knocked again, and then threw open the door, bending himself double as he did so. Hornblower, at Hernandez' gesture, strode into the room, Hernandez behind him, and the major-domo closed the door. It was a long room, lime-washed to a glittering white, whose ceiling was supported by thick wooden beams, painted and carved. Towards the farther end, solitary in the bleak bareness of the room, stood a treble dais, and in a canopied chair on the dais sat the man Hornblower had been sent half round the world to see.

He did not seem very impressive or dignified: a small swarthy man, restless and fidgety, with piercing black eyes and lank black hair beginning to turn grey. From his appearance one might have guessed at only a small admixture of Indian blood in his European ancestry, and he was dressed in European fashion, in a red coat laced with gold, a white stock, and white breeches and stockings; there were gold buckles on his shoes. Hernandez cringed before him.

'You have been a long time,' snapped Alvarado. 'Eleven men have been flogged during your absence.'

'Supremo,' sighed Hernandez – his teeth were chattering with fright – 'the captain came instantly on hearing your summons.'

Alvarado turned his piercing eyes upon Hornblower, who bowed stiffly. His mind was playing with the suspicion that the eleven men who had been flogged had suffered, unaccountably, because of the length of time it took to ride a horse from the beach to the house.

'Captain Horatio Hornblower, of His Britannic Majesty's frigate *Lydia*, at your service, sir,' he said.

'You have brought me arms and powder?'

'They are in the ship.'

'That is well. You will make arrangements with General Hernandez here for landing them.'

Hornblower thought of his frigate's almost empty storerooms; and he had three hundred and eighty men to feed. Moreover, as with every ship's captain, he was already feeling irritation at dependence on the shore. He would be restless and uncomfortable until the *Lydia* was fully charged again with food and water and wood and every other necessary, sufficient to take her back round the Horn at least as far as the West Indies or St Helena, if not home.

'I can hand nothing over, sir, until my ship's needs are satisfied,' he said. He heard Hernandez drawing his breath sharply at this sacrilegious temporising in the face of orders from el Supremo. The latter's eyebrows came together; for a moment it seemed likely that he would attempt to impose his imperious will upon the captain, but immediately afterwards his expression cleared as he realised the folly of quarrelling with his new ally.

'Certainly,' he said. 'Please make known to General Hernandez what you require, and he will supply you.'

Hornblower had had dealing with officers of the Spanish services, and knew what they could accomplish in the way of fair promises not carried out, and procrastination and shiftiness and double-dealing. He guessed that Spanish American rebel officers would be proportionately less trustworthy. He decided to make known his wants now, so that there might be a fair chance of seeing a part at least of his demands satisfied in the near future.

'My water-casks must be refilled tomorrow,' he said.

Hernandez nodded.

'There is a spring close to where we landed. If you wish, I will have men to help you.'

'Thank you, but that will not be necessary. My ship's crew will attend to it. Besides water I need—'

Hornblower's mind began to total up all the multifarious wants of a frigate seven months at sea.

'Yes, señor?'

'I shall need two hundred bullocks. Two hundred and fifty if they are thin and small. Five hundred pigs. One hundred quintals of salt. Forty tons of ship's bread, and if biscuit is unobtainable I shall need the equivalent amount of flour, with ovens and fuel provided to bake it. The juice of forty thousand lemons, oranges or limes – I can supply the casks to contain it. Ten tons of sugar. Five tons of tobacco. A ton of coffee. You grow potatoes on this coast, do you not? Then twenty tons of potatoes will suffice.'

Hernandez' face had grown longer and longer during this formidable recital.

'But, captain—' he ventured to protest, but Hornblower cut him short.

'Then for our current needs, while we are in harbour,' he went on 'I shall need five bullocks a day, two dozen chickens, as many eggs as you can provide, and sufficient fresh vegetables for the daily consumption of my ship's company.'

By nature Hornblower was the mildest of men, but in any matter regarding his ship, fear of being deemed a failure drove him into unexpected hardness and temerity.

'Two hundred bullocks!' said the wretched Hernandez. 'Five hundred pigs?'

'That is what I said,' replied Hornblower, inexorably. 'Two hundred *fat* bullocks.'

At this point el Supremo intervened.

'See that the captain's wants are satisfied,' he said, with an impatient wave of his hand. 'Start now.'

Hernandez only hesitated for a further tenth of a second, and then retired. The big brass-bound door closed silently behind him.

'That is the only way to deal with these people,' said el Supremo, lightly. 'They are no better than beasts. Any kind of refinement is wasted upon them. Doubtless you saw on your way here various criminals suffering punishment?'

'I did.'

'My ancestors on earth,' said el Supremo 'went to much trouble in arranging elaborate punishments. They burned people to death with elaborate ceremonial. They cut out their hearts to the accompaniment of music and dances, or pressed them to death in wrappings of raw hide exposed to the sun. I find all that quite unnecessary. A simple order to have the man tied up to die of thirst is sufficient. The man dies, and there is an end of him.'

'Yes,' said Hornblower.

'They are incapable of absorbing even the simplest of conceptions. There are some who to this very day cannot understand the very obvious principle that the blood of Alvarado and Moctezuma must be divine. They still cling to their absurd Christs and Virgins.'

'Indeed?' said Hornblower.

'One of my earliest lieutenants could not shake himself free from the influence of early education. When I announced my divinity he actually made suggestions that missionaries should be sent out to preach to the tribes so as to convert them, as though I were putting forward a new religion. He could never realise that it was not a matter of opinion but a matter of fact. He was, of course, one of the first to die of thirst.'

'Of course.'

Hornblower was utterly bewildered by all this. But he clung to the fact that he had to ally himself to this madman. The revictualling of the *Lydia* depended upon his acting in concert with him, if nothing else did – and that was a matter of the most vital primary importance.

'Your King George must have been delighted to hear that I had decided to act in concert with him,' continued el Supremo.

'He charged me with messages to you assuring you of his friendship,' said Hornblower cautiously.

'Of course,' said el Supremo 'he would not venture to push himself forward beyond that point. The blood of the family of Guelph naturally cannot compare with that of Alvarado.'

'Ha – h'm,' said Hornblower. He found that noncommittal noise as useful in conversation with el Supremo as with Lieutenant Bush. El Supremo's brows approached each other a trifle.

'I suppose you are aware,' he said a little sternly, 'of the history of the family of Alvarado? You know who was the first of that name to reach this country?'

'He was Cortez' lieutenant—' began Hornblower.

'Lieutenant? Nothing of the sort. I am surprised that you should believe such lies. He was the leader of the Conquistadores; it is only by the falsification of history that Cortez is represented as in command. Alvarado conquered Mexico, and from Mexico he descended upon this coast and conquered it all, as far as the Isthmus. He married the daughter of Moctezuma the last of the Emperors; and as a direct descendant from that union I have chosen to select from my family names those of Alvarado and Moctezuma. But in Europe; long before the head of the house came to the Americas, the name of Alvarado can be traced back, beyond the Hapsburgs and the Visigoths, beyond the Romans and the empire of Alexander, to the ultimate sources of time. It is only natural, therefore, that in this present generation the family should have attained to the divine state in my person. I find it satisfactory that you agree with me, Captain – Captain—'

'Hornblower.'

'I thank you. And now I think we had better, Captain Hornblower, discuss the plans for the extension of my Empire.'

'As you please,' said Hornblower. He felt he must at least agree with this madman until the *Lydia* was revictualled, although his already faint hope of heading a successful insurrection in this country was fast becoming fainter.

'The Bourbon who calls himself King of Spain,' said el Supremo, 'maintains in this country an official who calls himself Captain General of Nicaragua. I sent to this gentleman some time ago a message ordering him to announce his fealty to me. This he had not done, and he was even misguided enough to hang my messenger publicly in Managua. Of the insolent men whom he subsequently sent to secure my divine person some were killed on the road and some died while attached to stakes, while a few were fortunate enough to see the light and are now included in my army. The Captain General is now, I hear, at the head of an army of three hundred men in the city of El Salvador. When you have landed the weapons consigned to me I propose to move on this town, which I shall burn, along with the Captain General and the unenlightened among his men. Perhaps, Captain, you will accompany me? A burning town is worth seeing.'

'My ship must be revictualled first,' said Hornblower, sturdily.

'I have given the orders for that,' replied el Supremo with a trace of impatience.

'And further,' continued Hornblower 'it will be my duty first to ascertain the whereabouts of a Spanish ship of war, the *Natividad*, which I believe to be on this station. Before I can engage in any operations on land I must see that she can do no harm to my ship. I must either capture her or know for certain that she is too distant to interfere.'

'Then you had better capture her, captain. I expect, from the information I have received, she will be sailing into the bay here at any moment.'

'Then I must go back to my ship immediately,' said Hornblower, all agitation. The possibility that his frigate might be attacked in his absence by a fifty-gun ship threw him into a seething panic. What would the Lords of the Admiralty say if the *Lydia* were lost while her captain was on shore?

'There is food being brought in. Behold,' said el Supremo.

The door at the end of the hall was flung open as he spoke. A crowd of attendants began to walk slowly in, carrying a large table covered with silver dishes, and bearing four large silver candelabra each supporting five lighted candles.

'Your pardon, but I cannot wait for food. I must not,' said Hornblower.

'As you will,' said el Supremo indifferently. 'Alfonso!'

The negroid major-domo came forward, bowing.

'See that Captain Hornblower goes back to his ship.'

El Supremo had no sooner spoken the words than he relapsed into an attitude of contemplation. The bustle attendant upon the bringing in of the banquet he allowed to pass unheeded.

He did not bestow another glance on Hornblower, who stood before him, regretting already his precipitation in deciding to rejoin his ship, anxious to cause no offence by a breach of good manners, worried by the need to revictual the *Lydia*, and acutely conscious that his present attitude of uncertainty before a man who was paying him no attention whatever was quite undignified.

'This way, señor,' said Alfonso, at his elbow, while el Supremo still gazed blankly over his head. Hornblower yielded, and followed the major-domo out to the patio.

Two men and three horses awaited him there, in the half light. Without a word, bewildered by this sudden turn of events, Hornblower set his foot in the linked hands of a half-naked slave who knelt at his horse's side and swung himself up into the saddle. The escort clattered before him out through the gates, and he followed them; night was falling fast.

At the corner of the path the wide bay opened before them. A young moon was fast fading down th sky. A shadowy shape in the centre of the silver water showed where the *Lydia* swung to her anchor – she, at least, was something solid and matter-of-fact in this mad world. Eastward a mountain top suddenly glowed red, illuminating the clouds above it, and then died away into darkness. They rode at a sharp trot down the steep path, past the moaning men tied to the stakes, past the stinking corpses, and into the little town. Here there was neither light nor movement; Hornblower had to leave his horse to the task of following the escort round the corners. The sound of the horses' hoofs ceased as they reached the soft sand of the beach; and simultaneously he heard the pitiful moaning of the first man he had seen tied to a stake and saw the faint phosphorescence of the edge of the sea.

He felt his way in the darkness into the waiting boat, and sat on a thwart while to the accompaniment of an explosion of orders the unseen crew pushed off. There was not a breath of wind – the sea breeze had died with the sunset and the land breeze had not yet sprung up. The unseen crew tugged at six oars, and the water sprang into view, the foam faintly visible as each stroke waked the phosphorescence. Slowly they made their way out into the bay to the rhythmical sound of the oars. Far out across the water he could see the faint loom of the *Lydia*, and a minute later he heard the welcome sound of Bush's voice as he hailed.

'Boat ahoy!'

Hornblower made a speaking trumpet of his hands and hailed back '*Lydia!*' The captain of a King's ship calls himself by the name of that ship when he is on board a small boat.

Hornblower could hear all the expected noises now, could see all the expected sights; the bustle and clatter as boatswain's mate and sideboys ran to the gangway, the measured tramp of the marines, the flickering of lanterns. The boat ran alongside and he sprang to the ladder. It was good to feel solid oak under his feet again. The pipes of the boatswain's mates twittered in chorus; the marines brought their muskets to the present, and Bush was at the gangway to receive him, with all the pomp and ceremony due to a Captain arriving on board.

Hornblower saw, by the lantern light, the relief in Bush's honest face. He glanced round the decks; one watch, wrapped in blankets, was lying on the bare boards of the deck, while the other squatted by the guns ready for action. Bush had very properly maintained all precautions while thus at anchor in a presumably hostile port.

'Very good, Mr Bush,' said Hornblower. Then he became conscious that his white breeches were stained by the dirty saddle, and that his best silk stockings were in threads about his calves. He felt discontented with his appearance; he was ashamed of the fact that he had come back to his ship in this undignified fashion, and without, as far as he knew, having settled anything for the future. He was angry with himself; he feared lest Bush should have a worse opinion of him should he come to know the facts.

He felt his cheeks go hot with self-consciousness, and he took refuge, as ever, in uncommunicativeness.

'Ha – h'm,' he rasped. 'Call me if there is anything unusual to justify it.'

With that, and no other word, he turned and went below to his cabin, where canvas screens replaced the torn-down bulkheads.

Bush stared at his disappearing form. The volcanoes flicked and glowed round the bay. The crew, excited at their arrival in this strange land and anxious to hear about the future, saw themselves doomed to disappointment, just like the officers, who watched with dropped jaws their captain descending the companion ladder.

For one brief instant Hornblower felt that his dramatic appearance and exit compensated him for his consciousness of failure, but it was only for an instant. Seated on his cot, having sent away Polwheal, he felt his spirits fall again. His weary mind set itself vaguely again to debate the question of whether he would be able to obtain stores on the morrow. He fretted about whether he would be able to raise a rebellion successful enough to satisfy the Admiralty. He fretted about the approaching duel with the *Natividad*.

And throughout these considerations he continually found himself blushing again at the recollection of his abrupt dismissal by el Supremo. He felt that there were few captains in His Britannic Majesty's service who would have submitted so meekly to such cavalier treatment.

'But what the devil could I have *done*?' he asked himself pathetically.

Without turning out his lantern, he lay on his cot sweating in the still tropical night while his mind raced back and forth through past and future.

And then the canvas screen flapped. A little breath of wind came stealing along the decks. His sailor's instincts kept him informed of how the *Lydia* was swinging to her anchor. He felt the tiny tremor which ran through the ship as she brought up

short to her anchor cable in a new direction. The land breeze had
begun at last. The ship was cooler at once. Hornblower wriggled
over on to his side, and slept.

CHAPTER V

Those doubts and fears which encompassed Hornblower while he was trying to go to sleep the night before vanished with the day. Hornblower felt a new strength running through his veins when he awoke. His mind was teeming with plans as he drank the coffee which Polwheal brought him at dawn, and for the first time for weeks he dispensed with his morning walk on the quarterdeck. He had decided as he stepped on the deck that at least he could fill the water casks and restock with fuel, and his first orders sent parties of men hurriedly to the tackles to hoist out the launch and lower the quarter boats. Soon they were off for the shore, charged with the empty casks and manned by crews of excited chattering men; in the bows of each boat sat two marines in their red coats with their muskets loaded and bayonets fixed, and in their ears echoing their final orders from their sergeant, to the effect that if a single sailor succeeded in deserting while on shore every man among them would have his back well scratched with the cat.

An hour later the launch came back under sail, deep laden with her water casks full, and while the casks were being swayed out of her and lowered into the hold, Mr Midshipman Hooker came running up to Hornblower and touched his hat.

'The beef cattle are coming down to the shore, sir,' he said.

Hornblower had to struggle hard to keep his face immobile and to receive the news as if he expected it.

'How many?' he snapped; it seemed a useful question to ask in order to waste time, but the answer was more surprising still.

'Hundreds, sir. There's a Dago in charge with a lot to say, but there's no one ashore who can speak his lingo.'

'Send him out to me when you go ashore again,' said Hornblower.

Hornblower spent the interval granted him in making up his mind. He hailed the lookout at the main royal masthead to ensure that a careful watch was kept to seaward. On the one hand there was the chance that the *Natividad* might come sailing in from the Pacific, in which case the *Lydia*, caught with half her crew ashore, would have no time to clear from the bay and would have to fight in confined waters and with the odds necessarily against her. On the other hand there was the opportunity of filling up completely with stores and regaining entire independence of the shore. From what Hornblower had seen of conditions prevailing there he judged that to postpone regaining that independence would be dangerous in the extreme; at any moment Don Julian Alvarado's rebellion might come to a hurried and bloody ending.

It was Hernandez who came out to him, in the same boat with the two tiny lateen sails in which Hornblower had been ferried across last night. They exchanged salutes on the quarterdeck.

'There are four hundred cattle awaiting your orders, Captain,' said Hernandez. 'My men are driving them down to the beach.'

'Good,' said Hornblower, his mind still not made up.

'I am afraid it will take longer to assemble the pigs,' went on Hernandez. 'My men are sweeping the country for them, but pigs are slow animals to drive.'

'Yes,' said Hornblower.

'With regard to the salt, it will not be easy to collect the hundred quintals you asked for. Until our lord declared his divinity, salt was a royal monopoly and scarce in consequence, but I have sent a party to the salt pans at Jiquilisco and hope to find sufficient there.'

'Yes,' said Hornblower. He remembered demanding salt, but he had no distinct recollection of the quantity he had asked for.

'The women are out collecting the lemons, oranges and limes which you ordered,' continued Hernandez, 'but I am afraid it will be two days before we shall have them all ready.'

'Ha – h'm,' said Hornblower.

'The sugar is ready at el Supremo's mill, however. And with regard to the tobacco, señor, there is a good deal in store. What special kind do you prefer? For some time we have only been rolling cigars for our own consumption, but I can set the women to work again after the fruit has been collected.'

'Ha – h'm,' said Hornblower again, suppressing just in time the cry of delight which nearly escaped him involuntarily at the mention of cigars – it was three months since he had last smoked one. Virginia pigtail twist was what his men used, but that, of course, would be unobtainable on this coast. However, he had often seen British sailors chewing and enjoying the half-cured native leaf.

'Send as many cigars as will be convenient to you,' he said, lightly. 'For the rest, it is of no importance what you send.'

Hernandez bowed.

'Thank you, señor. The coffee, the vegetables and the eggs will, of course, be easy to supply. But with regard to the bread—'

'Well?'

Hernandez was obviously nervous about what he was going to say next.

'Your excellency will forgive me, but in this country we have only maize. There is a little wheat grown in the tierra templada, but it rests still in the hands of the unenlightened. Would maize flour suffice?'

Hernandez' face was working with anxiety as he gazed at Hornblower. It was only then that Hornblower realised that Hernandez was in terror of his life, and that el Supremo's light-hearted endorsement of the requisitions he had made was far more potent than any stamped and sealed order addressed to a Spanish official.

'This is very serious,' said Hornblower sternly. 'My English sailors are unaccustomed to maize flour.'

'I know that,' said Hernandez, his interlocked fingers working galvanically. 'But I assure your excellency that I can only obtain wheat flour for them by fighting for it, and I know that el Supremo would not like me to fight at present. El Supremo will be angry.'

Hornblower remembered the abject fright with which Hernandez had regarded el Supremo the night before. The man was in terror lest he should be denounced as having failed to execute his orders. And then, suddenly, Hornblower remembered something he had unaccountably forgotten to ask for – something more important, if possible, than tobacco or fruit, and certainly far more important than the difference between maize flour and wheat.

'Very well,' he said. 'I will agree to use maize flour. But in consequence of this deficiency there is something else I must ask for.'

'Certainly, Captain. I will supply whatever you ask. You have only to name it.'

'I want drink for my men,' said Hornblower. 'Is there wine to be had here? Ardent spirits?'

'There is a little wine, your excellency. Only a little. The people on this coast drink an ardent spirit with which you are perhaps not acquainted. It is good when of good quality. It is distilled from the waste of the sugar mills, from the treacle, your excellency.'

'Rum, by God!' exclaimed Hornblower.

'Yes, señor, rum. Would that be of any use to your excellency?'

'I shall accept it in lieu of anything better,' said Hornblower sternly.

His heart was leaping with joy. It would appear like a miracle to his officers that he should conjure rum and tobacco from this volcano-riddled coast.

'Thank you, Captain. And shall we begin to slaughter the cattle now?'

That was the question on which Hornblower had been postponing a decision ever since he had heard about the arrival of the cattle on the beach. Hornblower looked up at the lookout at the masthead. He tested the strength of the wind. He gazed out to sea before he took the plunge.

'Very well,' he said at length. 'We will start now.'

The sea breeze was not nearly as strong as yesterday, and the weaker the breeze, the less chance there was of the *Natividad* coming in to interrupt the *Lydia*'s revictualling. And as events turned out the *Lydia* completed the work undisturbed. For two days the boats plied back and forth between the beach and the ship. They came back piled high with bloody joints of meat; the sand of the shore ran red with the blood of the slaughtered animals, while the half-tame vultures gorged themselves into a coma in the piled offal. On board the ship the purser and his crew toiled like slaves in the roasting heat, cramming the brine barrels with the meat and tugging them into position in the storerooms. The cooper and his mates worked for two days with hardly a break, making and repairing casks. Sacks of flour, ankers of rum, bales of tobacco – the hands at the tackles sweated as they swayed these up from the boats. The *Lydia* was gorging herself full.

So obvious were the good intentions of those on shore that Hornblower was able to give orders that the cargo consigned to this coast should be released, and so the boats which bore the meat and flour to the ship returned laden with cases of muskets and kegs of powder and shot. Hornblower had his gig hoisted out, and was rowed periodically round his ship inspecting her trim, in the anticipation lest at any moment he would have to hoist up his anchor and beat out to sea to fight the *Natividad*.

The work proceeded by night as well as by day; in fifteen years at sea – every one a year of warfare – Hornblower had seen many opportunities lost as a result of some trivial lack of energy, some omission to drive a crew into exerting the last ounce of its strength. He had lost opportunities himself like that, for that matter. He still felt a revulsion of shame at the recollection of how he had missed that privateer off the Azores, for example. For fear of standing condemned again in his own eyes he drove his men until they dropped.

There was no time for enjoyment of the pleasures of land at the moment. The shore party did indeed cook their rations before a huge bonfire, and revel in roast fresh meat after seven months of boiled salt meat, but with the characteristic contrariness of British sailors they turned with revulsion from the delicious fruit which was offered them – bananas and pawpaws, pineapples and guavas, and considered themselves the victims of sharp practice because these were substituted for their regulation ration of boiled dried peas.

And then, on the second evening, as Hornblower walked the quarterdeck enjoying the sea breeze at its freshest, and revelling in the thought that he was free of the land, if necessary, for another six months, and looking forward with the sheerest joy to his imminent dinner of roast fowl, there came the sound of firing from the beach. A scattering volley at first; a few dropping shots, and then another ragged volley. Hornblower forgot his dinner, his feeling of wellbeing, everything. Trouble on the mainland, of whatever sort, meant that the success of his mission was being imperilled. In hot haste he called for his gig, and he was pulled to the shore by a crew who made the stout oars bend as they flung their weight on the handles in response to the profane urgings of Coxswain Brown.

The scene that greeted his eyes as he rounded the point excited his worst apprehensions. The whole landing party was clubbed together on the beach; the dozen marines were in line on one flank, reloading their muskets; the sailors were bunched beside them armed with whatever weapons had come to their hands. In a wide semi-circle round them were the inhabitants, brandishing swords and muskets, and in the no man's land between the two parties lay one or two corpses. At the water's edge, behind the sailors, lay one of the hands with two of his mates bending over him. He was propped up on his elbow and he was vomiting floods of blood.

Hornblower sprang into the shallows; he paid no attention to the wounded sailor, but pushed his way through the mob before him. As he emerged into the open there came a puff of smoke from the half circle up the beach and a bullet sang over his head. He paid no attention to that either.

'Put those muskets down!' he roared at the marines, and he turned towards the gesticulating inhabitants and held up his hand palm forward, in the universal and instinctive gesture of peace. There was no room in his mind for thought of personal danger, so hot was he with anger at the thought that someone was botching his chance of success.

'What's the meaning of this?' he demanded.

Galbraith was in command. He was about to speak, but he was given no opportunity. One of the sailors who had been attending to the dying man came pushing forward, discipline forgotten in the blind whirl of sentimental indignation which Hornblower instantly recognised as characteristic of the lower deck – and which he despised and distrusted.

'They been torturing a poor devil up there, sir,' he said. 'Lashed him to a spar and left him to die of thirst.'

'Silence!' bellowed Hornblower, beside himself with rage not merely at this breach of discipline but at realising the difficulties ahead of him. 'Mr Galbraith!'

Galbraith was slow of speech and of mind.

'I don't know how it started, sir,' he began; although he had been at sea since childhood there was still a trace of Scotch in his accent. 'A party came running back from up there. They had Smith with them, wounded.'

'He's dead now,' put in a voice.

'Silence!' roared Hornblower again.

'I saw they were going to attack us, and so I had the marines fire, sir,' went on Galbraith.

'I'll speak to you later, Mr Galbraith,' snapped Hornblower. 'You, Jenkins. And you, Poole. What were you doing up there?'

'Well, sir, it was like this, sir—' began Jenkins. He was sheepish and crestfallen now. Hornblower had pricked the bubble of his indignation and he was being publicly convicted of a breach of orders.

'You knew the order that no one was to go beyond the creek?'

'Yessir.'

'Tomorrow morning I'll show you what orders mean, and you, too, Poole. Where's the sergeant of marines?'

'Here, sir.'

'A fine guard you keep, sergeant, to let these men get by. What were your pickets about?'

The sergeant could say nothing; he could only stand rigidly at attention in face of this incontrovertible proof of his being found wanting.

'Mr Simmonds will speak to you in the morning,' went on Hornblower. 'I don't expect you'll keep those stripes on your arm much longer.'

Hornblower glowered round at the landing party. His fierce rebukes had them all cowed and subservient now, and he felt his anger ebbing away as he realised that he had managed this without having to say a word in extenuation of Spanish-American justice. He turned to greet Hernandez, who had come riding up as fast as his little horse would gallop, reining up on his haunches in a shower of sand.

'Did el Supremo give orders for this attack on my men?' asked Hornblower, getting in the first broadside.

'No, Captain,' said Hernandez, and Hornblower rejoiced to see how he winced at the mention of el Supremo's name.

'I think he will not be too pleased with you when I tell him about this,' went on Hornblower.

'Your men tried to release a man condemned to death,' said Hernandez, half sullenly, half apologetically. He was clearly not too sure of his ground, and was nervous about what would be Alvarado's attitude towards this incident. Hornblower kept a rasp in his voice as he went on speaking. None of the Englishmen round him, as far as he knew, could speak Spanish, but he was anxious for his crew to believe (now that discipline was restored) that he was wholeheartedly on their side.

'That does not permit your men to kill mine,' he said.

'They are angry and discontented,' said Hernandez. 'The whole country has been swept to find food for you. The man your men tried to save was condemned for driving his pigs into the bush to keep them from being taken and given to you.'

Hernandez made this last speech reproachfully and with a hint of anger; Hornblower was anxious to be conciliatory if that were possible without exasperating his own men. Hornblower had in mind the plan of leading Hernandez out of earshot of the Englishmen, and then softening his tone, but before he could act upon it his attention was caught by the sight of a horseman galloping down the beach at full speed, waving his wide straw hat. Every eye turned towards this new arrival – a peon of the ordinary Indian type. Breathlessly he announced his news.

'A ship – a ship coming!'

He was so excited that he lapsed into the Indian speech, and Hornblower could not understand his further explanations. Hernandez had to interpret for him.

'This man has been keeping watch on the top of the mountain up there,' he said. 'He says that from there he could see the sails of a ship coming towards the bay.'

He addressed several more questions rapidly, one after the other, to the lookout, and was answered with nods and gesticulations and a torrent of Indian speech.

'He says,' went on Hernandez, 'that he has often seen the *Natividad* before, and he is sure this is the same ship, and she is undoubtedly coming in here.'

'How far off is she?' asked Hornblower and Hernandez translated the answer.

'A long way, seven leagues or more,' he said. 'She is coming from the south-eastward – from Panama.'

Hornblower pulled at his chin, deep in thought.

'She'll carry the sea breeze down with her until sunset,' he muttered to himself, and glanced up at the sun. 'That will be another hour. An hour after that she'll get the land breeze. She'll be able to hold her course, close hauled. She could be here in the bay by midnight.'

A stream of plans and ideas was flooding into his mind. Against the possibility of the ship's arrival in the dark must be balanced what he knew of the Spanish habit at sea of snugging down for the night, and of attempting no piece of seamanship at all complicated save under the best possible conditions. He wished he knew more about the Spanish captain.

'Has this ship, the *Natividad*, often come into this bay?' he asked.

'Yes, Captain, often.'

'Is her captain a good seaman?'

'Oh yes, Captain, very good.'

'Ha – h'm,' said Hornblower. A landsman's opinion of the seamanship of a frigate captain might not be worth much, but still it was an indication.

Hornblower tugged at his chin again. He had fought in ten single-ship actions. If he took the *Lydia* to sea and engaged the *Natividad* on open water the two ships might well batter each other into wrecks. Rigging and spars and hulls and sails would be shot to pieces. The *Lydia* would have a good many casualties which would be quite irreplaceable here in the Pacific. She would expend her priceless ammunition. On the other hand, if he stayed in the bay and yet the plan he had in mind did not succeed – if the *Natividad* waited off shore until the morning – he would have to beat his way out of the bay against the sea breeze, presenting the Spaniards with every possible advantage as he came out to fight them. The *Natividad*'s superiority of force was already such that it was rash to oppose the *Lydia* to her. Could he dare to risk increasing the odds? But the possible gains were so enormous that he made up his mind to run the risk.

CHAPTER VI

Ghostlike in the moonlight, with the first puffs of the land breeze, the *Lydia* glided across the bay. Hornblower had not ventured to hoist sail, lest a gleam of canvas might be visible to the distant ship at sea. The launch and the cutter towed the ship, sounding as they went, into the deep water at the foot of the island at the entrance of the bay – Manguera Island, Hernandez called it when Hornblower had cautiously sketched out his plan to him. For an hour the men laboured at the oars, although Hornblower did his best to aid them, standing by the wheel and making as much use as possible of the leeway acquired by the ship through the force of the puffs of wind on the *Lydia*'s rigging. They reached the new anchorage at last, and the anchor splashed into the water.

'Have that cable buoyed and ready to slip, Mr Bush,' said Hornblower.

'Aye aye, sir.'

'Call the boats alongside. I want the men to rest.'

'Aye aye, sir.'

'Mr Gerard, you have charge of the deck. See that the lookouts keep awake. I want Mr Bush and Mr Galbraith to come below with me.'

'Aye aye, sir.'

The ship was seething quietly with excitement. Everyone on board had guessed the captain's plan, even though the details of its execution, which he was now explaining to his lieutenants, were still unknown. In the two hours which had elapsed since the arrival of the news of the *Natividad*'s approach, Hornblower's mind had worked busily at the perfection of his plan. Nothing must go wrong. Everything that could possibly contribute to success must be done.

'That is all understood?' he asked finally; he stood stooping under the deck beams in his screened-off cabin while his lieutenants fiddled awkwardly with their hats.

'Aye aye, sir.'

'Very good,' said Hornblower, dismissing them. But within five minutes impatience and anxiety drove him up on deck again.

'Masthead, there? What can you see of the enemy?'

'She's just come up over the island, sir. She's more than hull down. I can only see her torps'ls, sir, below her t'garns.'

'What's her course?'

'She's holding her wind, sir. She ought to make the bay on this tack.

'Ha – h'm,' said Hornblower, and went below again.

It would be four hours at least before the *Natividad* reached the entrance, and before he could take any further action. He found himself pacing, stoop-shouldered, up and down the tiny limits of his cabin, and checked himself furiously. The iron-nerved captain of his dreams would not allow himself to work himself into this sort of fever, even though his professional reputation was to be at stake in four hours' time. He must show the ship that he, too, could face uncertainty with indifference.

'Pass the word for Polwheal!' he snapped, coming out through the screen and addressing a group by a main deck gun; and when Polwheal appeared he went on 'My compliments to Mr Bush, and tell him that if he can spare Mr Galbraith and Mr Clay and Mr Savage from their duties I would be glad if they would sup with me and have a hand of whist.'

Galbraith was nervous, too. Not merely was he anticipating a battle, but hanging over his head there was still the promised reprimand for his part in the skirmish of the afternoon. His raw-boned Scotch figure moved restlessly, and his face was flushed over his high cheekbones. Even the two midshipmen were subdued as well as fidgety.

Hornblower compelled himself to play the part of the courtly host, while every word he uttered was designed to increase his reputation for imperturbability. He apologised for the short-comings of the supper – the ship being cleared for action involved the extinction of all fires and the consequent necessity for serving cold food. But the sight of the cold roast chickens, the cold roast pork, the golden cakes of maize, the dishes of fruit, roused Mr Midshipman Savage's sixteen-year-old appetite and caused him to forget his embarrassment.'

'This is better than rats, sir,' he said, rubbing his hands.

'Rats?' asked Hornblower, vaguely. For all his appearance and attention his thoughts were up on deck, and not in the cabin.

'Yes, sir. Until we made this harbour rats had become a favourite dish in the midshipmen's berth.'

'That they had,' echoed Clay. He carved himself substantial slices of cold pork, and plenty of crackling, and added them to the half chicken on his plate. 'I was paying that thief Bailey threepence apiece for prime rats.'

Desperately Hornblower jerked his mind away from the approaching *Natividad* and delved into the past when he had been a half-starved midshipman, homesick and seasick. His seniors then had eaten rats with gusto, and maintained that a biscuit-fed rat was far more delicate a dish than beef two years in cask. He had never been able to stomach them himself, but he would not admit it to these boys.

'Threepence apiece for rats seems a trifle dear,' he said. 'I can't remember paying as much as that when I was a midshipman.'

'Why, sir, did you ever eat them yourself?' asked Savage, amazed.

In reply to this direct question Hornblower could only lie.

'Of course,' he said. 'Midshipmen's berths were much the same twenty years ago as now. I always maintained that a rat who had had the run of the bread-locker all his life made a dish fit for a king, let alone a midshipman.'

'God bless my soul!' gasped Clay, laying down his knife and fork. He had never thought for a moment that this stern and inflexible captain of his had once been a rat-eating midshipman.

The two boys blinked at their captain with admiration. This little human touch had won their hearts completely, as Hornblower had known it would. At the end of the table Galbraith sighed audibly. He had been eating rats himself only three days ago, but he knew full well that to admit it would not increase the boys' respect for him, but would rather diminish it, for he was that sort of officer. Hornblower had to make Galbraith feel at home, too.

'A glass of wine with you, Mr Galbraith,' he said, raising his glass. 'I must apologise because this is not my best Madeira, but I am keeping the last two bottles for when I entertain the Spanish captain as our prisoner tomorrow. To our victories of the future!'

The glasses were drained, and constraint dwindled. Hornblower had spoken of '*our* prisoner' when most captains would have said '*my* prisoner'. And he had said '*our* victories'. The strict cold captain, the stern disciplinarian, had for a moment revealed human characteristics and had admitted his inferiors to his fellowship. Any one of the three junior officers would at that moment have laid down his life for his captain – and Hornblower, looking round at their flushed faces, was aware of it. It gratified him at the same moment as it irritated him; but with a battle in the immediate future which might well be an affair of the utmost desperation, he knew that he must have behind him a crew not merely loyal but enthusiastic.

Another midshipman, young Knyvett, came into the cabin.

'Mr Bush's compliments, sir, and the enemy is hull up from the masthead now, sir.'

'Is she holding her course for the bay?'

'Yes, sir. Mr Bush says two hours ought to see her within range.'

'Thank you, Mr Knyvett,' said Hornblower, dismissing him. The reminder that in two hours he would be at grips with a fifty-gun ship set his heart beating faster again. It took a convulsive effort to maintain an unmoved countenance.

'We still have ample time for our rubber, gentlemen,' said Hornblower.

The weekly evening of whist which Captain Hornblower played with his officers was for these latter – especially the midshipmen – a sore trial. Hornblower himself was a keen good player; his close observation and his acute study of the psychology of his juniors were of great help to him. But to some of his officers, without card sense, and floundering helplessly with no memory for the cards that had been played, Hornblower's card evenings were periods of torment.

Polwheal cleared the table, spread the green tablecloth and brought the cards. When play began Hornblower found it easier to forget about the approaching battle. Whist was enough of a passion with him to claim most of his attention whatever the distraction. It was only during the intervals of play, during the deals and while making the score, that he found his heart beating faster again and felt the blood surging up in his throat. He marked the fall of the cards with close attention, making allowances for Savage's schoolboy tendency to dash out his aces, and for the fact that Galbraith invariably forgot, until it was too late, to signal a short suit. One rubber ended quickly; there was almost dismay on the faces of the other three as Hornblower proffered the cards for cutting for a second one. He kept his face expressionless.

'You really must remember, Clay,' he said 'to lead the king from a sequence of king, queen, knave. The whole art of leading is based upon that principle.'

'Aye aye, sir,' said Clay, rolling his eyes drolly at Savage, but Hornblower looked up sharply and Clay hurriedly composed his expression. Play continued – and to all of them seemed interminable. It came to an end at last, however.

'Rubber,' announced Hornblower, marking up the score. 'I think, gentlemen, that it is almost time that we went on deck.'

There was a general sigh of relief and a scraping of feet on the deck. But at all costs Hornblower felt that he must consolidate his reputation for imperturbability.

'The rubber would not be over,' he said dryly 'if Mr Savage had paid attention to the score. It being nine, Mr Savage and Mr

Galbraith had only to win the odd trick to secure the rubber. Hence Mr Savage, at the eighth trick, should have played his ace of hearts instead of risking the finesse. I grant that if the finesse had been successful he would have won two more tricks, but—'

Hornblower droned on, while the other three writhed in their chairs. Yet they glanced at each other with admiration for him in their eyes as he preceded them up the companion ladder.

Up on deck, everything was deathly still as the crew lay at their posts. The moon was setting fast, but there was ample light still as soon as the eye grew accustomed to it. Bush touched his hat to the captain.

'The enemy is still heading for the bay, sir,' he said hoarsely.

'Send the crews into the launch and cutter again,' replied Hornblower. He climbed the mizzen rigging to the mizzen topgallant yard. From here, he could just see over the island; a mile away, with the setting moon behind her, he could see the white canvas of the *Natividad* as she stood in, close hauled, across the entrance. He struggled with his agitation as he endeavoured to predict her movements. There was small chance of her noticing, against the dark sky, the topgallant masts of the *Lydia*, and it was on the assumption that she would not that all his plans were based. She must go about soon, and her new course would bring her directly to the island. Perhaps she would weather it, but not likely. She would have to go about again to enter the bay, and that would be his opportunity. As he watched, he saw her canvas gleam brighter for a space and then darken again as she came round. She was heading for the middle of the entrance, but her leeway and the beginning of the ebb tide would carry her back to the island. He went down again to the deck.

'Mr Bush,' he said, 'send the hands aloft ready to set sail.'

The ship was filled with gentle noises as bare feet padded over the deck and up the rigging. Hornblower brought the silver whistle out of his pocket. He did not trouble to ask whether everyone was ready for the signal and properly instructed in the part he had to play; Bush and Gerard were efficient officers.

'I am going for'ard, now, Mr Bush,' he said. 'I shall try and get back to the quarterdeck in time, but you know my orders if I do not.'

'Aye aye, sir.'

Hornblower hurried forward along the gangway, past the forecastle carronades with their crews crouching round them, and swung himself over on to the bowsprit. From the sprit sail yard he could see round the corner of the island; the *Natividad* was heading straight for him. He could see the glimmer of phosphorescent foam about her cutwater. He could almost hear the sound of her passage through the water. He swallowed hard, and then all his excitement vanished and he was left deadly cool. He had forgotten about himself, and his mind was making calculations of time and space like a machine. Now he could hear the voice of a man at the lead on board the *Natividad*, although he could distinguish no word. The Spaniard was coming very close. By now he could hear the babble of the Spanish crew, everyone busy talking like every Spaniard, and no one looking out sufficiently well to catch sight of the *Lydia*'s bare spars. Then he heard orders being shouted from the *Natividad*'s deck; she was going about. At the very first sound he put the whistle to his lips and blew, and the whole of the *Lydia* sprang into activity. Sail was loosed from every yard simultaneously. The cable was slipped, the boats were cast off. Hornblower, racing aft again, collided with the hands at the braces as the ship paid off. He picked himself off the deck and ran on, while the *Lydia* gathered way and surged forward. He reached the wheel in time.

'Steady!' he called to the quartermaster. 'Port a little! A little more! Now, hard-a-starboard!'

So quickly had it all happened that the Spaniard had only just gone about and had gathered no way on her new course when the *Lydia* came leaping upon her out of the blackness behind the island and rasped alongside. Months of drill bore their fruit in the English ship. The guns crashed out in a single shattering broadside as the ships touched, sweeping the deck of the *Natividad* with grape. Overhead the topmen ran out along the yards and lashed the ships together. On deck the cheering boarders came rushing to the portside gangway.

On board the Spaniard there was utter surprise. One moment all hands had been engrossed with the work of the ship, and the next, seemingly, an unknown enemy had come crashing alongside; the night had been torn to shreds with the flare of hostile guns; on every hand men had been struck down by the hurtling shot, and now an armed host, yelling like fiends from the pit, came pouring on to the deck. Not the most disciplined and experienced crew could have withstood the shock of that surprise. During the twenty years the *Natividad* had sailed the Pacific coast no enemy had been nearer to her than four thousand miles of sea.

Yet even then there were some stout hearts who attempted resistance. These were officers who drew their swords; on the high quarterdeck there was an armed detachment who had been served out with weapons in consequence of the rumours of rebellion on shore; there were a few men who grasped capstan bars and belaying pins; but the upper deck was swept clear immediately by the wave of boarders with their pikes and cutlasses. A single pistol flashed and exploded. The Spaniards who offered resistance were struck down or chased below; the others were herded together under guard.

And on the lower deck the men sought blindly round for leaders, for means of resistance. They were gathering together in the darkness ready to oppose the enemy above them, and to defend the hatchways, when suddenly a new yelling burst out behind them. Gerard's two boats' crews had reached the *Natividad*'s port side, and prising open the lower deck ports, came swarming in, yelling like fiends as their orders bid them do – Hornblower had foreseen that the moral effect of a surprise attack would be intensified, especially against undisciplined Spaniards, if the attackers made as much noise as possible. At this new surprise the resistance of the lower deck broke down completely, and Hornblower's prescience in detaching the two boats' crews to make this diversion was justified.

CHAPTER VII

The Captain of the *Lydia* was taking his usual morning walk on the quarterdeck of his ship. Half a dozen Spanish officers had attempted, on his first appearance, to greet him with formal courtesy, but they had been hustled away by the *Lydia*'s crew, indignant that their captain's walk, sacrosanct after so many months, should be disturbed by mere prisoners.

The captain had a good deal to think about, too – so much, in fact, that he could spare no time to rejoice in the knowledge that his frigate last night, in capturing a two-decker without losing a man, had accomplished a feat without precedent in the long annals of British naval history. He wanted instead to think about his next move. With the capture of the *Natividad* he was lord of the South Sea. He knew well enough that the communications by land were so difficult that the whole trade – the whole life, it might be said – of the country depended upon the coastwise traffic; and now not a boat could move without his licence. In fifteen years of warfare he had learned the lessons of sea power. There was at least a chance now that with Alvarado's aid he might set the whole of Central America into such a flame that the Spanish Government would rue the day when they had decided to throw in their lot with Bonaparte.

Hornblower paced up and down the sanded deck. There were other possibilities, too. North-westward along the coast lay Acapulco, whither came and whence departed yearly galleons bearing a million sterling in treasure. The capture of a galleon would at a stroke make him a wealthy man – he could buy an estate in England then; could buy a whole village and be a squire, with the country folk touching their hats to him as he drove by in his coach. Maria would like that, although he could not imagine Maria playing the part of a great lady with any grace.

Hornblower tore his mind away from the contemplation of Maria snatched from her Southsea lodgings and settled in a country home. To the east was Panama, with its stored silver from Peru, its pearling fleet, its whitewashed golden altar which had escaped Morgan but would not escape him. A blow there, at the central knot of the transcontinental communications, would be the best strategy perhaps, as well as being potentially profitable. He tried to think about Panama.

Forward Sullivan, the red-haired Irish vagabond, was perched on a carronade slide with his fiddle, and round him a dozen sailors, their horny feet flapping on the deck, were setting to partners. Twenty-five guineas apiece, at least, the men would get as prize money for the capture of *Natividad*, and they were already spending it in imagination. He looked across to where the *Natividad* swung at anchor. Her waist was black with her crew, crammed on her upper deck. On her old-fashioned poop and quarterdeck he could see the red coats and shakoes of his marines, and he could see, too, the carronades pointing down into the waist and the men posted beside them with lighted matches. Gerard, whom he had left on board as prizemaster, had served in a Liverpool slaver in his day and knew well how to keep a ship full of hostile humanity in subjection – although, parted from their officers, Hornblower for one did not anticipate trouble from the crew.

Hornblower knew that he must make up his mind about what to do with the *Natividad*, and more especially with his prisoners. He could not hand them over to the tender mercies of el Supremo; his own crew would hardly permit that. He tried to think about the problem. A long line of pelicans came flying by, more rigid in their formation than the Channel fleet at drill. A frigate bird, superb with its forked tail, came wheeling above them with motionless wings, and having obviously decided that they were not worth plundering, swooped away again towards the island where the cormorants were fishing industriously. The sun was already hot and the water of the bay was as blue as the sky above.

Hornblower cursed sun and pelicans and frigate birds as he tried to concentrate on the problems before him. He paced moodily up and down the deck another half dozen times. Then Midshipman Knyvett barred his way, touching his hat.

'What the devil is it now?' snapped Hornblower.

'Boat coming alongside, sir. Mr – Mr Hernandez on board.'

That was only to be expected.

'Very good,' said Hornblower, and went down the gangway to greet Hernandez as he came up the side. Hernandez wasted no time on felicitations for the late victory. In the service of el Supremo apparently even Spanish-Americans grew abrupt and businesslike.

'El Supremo wishes to see you at once, Captain,' said Hernandez. 'My boat is waiting.'

'Indeed,' said Hornblower. He knew well that dozens of his brother captains in the British service would be infuriated at such a cavalier message. He toyed with the idea of sending back to tell el Supremo to come out to the ship himself if he wanted to interview her captain. But he knew that it would be foolish to imperil his cordial relations with the shore, upon which so much of his success depended, upon a mere question of dignity. The captain of the *Natividad* could afford to overlook the presumption of others.

A compromise suggested itself to him; he could keep Hernandez waiting for an hour or two so as to bolster up his own dignity. But his commonsense rejected the notion. Hornblower hated compromises, and this one would only (like most compromises) irritate one side and do no good to the other. Far better to put his pride in his pocket and to come at once.

'Certainly,' he said. 'My duties leave me free at the moment.'

But this time, at least there was no need to dress up for the occasion. There was no call to put on his best silk stockings and his buckled shoes. The capture of the *Natividad* was a clearer proof of his *bona fides* than any gold-hilted sword.

It was only while giving final orders to Bush that Hornblower remembered that last night's success gave him adequate grounds

for not flogging the erring Jenkins and Poole, and for not repri-
manding Galbraith. That was an enormous relief, anyway. It
helped to clear away the clouds of depression which always
tended to settle on him after every success. It cheered him up as
he mounted the minute horse which awaited him on shore, and
rode past the mountain of stinking animal intestines, and along
the avenue of dead men, up to el Supremo's house.

The appearance of el Supremo, sitting in his canopied chair
on his dais, seemed for all the world to indicate that he had been
sitting there, immobile, since the occasion four days ago (it
seemed more like a month) when Hornblower had left him.

'So you have already done what I wished you to do, Captain?'
were his opening words.

'I captured the *Natividad* last night,' said Hornblower.

'And the provisioning of your ship is, I understand, complete?'

'Yes.'

'Then,' said el Supremo, 'you have done what I wanted. That
is what I said before.'

In the face of such sublime self-assurance there was no point
in arguing.

'This afternoon,' said el Supremo, 'I shall proceed with my
plan for the capture of the city of El Salvador and the man who
calls himself Captain General of Nicaragua.'

'Yes?' said Hornblower.

'There are fewer difficulties before me now, Captain. You may
not be aware that the roads between here and El Salvador are
not as good as roads might be. At one place the path goes up
one hundred and twenty-seven steps cut in the lava between two
precipices. It is difficult for a mule, to say nothing of a horse, to
make the journey, and an evilly disposed person armed with a
musket could cause much trouble.'

'I expect he could,' said Hornblower.

'However,' said el Supremo, 'El Salvador lies less than ten
miles from the sea, and there is a good road from the city to its
port of La Libertad. This afternoon I shall sail with five hundred

men in the two ships to La Libertad. As this town is no more
than a hundred miles away I shall reach there at dawn tomorrow.
Tomorrow evening I shall dine in El Salvador.'

'Ho – h'm,' said Hornblower. He was wondering how best to
present in argument the difficulties he could see ahead.

'You killed very few of the crew of the *Natividad*, Captain?'
asked el Supremo, and thereby approaching directly some of the
difficulties Hornblower had in mind.

'Eleven killed,' said Hornblower. 'And eighteen wounded, of
whom four seem unlikely to recover.'

'So you left enough to work the ship?'

'Ample, señor, if — '

'That is what I wanted. And, Captain, human beings in
addressing me do not use the expression 'senor'. That is insuf-
ficiently honorific. I am el Supremo.'

Hornblower could only bow in reply. El Supremo's marvellous
manner was like a stone wall.

'The navigating officers are still alive?' went on el Supremo.

'Yes,' said Hornblower; and, because he could see trouble
close ahead and was anxious to keep it to a minimum, he added,
with a gulp, 'Supremo.'

'Then,' said el Supremo, 'I will take the *Natividad* into my
service. I will kill the executive officers and replace them with men
of my own. The others and the common sailors will serve me.'

There was nothing intrinsically impossible in what el Supremo
suggested; Hornblower knew from experience that the Spanish
navy, old fashioned as always, maintained a rigid distinction
(such as was fast dying out in our own service) between the
officers who worked the ship and the gentlemen who commanded
it. And Hornblower had no doubt whatever as to what choice the
seamen and sailing master would make if asked to choose between
death by torture and serving el Supremo.

Nor could it be denied that el Supremo's suggestion was in
many ways a good one; to transport five hundred men in the
Lydia alone would be difficult, to say the least, while the *Lydia*

by herself would find it impossible to blockade completely all
the thousand miles of coast – two ships would cause far more
than twice as much trouble to the enemy in that way. Yet to hand
over the *Natividad* meant starting an endless and probably unsuccessful argument with the lords of the Admiralty on the question
of prize money. And he could not in honour hand over the Spanish
officers to the death el Supremo had in mind for them. He had
to think quickly.

'The *Natividad* is the prize of my King,' he said. 'Perhaps he
would not be pleased if I let her go.'

'He certainly would be displeased if he knew you had offended
me,' said el Supremo. His eyebrows came closer together, and
Hornblower heard Hernandez beside him take a quick breath. 'I
have noticed before, Captain Hornblower, that you have verged
upon disrespect towards me, and I have been mild enough to
attribute it to your foreign breeding.'

Hornblower was still thinking hurriedly. A little more oppo-
sition would cause this madman to order him out for execution,
and if her captain were killed the *Lydia* would certainly not fight
for el Supremo. There would indeed be a complicated situation
in the Pacific, and the *Lydia*, with friends neither among the
rebels nor among the government, would probably never reach
home again – especially with the unimaginative Bush in command.
England would lose a fine frigate and a fine opportunity. He must
sacrifice his prize money, the thousand pounds or so with which
he had wanted to dazzle Maria's eyes. But at all costs he must
keep his prisoners alive.

'I am sure it is my foreign breeding which is to blame,
Supremo,' he said. 'It is difficult for me to express in a foreign
tongue all the delicate shades of meaning which it is necessary
to convey. How could it possibly be imagined that I could be
lacking in respect to el Supremo?'

El Supremo nodded. It was satisfactory to see that a madman
who attributed almightiness to himself was naturally inclined to
accept the grossest flattery at its face value.

'The ship is yours, Supremo,' went on Hornblower, 'she has been yours since my men first set foot on her deck last night. And when in the future a vast Armada sails the Pacific under el Supremo's direction I only wish it to be remembered that the first ship of that fleet was taken from the Spaniards by Captain Hornblower at el Supremo's orders.'

El Supremo nodded again, and then turned to Hernandez.

'General,' he said, 'make arrangements for five hundred men to go on board the ships at noon. I will sail with them and so will you.'

Hernandez bowed and departed; it was easy to see that there was no chance of el Supremo doubting his own divinity as a result of disrespect or hesitation on the part of his subordinates. His lightest order, whether it dealt with a thousand pigs or five hundred men, was obeyed instantly. Hornblower made his next move at once.

'Is the *Lydia*,' he asked, 'to have the honour of carrying el Supremo to La Libertad? My crew would greatly appreciate the distinction.'

'I am sure they would,' said el Supremo.

'I hardly venture to ask it,' said Hornblower, 'but could my officers and I aspire to the honour of your dining with us before our departure?'

El Supremo considered for a moment.

'Yes,' he said, and Hornblower had to suppress the sigh of relief he was on the point of drawing. Once el Supremo was on board the *Lydia* it might be possible to deal with him with less difficulty.

El Supremo clapped his hands, and instantly, as though by clockwork, a knocking at the brass-studded door heralded the arrival of the swarthy major-domo. He received in a single sentence orders for the transfer of el Supremo's household to the *Lydia*.

'Perhaps,' said Hornblower, 'you will permit me to return to my ship now to make arrangements for your reception, Supremo.' He received another nod in reply.

'At what time shall I be at the beach to receive you?'

'At eleven.'

Hornblower, as he came out into the patio, thought with sympathy of the Oriental vizier who never came out of the royal presence without feeling to see if his head were still on his shoulders. And on the *Lydia*'s deck, the moment the twittering of the pipes had died away, Hornblower was giving his orders.

'Have those men taken below at once,' he said to Bush, pointing to the Spanish prisoners. 'Put them in the cable tier under guard. Call the armourer and have them put in irons.'

Bush made no attempt to conceal his surprise, but Hornblower wasted no time on explanations to him.

'Señores,' he said, as the officers came by him. 'You are going to be harshly treated. But believe me, if you are as much as seen during the next few days you will be killed. I am saving your lives for you.'

Next Hornblower turned back to his first lieutenant.

'Call all hands, Mr Bush.'

The ship was filled with the sound of horny feet pattering over pine boards.

'Men!' said Hornblower. 'There is coming aboard today a prince of this country who is in alliance with our own gracious King. Whatever happens – mark my words, *whatever happens* – he is to be treated with respect. I will flog the man who laughs, or the man who does not behave towards Senor el Supremo as he would to me. And we shall be sailing tonight with this gentleman's troops on board. You will look after them as if they were Englishmen. And better than that. You would play tricks on English soldiers. The first man to play a trick on any of these men I shall flog within the hour. Forget their colour. Forget their clothes. Forget that they cannot speak English, and remember only what I say to you. You can pipe down now, Mr Bush.'

Down in the cabin Polwheal was waiting faithfully with the dressing gown and towel for his captain's bath, which ought according to timetable have been taken two hours back.

'Put out my best uniform again,' snapped Hornblower. 'And I want the after cabin ready for a state dinner for eight at six bells. Go for'ard and bring my cook to me.'

There was plenty to do. Bush and Rayner the first and fourth lieutenants, and Simmonds the marine officer, and Crystal the master, had to be invited to the dinner and warned to be ready in full dress. Plans had to be made for the accommodation of five hundred men on board the two frigates.

Hornblower was just looking across to the *Natividad*, where she swung with her white ensign over the red and gold of Spain, wondering what steps he should take with regard to her, when a boat came running gaily out to him from the shore. The leader of the party which came on board was a youngish man of less than middle height, slight of figure and lithe as a monkey, with a mobile smile and an expression of indefeatable good humour. He looked more Spanish than American. Bush brought him up to where Hornblower impatiently trod his quarterdeck. Making a cordial bow, the newcomer introduced himself.

'I am Vice-Admiral Don Cristobal de Crespo,' he said. Hornblower could not help but look him up and down. The Vice-Admiral wore gold earrings, and his gold-embroidered coat did not conceal the raggedness of the grey shirt beneath. At least he wore boots, of soft brown leather, into which were tucked his patched white trousers.

'Of el Supremo's service?' asked Hornblower.

'Of course. May I introduce my officers. Ship-captain Andrade. Frigate-captain Castro. Corvette-captain Carrera. Lieutenants Barrios and Barillas and Cerno. Aspirants Diaz—'

The dozen officers introduced under these resounding titles were barefooted Indians, the red sashes round their waists stuck full of pistols and knives. They bowed awkwardly to Hornblower; one or two of them wore expressions of brutish cruelty.

'I have come,' said Crespo, amiably, 'to hoist my flag in my new ship *Natividad*. It is el Supremo's wish that you should salute it with the eleven guns due to a vice-admiral.'

Hornblower's jaw dropped a little at that. His years of service had grained into him despite himself a deep respect for the details of naval pageantry, and he was irked by the prospect of giving this ragged-shirted rascal as many guns as Nelson ever had. With an effort he swallowed his resentment. He knew he had to go through with the farce to the bitter end if he was to glean any success. With an empire at stake it would be foolish to strain at points of ceremony.

'Certainly, Admiral,' he said. 'It gives me great happiness to be one of the first to congratulate you upon your appointment.'

'Thank you, Captain. There will be one or two details to attend to first,' said the vice-admiral. 'May I ask if the executive officers of the *Natividad* are on board here or are still in the *Natividad*?'

'I greatly regret,' said Hornblower, 'that I dropped them overboard this morning after courtmartial.'

'That is indeed a pity,' said Crespo. 'I have el Supremo's orders to hang them at the *Natividad*'s yardarms. You did not leave even one?'

'No one, Admiral. I am sorry that I received no orders from el Supremo on the subject.'

'There is no help for it, then. Doubtless there will be others. I will go on board my ship, then. Perhaps you will be good enough to accompany me so as to give orders to your prize crew?'

'Certainly, Admiral.'

Hornblower was curious to see how el Supremo's subordinates would deal with the problem of changing the allegiance of a whole ship's crew. He gave hurried orders to the gunner for the saluting of the flag when it should be hoisted in the *Natividad*, and went down into the boat with the new officers.

On board the *Natividad* Crespo swaggered on to the quarter-deck. The Spanish sailing master and his mates were grouped there, and under their startled eyes he walked up to the image of the Virgin and Child beside the taffrail and tossed it overboard. At a sign from him one of the aspirants hauled down the Spanish and British ensigns from the peak. Then he turned upon the navigating officers. It was a dramatic scene on that crowded quarterdeck in the brilliant sunshine. The British marines stood in rigid line in their red coats, with ordered arms. The British seamen stood by their carronades, matches smouldering, for no orders had yet relieved them of their duty. Gerard came over and stood beside Hornblower.

'Which is the sailing master?' demanded Crespo.

'I am,' quavered one of the Spaniards.

'Are you his mates?' rasped Crespo, and received frightened nods in reply.

All trace of humour had disappeared from Crespo's expression. He seemed to expand and dilate with cold anger.

'You,' he said, pointing at the youngest. 'You will now hold up your hand and declare your faith in our lord el Supremo. Hold up your hand.'

The boy obeyed as if in a trance.

'Now repeat after me. "I swear—"'

The boy's face was white. He tried to look round at his superior officer, but his gaze was held by Crespo's glaring eyes.

'"I swear,"' said Crespo, more menacingly. The boy's mouth opened and shut without a sound. Then convulsively he freed himself from the hypnotic stare. His hand wavered and came down, and he looked away from Crespo's pointing right forefinger. Instantly Crespo's left hand shot out; so quick was the motion that no one could see until afterwards that it held a pistol from his sash. The shot rang out, and the boy, with a pistol ball in his stomach, fell to the deck writhing in agony. Crespo disregarded his convulsions and turned to the next man.

'*You* will now swear,' he said.

He swore at once, repeating Crespo's words in quavering tones. The half-dozen sentences were very much to the point; they declared the omnipotence of el Supremo, testified to the speaker's faith, and in a single sweeping blasphemy denied the existence of God and the virginity of the Mother of God. The others followed his example, repeating the words of the oath one after the other, while no one paid any attention to the dying boy at their feet. Crespo only condescended to notice him after the conclusion of the ceremony.

'Throw that overboard,' he said curtly. The officers only hesitated a moment under his gaze, and then one stooped and lifted the boy by his shoulders, another by his feet, and they flung the still-living body over the rail.

Crespo waited for the splash, and then walked forward to the quarterdeck rail with its peeling gilt. The herded crew in the waist listened dumbly to his uplifted voice. Hornblower, gazing down at them, saw that there would be small resistance to Crespo's missionary efforts. To a man the crew were of non-European blood; presumably during the many years of the *Natividad*'s commission in the Pacific the original European crew had quite died out. Only officers had been replaced from Spain; fresh hands had been recruited from the native races. There were Chinese among them, as Hornblower recognised, and negroes, and some whose physiognomy was unfamiliar to him – Filipinos.

In five minutes of brilliant speaking Crespo had won them all over. He made no more attempt to enunciate the divinity of el Supremo than was involved in the mention of his name. El Supremo, he said, was at the head of a movement which was sweeping the Spaniards from the dominion of America. Within the year the whole of the New World from Mexico to Peru would be at his feet. There would be an end of Spanish misrule, or brutal domination, of slavery in mine and field. There would be land for the asking for everybody, freedom and happiness under the benign supervision of el Supremo. Who would follow him?

They all would seemingly. Crespo had them all cheering wildly at the end of his speech. Crespo came back to Hornblower.

'Thank you, Captain,' he said. 'I think there is no more need for the presence of your prize crew. My officers and I will be able to attend to any insubordination which may arise later.'

'I think you will be quite able to,' said Hornblower, a little bitterly.

'Some of them may not easily be enlightened when the time comes for that,' said Crespo, grinning.

Pulling back to the *Lydia*, Hornblower thought bitterly about the murder of the Spanish master's mate. It was a crime which he ought to have prevented – he had gone on board the *Natividad* expressly to prevent cruelty and he had failed. Yet he realised that that kind of cruelty would not have the bad effect on his own men that a cold-blooded hanging of the officers would have done. The crew of the *Natividad was* being forced to serve a new master against *their* will – but the press gang had done the same for three-quarters of the crew of the *Lydia*. Flogging and death were the punishments meted out to Englishmen who refused to obey the orders of officers who had arbitrarily assumed command over them – English sailors were not likely to fret unduly over Dagoes in the same position, even though with English lower-class lack of logic they would have been moved to protest against a formal hanging of officers.

His train of thought was suddenly interrupted by the sound of a gun from the *Natividad*, instantly answered by another from the *Lydia*. He almost sprang to his feet in the sternsheets of the launch, but a glance over his shoulder reassured him. A new flag was now flying from the *Natividad*'s peak. Blue with a yellow star in the middle, he saw. The sound of the saluting guns rolled slowly round the bay; the salute was still being fired as he went up the *Lydia*'s side. Mr Marsh, the gunner, was pacing up and down the foredeck mumbling to himself – Hornblower guessed at the jargon.

'If I hadn't been a born bloody fool I shouldn't be here. Fire *seven*. I've left my wife; I've left my home and everything that's dear. Fire *eight*.'

Half an hour later, Hornblower was at the beach to meet el Supremo, who came riding down, punctual to the minute, a ragged retinue of a dozen riding with him. El Supremo did not condescend to present his suite to the captain, but bowed and stepped straight into the launch; his suite introduced themselves, in a string of meaningless names, in turn as they came up to Hornblower. They were all nearly pure Indians; they were all Generals save for one or two Colonels, and they were all clearly most devotedly attached to their master. Their whole bearing, every little action of theirs, indicated not merely their fear of him but their admiration – their love, it might be said.

At the gangway, sideboys and boatswain's mates and marines were ready to receive el Supremo with distinguished military formality, but el Supremo astonished Hornblower as he was about to go up the ladder, with the casual words –

'The correct salute for me, Captain, is twenty-three guns.'

That was two more guns than His Majesty King George himself would receive. Hornblower stared for a moment, thought wildly of how he could refuse, and finally salved his conscience with the notion that a salute of that number of guns would be entirely meaningless. He sent a message hurriedly to Mr Marsh ordering twenty-three guns – it was odd, the way in which the ship's boy almost reduplicated Hornblower's reactions, by staring, composing his features, and hurrying off comforted by the thought that it was the Captain's reponsibility and not his own. And Hornblower could hardly repress a grin as he thought of Marsh's certain astonishment, and the boiling exasperation in his voice when he reached – 'If I hadn't been a born bloody fool I shouldn't be here. Fire *twenty-three*.'

El Supremo stepped on to the quarterdeck with a keen glance round him, and then, while Hornblower looked at him, the interest faded from his face and he lapsed into the condition of abstracted indifference in which Hornblower had seen him before. He seemed to listen, but he looked over the heads of Bush and Gerard and the others as Hornblower presented them. He shook his head without a word when Hornblower suggested that he might care to inspect the ship. There was a little awkward pause, which was broken by Bush addressing his captain.

'*Natividad* hoisting another flag to the main yardarm, sir. No it's not, it's—'

It was the body of a man, black against the blue sky, rising slowly, jerking and twisting as it rose. A moment later another body rose at the other end of the yard. All eyes instinctively turned towards el Supremo. He was still gazing away into the distance, his eyes focused on nothing, yet everyone knew he had seen. The English officers cast a hasty glance at their captain for guidance, and followed his lead in lapsing into an uncomfortable pose of having noticed nothing. Disciplinary measures in a ship of another nation could be no affair of theirs.

'Dinner will be served shortly, Supremo,' said Hornblower with a gulp. 'Would you care to come below?'

Still without a word, el Supremo walked over to the companion and led the way. Down below his lack of stature was made apparent by the fact that he could walk upright. As a matter of fact, his head just brushed the deck beams above him, but the nearness of the beams did nothing to make him stoop as he walked. Hornblower became conscious of a ridiculous feeling that el Supremo would never need to stoop, that the deck beams would raise themselves as he passed rather than commit the sacrilege of bumping his head – that was how el Supremo's quiet dignity of carriage affected him.

Polwheal and the stewards assisting him, in their best clothes, held aside the screens which still took the place of the discarded bulkheads, but at the entrance to the cabin el Supremo stopped for a moment and said the first words which had passed his lips since he came on board.

'I will dine alone here,' he said. 'Let the food be brought to me.' None of his suite saw anything in the least odd about his request Hornblower, watching their expressions, was quite sure that their unconcern was in no way assumed. El Supremo might have been merely blowing his noise for all the surprise they evinced.

It was all a horrible nuisance, of course. Hornblower and his other guests had to dine in makeshift fashion in the gunroom mess, and his one linen tablecloth and his one set of linen napkins, and the two last bottles of his old Madeira remained in the after cabin for el Supremo's use. Nor was the meal improved by the silence that prevailed most of the time; el Supremo's suite were not in the least talkative, and Hornblower was the only Englishman with conversational Spanish. Bush tried twice, valiantly, to make polite speeches to his neighbours, putting a terminal 'o' on the ends of his English words in the hope that so they might be transmuted into Spanish, but the blank stares of the men he addressed reduced him quickly to stammering inarticulation.

Dinner was hardly finished; everyone had hardly lighted the loose brown cigars which had been part of the stores handed over to the *Lydia* when a new messenger arrived from the shore and was brought in by the bewildered officer of the watch who could not understand his jabbering talk. The troops were ready to come on board. With relief Hornblower put away his napkin and went on deck, followed by the others.

The men whom the launch and the cutter, plying steadily between ship and shore, brought out, were typical Central American soldiers, barefooted and ragged, swarthy and lank-haired. Each man carried a bright new musket and a bulging cartridge pouch, but these were merely what Hornblower had brought for them; most of the men carried in their hands cotton bags presumably filled with provisions – some bore melons and bunches of bananas in addition. The crew herded them on to the main deck; they looked about them curiously and chattered volubly, but they were amenable enough, squatting in gossiping groups between the guns where the grinning crew pushed them. They sat on the planking and most of them incontinently began to eat; Hornblower suspected them to be half starved and to be devouring the rations which were expected to last them for several days.

When the last man was on board, Hornblower looked across to the *Natividad*; it appeared as if her share of the expeditionary force was already embarked. Suddenly the babble on the main deck died away completely, to be succeeded by a silence surprising in its intensity. Next moment el Supremo came on the quarterdeck – it must have been his appearance from the after cabin which had quelled the noise.

'We shall sail for La Libertad, Captain,' he said.

'Yes, Supremo,' replied Hornblower. He was glad that el Supremo had made his appearance when he did; a few seconds later and the ship's officers would have seen that their captain was awaiting his orders, and that would never have done.

'We will weigh anchor, Mr Bush,' said Hornblower.

CHAPTER VIII

The voyage up the coast was completed. La Libertad had fallen, and el Supremo and his men had vanished into the tangle of volcanoes surrounding the city of the Holy Saviour. Once again in the early morning Captain Hornblower was pacing the quarterdeck of His Britannic Majesty's thirty-six-gun frigate *Lydia*, and Lieutenant Bush, as officer of the watch, was standing by the wheel rigidly taking no notice of him.

Hornblower was gazing round him, and filling his lungs deep with air at every respiration as he walked. He noticed that he was doing this, and grinned to himself at the realisation that what he was doing was to savour the sweet air of liberty. For a space he was free from the nightmare influence of el Supremo and his cut-throat methods, and the feeling of relief was inexpressible. He was his own master again, free to walk his quarterdeck undisturbed. The sky was blue, the sea was blue and silver – Hornblower caught himself making the old comparison with heraldic argent and azure, and knew that he was himself again; he smiled once more out of sheer high spirits, looking out to sea, nevertheless, so that his subordinates should not see that their captain was walking the deck grinning like a Cheshire cat.

There was just the gentlest wind abeam pushing the *Lydia* along at three or four knots; peeping over the horizon on the port side were the tops of the interminable volcanoes which formed the backbone of his wild dream of conquering Central America; perhaps after all there might be some solid foundation in the hope that good communications might be opened across the Isthmus – by Panama if the Nicaraguan scheme proved impracticable. That would make a profound difference to the world. It would bring Van Diemen's Land and the Moluccas into closer relation to the civilised world. It would open the Pacific to England by evading the difficulties of the journey round the Horn or by the Cape of Good Hope and India, and in that case the Pacific might see squadrons of ships of the line cruising where hardly a frigate had penetrated up to that moment. The Spanish Empire of Mexico and California might acquire a new importance.

Hornblower told himself hastily that all this was only a wild dream at present. As a kind of punishment for dreaming he began to take himself to task regarding his present movements, and to subject himself to a severe examination regarding the motives which had brought him southwards towards Panama. He knew full well that the main one was to shake himself free from el Supremo, but he tried to justify his action in the face of his self-accusation.

If el Supremo's attempt upon San Salvador should fail, the *Natividad* would suffice to bring off what few might survive of his army. The presence of the *Lydia* could in no way influence the land operations. If el Supremo should succeed it might be as well that while he was conquering Nicaragua there should be a diversion in Panama to distract the Spaniards and to prevent them from concentrating their whole strength upon him. It was only right that the *Lydia*'s crew should be given a chance of winning some prize money among the pearl fishers of the Gulf of Panama; that would compensate them for their probable loss of the prize money already gained – there would be no screwing money out of the Admiralty for the *Natividad*. The presence of the *Lydia* in the Gulf would hamper the transport of Spanish forces from Peru. Besides, the Admiralty would be glad of a survey of the Gulf and the Pearl Islands; Anson's charts were wanting in this respect. Yet for all these plausible arguments Hornblower knew quite well that why he had come this way was to get away from el Supremo.

A large flat ray, the size of a table top, suddenly leaped clear of the water close overside and fell flat upon the surface again with a loud smack, leaped clear again, and then vanished below, its pinky brown gleaming wet for a moment as the blue water closed over it. There were flying fish skimming the water in all directions, each leaving behind it a momentary dark furrow. Hornblower watched it all, carefree, delighted that he could allow his thoughts to wander and not feel constrained to keep them concentrated on a single subject. With a ship full of stores and a crew contented by their recent adventures he had no real care in the world. The Spanish prisoners whose lives he had saved from el Supremo were sunning themselves lazily on the forecastle.

'Sail ho!' came echoing down from the masthead.

The idlers thronged the bulwark, gazing over the hammock nettings; the seamen holystoning the deck surreptitiously worked more slowly in order to hear what was going on.

'Where away?' called Hornblower.

'On the port bow, sir. Lugger, sir, I think, an' standing straight for us, but she's right in the eye of the sun—'

'Yes, a lugger, sir,' squeaked midshipman Hooker from the fore topgallant masthead. 'Two masted. She's right to windward, running down to us, under all sail, sir.'

'Running down to us?' said Hornblower, mystified. He jumped up on the slide of the quarterdeck carronade nearest him, and stared into the sun and the wind under his hand, but at present there was still nothing to be seen from that low altitude.

'She's still holding her course, sir,' squeaked Hooker.

'Mr Bush,' said Hornblower. 'Back the mizzen tops'l.'

A pearling lugger from the Gulf of Panama, perhaps, and still ignorant of the presence of a British frigate in those waters; on the other hand she might be bearing a message from el Supremo – her course made that unlikely, but that might be explained. Then as the ship lifted, Hornblower saw a gleaming square of white rise for a second over the distant horizon and vanish again. As the minutes passed by the sails were more and more frequently to be seen, until at last from the deck the lugger was in plain view, nearly hull up, running goose-winged before the wind with her bow pointed straight at the *Lydia*.

'She's flying Spanish colours at the main, sir,' said Bush from behind his levelled telescope. Hornblower had suspected so for some time back, but had not been able to trust his eyesight.

'She's hauling 'em down, all the same,' he retorted, glad to be the first to notice it.

'So she is, sir,' said Bush, a little puzzled, and then – 'There they go again, sir. No! What do you make of that, sir?'

'White flag over Spanish colours now,' said Hornblower. 'That'll mean a parley. No, I don't trust 'em. Hoist the colours, Mr Bush, and send the hands to quarters. Run out the guns and send the prisoners below under guard again.'

He was not going to be caught unaware by any Spanish tricks. That lugger might be as full of men as an egg is of meat, and might spew up a host of boarders over the side of an unprepared ship. As the *Lydia*'s gun ports opened and she showed her teeth the lugger rounded-to just out of gunshot, and lay wallowing, hove-to.

'She's sending a boat, sir,' said Bush.

'So I see,' snapped Hornblower.

Two oars rowed a dinghy jerkily across the dancing water, and a man came scrambling up the ladder to the gangway – so many strange figures had mounted that ladder lately. This new arrival, Hornblower saw, wore the full dress of the Spanish royal navy, his epaulettes gleaming in the sun. He bowed and came forward.

'Captain Hornblower?' he asked.

'I am Captain Hornblower.'

'I have to welcome you as the new ally of Spain.'

Hornblower swallowed hard. This might be a ruse, but the moment he heard the words he felt instinctively that the man was speaking the truth. The whole happy world by which he had been encompassed up to that moment suddenly became dark with trouble. He could foresee endless worries piled upon him by some heedless action of the politicians.

'We have had the news for the last four days,' went on the Spanish officer. 'Last month Bonaparte stole our King Ferdinand from us and has named his brother Joseph King of Spain. The Junta of Government has signed a treaty of perpetual alliance and friendship with His Majesty of England. It is with great pleasure. Captain, that I have to inform you that all ports in the dominions of His Most Catholic Majesty are open to you after your most arduous voyage.'

Hornblower still stood dumb. It might all be lies, a ruse to lure the *Lydia* under the guns of Spanish shore batteries. Hornblower almost hoped it might be – better that than all the complications which would hem him in if it were the truth. The Spaniard interpreted his expression as implying disbelief.

'I have letters here,' he said, producing them from his breast. 'One from your admiral in the Leeward Islands, sent overland from Porto Bello, one from His Excellency the Viceroy of Peru, and one from the English lady in Panama.'

He tendered them with a further bow, and Hornblower, muttering an apology – his fluent Spanish had deserted him along with his wits – began to open them. Then he pulled himself up; on deck under the eye of the Spanish officer was no place to study these documents. With another muttered apology he fled below to the privacy of his cabin.

The stout canvas wrapper of the naval orders was genuine enough. He scrutinised the two seals carefully, and they showed no signs of having been tampered with; and the wrapper was correctly addressed in English script. He cut the wrapper open carefully and read the orders enclosed. They could leave him in no doubt. There was the signature – Thomas Troubridge, Rear Admiral, Bart. Hornblower had seen Troubridge's signature before, and recognised it. The orders were brief, as one would expect from Troubridge – an alliance having been concluded between His Majesty's Government and that of Spain, Captain Hornblower was directed and required to refrain from hostilities towards the Spanish possessions, and, having drawn upon the Spanish authorities for necessary stores, to proceed with all dispatch to England for further orders. It was a genuine document without any doubts at all. It was marked 'Copy No. 2'; presumably other copies had been distributed to other parts of the Spanish possessions to ensure that he received one.

The next letter was flamboyantly sealed and addressed – it was a letter of welcome from the Viceroy of Peru assuring him that all Spanish America was at his disposal, and hoping that he would make full use of all facilities so that he would speedily be ready to help the Spanish nation in its sacred mission of sweeping the French usurper back to his kennel.

'Ha – h'm,' said Hornblower – the Spanish viceroy did not know yet about the fate of the *Natividad*, nor about the new enterprise of el Supremo. He might not be so cordial when he heard about the *Lydia*'s part in these occurrences.

The third letter was sealed merely with a wafer and was addressed in a feminine hand. The Spanish officer had spoken about a letter from the English lady in Panama – what in the world was an English lady doing there? Hornblower slit open the letter and read it.

> The Citadel,
> Panama.
> Lady Barbara Wellesley presents her compliments to the captain of the English frigate. She requests that he will be so good as to convey her and her maid to Europe, because Lady Barbara finds that owing to an outbreak of yellow fever on the Spanish Main she cannot return home the way she would desire.

Hornblower folded the letter and tapped it on his thumbnail in meditation. The woman was asking an impossibility, of course. A crowded frigate sailing round the Horn was no place for females. She seemed to have no doubt about it, all the same; on the contrary, she seemed to assume that her request would be instantly granted. That name Wellesley, of course, gave the clue to that. It had been much before the public of late. Presumably the lady was a sister or an aunt to the two well-known Wellesleys – the Most Hon. the Marquis Wellesley, K.P., late Governor-General of India and now a member of the Cabinet, and General the Hon. Sir Arthur Wellesley, K.B., the victor of Assaye and now pointed at as England's greatest soldier after Sir John Moore. Hornblower had seen him once, and had noticed the high-arched arrogant nose and the imperious eye. If the woman had that blood in her she would be the sort to take things for granted. So she might, too. An impecunious frigate captain with no influence at all would be glad to render a service to a member of that family. Maria would be pleased as well as suspicious when she heard that he had been in correspondence with the daughter of an Earl, the sister of a Marquis.

But this was no time to stop and think about women. Hornblower locked the letters in his desk and ran up on deck; forcing a smile as he approached the Spanish captain.

'Greeting to the new allies,' he said. 'Señor, I am proud to be serving with Spain against the Corsican tyrant.'

The Spaniard bowed.

'We were very much afraid, Captain,' he said, 'lest you should fall in with the *Natividad* before you heard the news, because she has not heard it either. In that case your fine frigate would have come to serious harm.'

'Ha – h'm,' said Hornblower. This was more embarrassing than ever; he turned and snapped out an order to the midshipman of the watch. 'Bring the prisoners up from the cable tier. Quickly!'

The boy ran, and Hornblower turned back again to the Spanish officer.

'I regret to have to tell you, señor, that by evil chance the *Lydia* met the *Natividad* a week ago.'

The Spanish captain looked his surprise. He stared round the ship, at the meticulous good order, the well-set-up rigging. Even a Spaniard frigate captain could see that the frigate had not been engaged in a desperate action lately.

'But you did not fight her, Captain?' he said. 'Perhaps—'

The words died away on his lips as he caught sight of a melancholy procession approaching them along the gangway. He recognised the captain and the lieutenants of the *Natividad*. Hornblower plunged feverishly into an explanation of their presence; but it was not easy to tell a Spanish captain that the *Lydia* had captured a Spanish ship of twice her force without receiving a shot or a casualty – it was harder still to go on and explain that the ship was now sailing under the flag of rebels who had determined to destroy the Spanish power in the new world. The Spaniard turned white with rage and injured pride. He turned upon the captain of the *Natividad* and received confirmation of Hornblower's story from that wretched man's lips; his shoulders were bowed with sorrow as he told the story which would lead inevitably to his courtmartial and his ruin.

Bit by bit the newcomer from the lugger heard the truth about recent events, about the capture of the *Natividad*, and the success of el Supremo's rebellion. He realised that the whole of the Spanish overlordship of the Americas was in jeopardy, and as he realised that, a fresh and harassing aspect of the situation broke in upon him.

'The Manila galleon is at sea!' he exclaimed. 'She is due to arrive at Acapulco next month. The *Natividad* will intercept her.'

One ship a year crossed the wide Pacific from the Philippines, never bearing less than a million sterling in treasure. Her loss would cripple the bankrupt Spanish government hopelessly. The three captains exchanged glances – Hornblower was telling himself that this was why el Supremo had agreed so readily to the *Lydia* sailing south westward; he had doubtless been pleased at the thought of the *Natividad* to the north eastward acquiring this wealth for him. It would take the Spaniards months to bring round the Horn a ship capable of dealing with the *Natividad*, and in the interval el Supremo would enjoy all those advantages of sea power which Hornblower had foreseen for the *Lydia*. The rebellion would be so firmly rooted that nothing would put it down, especially as, apparently, the Spaniards of Spain were

engaged in a life-and-death struggle with Bonaparte and would
have neither ships nor men to spare for America. Hornblower
could see where lay his duty.

'Very well,' he announced abruptly. 'I will take my ship back
to fight the *Natividad*.'

All the Spanish officers looked their relief at that.

'Thank you, Captain,' said the officer of the lugger. 'You will
call in at Panama to consult the Viceroy first?'

'Yes,' snapped Hornblower.

In a world where news took months to travel, and where
complete upheavals of international relationships were not merely
possible but likely, he had learned now by bitter experience to
keep in the closest contact with the shore; his misery was in no
way allayed by the knowledge that the present difficulties were
occasioned merely by his strict obedience to orders – and he
knew, too, that the Lords of the Admiralty would not allow that
point to influence them in their opinion of a captain who could
cause such terrible trouble.

'Then,' said the captain of the lugger. 'I will bid you goodbye
for the time. If I reach Panama first, I will be able to arrange a
welcome for you. Perhaps you will allow my compatriots to
accompany me?'

'No I won't,' rasped Hornblower. 'And you, sir, will keep
under my lee until we drop anchor.'

The Spaniard shrugged and yielded. At sea one can hardly
argue with a captain whose guns are run out and whose broadside
could blow one's ship out of the water, especially as all
Englishmen were as mad and as domineering as el Supremo. The
Spaniard had not enough intuition to enable him to guess that
Hornblower still had a lurking fear that the whole business might
be a ruse to inveigle the *Lydia* helpless under the guns of Panama.

CHAPTER IX

It was not a ruse at all. In the morning, when the *Lydia* came stealing before a three knot breeze into the roadstead of Panama, the only guns fired were the salutes. Boatloads of rejoicing Spaniards came out to greet her, but the rejoicing was soon turned to wailing at the news that the *Natividad* now flew el Supremo's flag, that San Salvador had fallen, and that all Nicaragua was in a flame of rebellion. With cocked hat and gold-hilted sword ('a sword of the value of fifty guineas', the gift of the Patriotic Fund for Lieutenant Hornblower's part in the capture of the *Castilla* six years ago) Hornblower had made himself ready to go ashore and call upon the Governor and the Viceroy, when the arrival of yet one more boat was announced to him.

'There is a lady on board, sir,' said Gray, one of the master's mates, who brought the news.

'A lady?'

'Looks like an English lady, sir,' explained Gray. 'She seems to want to come aboard.'

Hornblower went on deck; close alongside a large rowing boat tossed and rolled; at the six oars sat swarthy Spanish Americans, bare armed and straw hatted, while another in the bows, boat hook in hand, stood waiting, face upturned for permission to hook on to the chains. In the stern sat a negress with a flaming red handkerchief over her shoulders, and beside her sat the English lady Gray had spoken about. Even as Hornblower looked, the bowman hooked on, and the boat closed in alongside, two men fending off. Somebody caught the rope ladder, and the next moment the lady, timing the movement perfectly, swung on to it and two seconds later came on deck.

Clearly she was an Englishwoman. She wore a wide shady hat trimmed with roses, in place of the eternal mantilla, and her

grey-blue silk dress was far finer than any Spanish black. Her
skin was fair despite its golden tan, and her eyes were grey-blue,
of just the same evasive shade as her silk dress. Her face was
too long for beauty and her nose too high arched, to say nothing
of her sunburn. Hornblower saw her at that moment as one of
the horsefaced mannish women whom he particularly disliked;
he told himself that all his inclinations were towards clinging
incompetence. Any woman who could transfer herself in that
fashion from boat to ship in an open roadstead, and could ascend
a rope ladder unassisted, must be too masculine for his taste.
Besides, an Englishwoman must be unsexed to be in Panama
without a male escort – the phrase 'globe trotting', with all its
disparaging implications, had not yet been invented, but it
expressed exactly Hornblower's feeling about her.

Hornblower held himself aloof as the visitor looked about
her. He was going to do nothing to help her. A wild squawk
from overside told that the negress had not been as handy with
the ladder, and directly afterwards this was confirmed by her
appearance on deck, wet from the waist down, water streaming
from her black gown on to the deck. The lady paid no attention
to the mishap to her maid; Gray was nearest to her and she
turned to him.

'Please be so good, sir,' she said, 'as to have my baggage
brought up out of the boat.'

Gray hesitated, and looked round over his shoulder at
Hornblower, stiff and unbending on the quarterdeck.

'The captain's here, ma'am,' he said.

'Yes,' said the lady. 'Please have my baggage brought up while
I speak to him.'

Hornblower was conscious of an internal struggle. He disliked
the aristocracy – it hurt him nowadays to remember that as the
doctor's son he had had to touch his cap to the squire. He felt
unhappy and awkward in the presence of the self-confident arro-
gance of blue blood and wealth. It irritated him to think that if
he offended this woman he might forfeit his career. Not even his

gold lace nor his presentation sword gave him confidence as she approached him. He took refuge in an icy formality.

'Are you the captain of this ship, sir?' she asked, as she came up. Her eyes looked boldly and frankly into his with no trace of downcast modesty.

'Captain Hornblower, at your service, ma'am,' he replied, with a stiff jerk of his neck which might charitably be thought a bow.

'Lady Barbara Wellesley,' was the reply, accompanied by a curtsy only just deep enough to keep the interview formal. 'I wrote you a note, Captain Hornblower, requesting a passage to England. I trust that you received it.'

'I did, ma'am. But I do not think it is wise for your ladyship to join this ship.'

The unhappy double mention of the word 'ship' in this sentence did nothing to make Hornblower feel less awkward.

'Please tell me why, sir.'

'Because, ma'am, we shall be clearing shortly to seek out an enemy and fight him. And after that, ma'am, we shall have to return to England round Cape Horn. Your ladyship would be well advised to make your way across the Isthmus. From Porto Bello you can easily reach Jamaica and engage a berth in the West India packet which is accustomed to female passengers.'

Lady Barbara's eyebrows arched themselves higher.

'In my letter,' she said, 'I informed you that there was yellow fever in Porto Bello. A thousand persons died there of it last week. It was on the outbreak of the disease that I removed from Porto Bello to Panama. At any day it may appear here as well.'

'May I ask why your ladyship was in Porto Bello, then?'

'Because, sir, the West India packet in which I was a female passenger was captured by a Spanish privateer and brought there. I regret, sir, that I cannot tell you the name of my grandmother's cook, but I shall be glad to answer any further questions which a gentleman of breeding would ask.'

Hornblower winced and then to his annoyance found himself blushing furiously. His dislike for arrogant blue blood was, if anything, intensified. But there was no denying that the woman's explanations were satisfactory enough – a visit to the West Indies could be made by any woman without unsexing herself, and she had clearly come to Porto Bello and Panama against her will. He was far more inclined now to grant her request – in fact he was about to do so, having strangely quite forgotten the approaching duel with the *Natividad* and the voyage round the Horn. He recalled them just as he was about to speak, so that he changed at a moment's notice what he was going to say and stammered and stuttered in consequence.

'B-but we are going out in this ship to fight,' he said. '*Natividad*'s got twice our force. It will be d-dangerous.'

Lady Barbara laughed at that – Hornblower noted the pleasing colour contrast between her white teeth and her golden sunburn; his own teeth were stained and ugly.

'I would far rather,' she said, 'be on board your ship, whomsoever you have got to fight, than be in Panama with the *vomito negro.*'

'But Cape Horn, ma'am?'

'I have no knowledge of this Cape Horn of yours. But I have twice rounded the Cape of Good Hope during my brother's Governor-Generalship, and I assure you, captain, I have never yet been seasick.'

Still Hornblower stammered and hesitated. He resented the presence of a woman on board his ship. Lady Barbara exactly voiced his thoughts – and as she did so her arched eyebrows came close together in a fashion oddly reminiscent of el Supremo although her eyes still laughed straight into his.

'Soon, Captain,' she said 'I will come to think that I shall be unwelcome on board. I can hardly imagine that a gentleman holding the King's commission would be discourteous to a woman, especially to a woman with my name.'

That was just the difficulty. No captain of small influence could afford to offend a Wellesley. Hornblower knew that if he did he might never command a ship again, and that he and

Maria would rot on the beach on half pay for the rest of their lives. At thirty-seven he still was not more than one-eighth the way up the captain's list – and the goodwill of the Wellesleys could easily keep him in employment until he attained flag rank. There was nothing for it but to swallow his resentment and to do all he could to earn that goodwill, diplomatically wringing advantage from his difficulties. He groped for a suitable speech.

'I was only doing my duty, ma'am,' he said, 'in pointing out the dangers to which you might be exposed. For myself there would be nothing that would give me greater pleasure than your presence on board my ship.'

Lady Barbara went down in a curtsy far deeper than her first, and at this moment Gray came up and touched his cap.

'Your baggage is all on board, ma'am,' he said.

They had hove the stuff up with a whip from the main yardarm, and now it littered the gangway – leather cases, ironbound wooden boxes, dome-topped trunks.

'Thank you, sir.' Lady Barbara brought out a flat leather purse from her pocket, and took from it a gold coin. 'Would you be so kind as to give this to the boat's crew?'

'Lord love you, ma'am, you don't need to give those Dago niggers gold. Silver's all they deserve.'

'Give them this, then, and thank you for your kindness.'

Gray hurried off, and Hornblower heard him bargaining in English with a boat's crew who knew no tongue but Spanish. The threat of having a cold shot hove down into the boat compelled it at length to shove off still spattering expostulation. A new little wave of irritation rose in Hornblower's mind. He disliked seeing his warrant officers running to do a woman's bidding, and his responsibilities were heavy, and he had been standing in a hot sun for half an hour.

'There will be no room in your cabin for a tenth of that baggage, ma'am,' he snapped.

Lady Barbara nodded gravely.

'I have dwelt in a cabin before this, sir. That sea chest there holds everything I shall need on board. The rest can be put where you will – until we reach England.'

Hornblower almost stamped on the deck with rage. He was unused to a woman who could display practical common-sense like this. It was infuriating that he could find no way of discomposing her – and then he saw her smiling, guessed that she was smiling at the evident struggle on his face, and blushed hotly again. He turned on his heel and led the way below without a word.

Lady Barbara looked round the captain's cabin with a whimsical smile, but she made no comment, not even when she surveyed the grim discomfort of the after-cabin.

'A frigate has few of the luxuries of an Indiaman you see, ma'am,' said Hornblower, bitterly. He was bitter because his poverty at the time when he commissioned the *Lydia* had allowed him to purchase none of the minor comforts which many frigate-captains could afford.

'I was just thinking when you spoke,' said Lady Barbara, gently, 'that it was scandalous that a King's officer should be treated worse than a fat John Company man. But I have only one thing to ask for which I do not see.'

'And that is, ma'am—?'

'A key for the lock on the cabin door.'

'I will have the armourer make you a key, ma'am. But there will be a sentry at this door night and day.'

The implications which Hornblower read into this request of Lady Barbara's angered him again. She was slandering both him and his ship.

'*Quis custodiet ipsos custodes?*' said Lady Barbara. 'It is not on my account, Captain, that I need a key. It is Hebe here whom I have to lock in unless she is directly under eye. She can no more keep from the men than a moth from a candle.'

The little negress grinned widely at this last speech, showing no resentment and a good deal of pride. She rolled her eyes at Polwheal, who was standing silently by.

'Where will she sleep, then?' asked Hornblower, disconcerted once more.

'On the floor of my cabin. And mark my words, Hebe, the first time I find you not there during the night I'll lace you so that you will have to sleep on your face.'

Hebe still grinned, although it was evident that she knew her mistress would carry out her threat. What mollified Hornblower was Lady Barbara's little slip in speaking of the 'floor' of her cabin instead of the deck. It showed that she was only a feeble woman after all.

'Very good,' he said. 'Polwheal, take my things into Mr Bush's cabin. Give Mr Bush my apologies and tell him he will have to berth in the wardroom. See that Lady Barbara has all that she wants, and ask Mr Gray with my compliments to attend to putting the baggage in my storeroom. You will forgive me, Lady Barbara, but I am already late in paying my call upon the Viceroy.'

CHAPTER X

The captain of the *Lydia* came on board again to the accompaniment of the usual twitterings of the pipes and the presenting of arms by the marine guard. He walked very carefully, for good news just arrived from Europe had made the Viceroy pressingly hospitable while the notification of the first case of yellow fever in Panama had made him apprehensive so that Hornblower had been compelled to drink one glass of wine too much. A naturally abstemious man, he hated the feeling of not being quite master of himself.

As always, he looked sharply round the deck as soon as his feet were on it. Lady Barbara was sitting in a hammock chair on the quarterdeck – someone must have had that chair made for her during the day; and someone had rigged for her a scrap of awning in the mizzen rigging so that she sat in the shade with Hebe crouching at her feet. She looked cool and comfortable, and smiled readily at him as he approached, but he looked away from her. He would not speak to her until his head was clearer.

'Call all hands to weigh anchor and make sail,' he said to Bush. 'We leave at once.'

He went below, checked himself with a gesture of annoyance at finding that habit had led him to the wrong cabin, and as he turned on his heel he hit his head a shattering crash on a deck beam. His new cabin, from which Bush had been evicted, was even smaller than the old one. Polwheal was waiting to help him change his clothes, and the sight of him reminded Hornblower of fresh troubles. He had been wearing his best gold-laced coat and white breeches when Lady Barbara came on board, but he could not afford to continue to wear them lest they should grow too shabby for use on ceremonial occasions. He would have to appear before this woman in future in his old patched coats and cheap duck trousers. She would sneer at his shabbiness and poverty.

He cursed the woman as he stripped off his clothes, all wet with sweat. Then a new trouble came into his mind. He had to leave Polwheal to keep watch while he had his shower bath under the pump lest she should surprise him there naked. He would have to issue orders to the crew so as to make sure that her fastidious eyes would not be offended by the state of undress which they habitually affected in the tropics. He combed his hair and cursed its curliness as drawing additional attention to the way his hair was receding from his forehead.

Then he hurried on deck; he was glad that the need for looking after the ship saved him from meeting Lady Barbara's eyes and seeing her reaction to his shabby clothes. He felt her gaze upon him, all the same, as he stood with his back to her attending to the business of getting under weigh. Half of one watch were at the capstan with all their weight upon the bars, their bare feet seeking holds on the smooth deck while Harrison bellowed encouragement and threats, and stimulated the laggards with cuts from his cane. Sullivan the mad fiddler, the two marine fifers and the two drummers were playing some lively tune – to Hornblower one tune was much the same as another – on the forecastle.

The cable came steadily in, the ship's boys with their nippers following it to the hatch coamings and scuttling back immediately to take a fresh hold on cable and messenger. But the measured clank-clank of the capstan grew slower and slower and then came to a dead stop.

'Heave, you bastards! Heave!' bellowed Harrison. 'Here, you fo'c'sle men, bear a hand! Now, heave!'

There were twenty more men thrusting at the bars now. Their added strength brought one more solemn clank from the capstan.

'Heave! Christ damn you, heave!'

Harrison's cane was falling briskly first here and then there.

'Heave!'

A shudder ran through the ship, the capstan swung round so sharply that the hands at the bars fell in a tumbling heap to the deck.

'Messenger's parted, sir,' hailed Gerard from the forecastle. 'The anchor's foul, I think, sir.'

'Hell fire!' said Hornblower to himself. He was certain that the woman in the hammock chair behind him was laughing at his predicament, with a foul anchor and the eyes of all Spanish America on him. But he was not going to abandon an anchor and cable to the Spaniards.

'Pass the small bower cable for a messenger,' he shouted.

That meant unbearably hot and unpleasant work for a score of men down in the cable tier rousing out the small bower cable and manhandling it up to the capstan. The calls and curses of the boatswain's mates came echoing back to the quarterdeck – the warrant officers were as acutely conscious of the indignity of the ship's position as was their captain. Hornblower could not pace the deck as he wished to do, for fear of meeting Lady Barbara's eyes. He could only stand and fume, wiping the sweat with his handkerchief from his face and neck.

'Messenger's ready, sir!' hailed Gerard.

'Put every man to the bars that there's place for. Mr Harrison, see that they heave!'

'Aye aye, sir!'

Br-r-r-rm. Boom! Br-r-r-rm. Boom! The drum rolled.

'Heave, you sons of bitches,' said Harrison, his cane going crack-crack-crack on the straining backs.

Clank! went the capstan. Clank-clank-clank.

Hornblower felt the deck inclining a trifle under his feet. The strain was dragging down the ship's bows, not bringing home the anchor.

'God—,' began Hornblower to himself, and then left the sentence uncompleted. Of the fifty-five oaths he had ready to employ not one was adequate to the occasion.

'Avast heaving!' he roared, and the sweating seamen eased their aching backs.

Hornblower tugged at his chin as though he wanted to pull it off. He would have to sail the anchor out of the ground – a delicate manoeuvre involving peril to masts and rigging, and which might end in a ridiculous fiasco. Up to the moment only a few knowing people in Panama could have guessed at the ship's predicament, but the moment sail was set, telescopes would be trained upon her from the city walls, and if the operation failed everyone would know and would be amused – and the *Lydia* might be delayed for hours repairing damage. But he was not going to abandon that anchor and cable.

He looked up at the vane at the masthead, and overside at the water; the wind was across the tide, which gave them a chance, at least. He issued his orders quietly, taking the utmost precaution to conceal his trepidation, and steadily keeping his back to Lady Barbara. The topmen raced aloft to set the fore topsail; with that and the driver he could get sternway upon the ship. Harrison stood by the capstan ready first to let the cable go with a run and then second to have it hove in like lightning when the ship came forward again. Bush had his men ready at the braces, and every idle hand was gathered round the capstan.

The cable roared out as the ship gathered sternway; Hornblower stood rooted to the quarterdeck feeling that he would give a week of his life for the chance to pace up and down without meeting Lady Barbara's eyes. With narrowed eyes he watched the progress of the ship, his mind juggling with a dozen factors at once – the drag of the cable on the bows, the pressure of the wind on the driver and the backed fore topsail, the set of the tide, the increasing sternway, the amount of cable still to run out. He picked his moment.

'Hard-a-starboard,' he rasped at the quartermaster at the wheel, and then to the hands forward 'Smartly with the braces now!'

With the rudder hard across the ship came round a trifle. The fore topsail came round. The jibs and fore staysails were set like lightning. There was a shuddering moment before the ship paid off. Her sternway checked, the ship hesitated, and then, joyfully, began slowly to move forward close hauled. Up aloft every sail that could draw was being set as Hornblower barked his orders.

The capstan clanked ecstatically as Harrison's men raced round with the bars gathering the cable again.

Hornblower had a moment to think now, with the ship gathering forward way. The drag of the cable would throw her all aback if he gave her the least chance. He was conscious of the rapid beating of his heart as he watched the main topsail for the first signs of flapping. It took all his force of will to keep his voice from shaking as he gave his orders to the helmsman. The cable was coming in fast; the next crisis was at hand, which would see the anchor out of the ground or the *Lydia* dismasted. He nerved himself for it, judged his moment, and then shouted for all sail to be got in.

All the long and painful drill to which Bush had subjected the crew bore its fruit now. Courses, topsails and topgallants were got in during the few seconds which were left, and as the last shred of canvas disappeared, a fresh order from Hornblower brought the ship round, pointing straight into the wind and towards the hidden anchor, the way she had gathered carrying her slowly forward. Hornblower strained his ears to listen to the capstan.

Clank-clank-clank-clank.

Harrison was driving his men round and round the capstan like madmen.

Clank-clank-clank.

The ship was moving perceptibly slower. He could not tell yet if all his effort was to end ignominiously in failure.

Clank-clank.

There came a wild yell from Harrison.

'Anchor's free, sir!'

'Set all sail, Mr Bush,' said Hornblower; Bush was making no attempt to conceal his admiration for a brilliant piece of seamanship, and Hornblower had to struggle hard to keep his voice at the hard mechanical pitch which would hide his elation and convince everyone that he had had no doubt from the very start of the success of his manoeuvre.

He set a compass course, and, as the ship came round and steadied upon it, he gave one final glance of inspection round the deck.

'Ha – h'm,' he rasped, and dived below, to where he could relax and recover, out of Bush's sight – and out of Lady Barbara's, too.

CHAPTER XI

Stretched flat on his back in his cabin, blowing thick greasy wreaths of smoke from one of General Hernandez' cigars towards the deck above him where sat Lady Barbara, Hornblower began slowly to recover from the strain of a very trying day. It had begun with the approach to Panama, with every nerve keyed up lest an ambush had been laid, and it had ended so far with this trying business of the fouled anchor. Between the two had come Lady Barbara's arrival and the interview with the Viceroy of New Granada.

The Viceroy had been a typical Spanish gentleman of the old school – Hornblower decided that he would rather have dealings with el Supremo any day of the week. El Supremo might have an unpleasant habit of barbarously putting men to death, but he found no difficulty in making up his mind and one could be confident that orders issued by him would be obeyed with equal promptitude. The Viceroy, on the other hand, while full of approval of Hornblower's suggestion that instant action against the rebels was necessary, had not been ready to act on it. He was obviously surprised at Hornblower's decision to sail from Panama on the same day as his arrival – he had expected the *Lydia* to stay for at least a week of fêtings and junketings and idleness. He had agreed that at least a thousand soldiers must be transported to the Nicaraguan coast – although a thousand soldiers constituted practically the whole of his command – but he had clearly intended to postpone until the morrow the issuing of the orders for that concentration.

Hornblower had had to use all his tact to persuade him to do it at once, to give his instructions from his very banqueting table, and to put his favourite aides-de-camp to the pain of riding with messages under a hot sun during the sacred hours of the siesta.

The banquet had in itself been trying; Hornblower felt as if there was no skin left on his palate, so highly peppered had been every dish. Both because of the spiciness of the food and the pressing hospitality of the Viceroy it had been hard to avoid drinking too much; in an age of hard drinking, Hornblower stood almost alone in his abstemiousness, from no conscientious motive but solely because he actively disliked the feeling of not having complete control of his judgement.

But he could not refuse that last glass of wine, seeing what news had just come in. He sat up on his cot with a jerk. That business with the anchor had driven the recollection out of his mind. Good manners compelled him to go and communicate the news to Lady Barbara, seeing how closely it concerned her. He ran up on deck, pitched his cigar overboard, and went towards her. Gerard, the officer of the watch, was in close conversation with her; Hornblower smiled grimly to himself when he saw Gerard hurriedly break off the conversation and move away.

She was still seated aft by the taffrail in her hammock chair, the negress at her feet. She seemed to be drinking in the cool wind against which the *Lydia* was standing out of the gulf, close hauled. On the starboard beam the sun was ready at the horizon, a disc of orange fire in the clear blue of the sky, and she was exposing her face to its level beams with a total disregard for her complexion which accounted for her sunburn and, presumably, for the fact that she was now twenty-seven and still unmarried despite a trip to India. Yet there was a serenity in her expression which seemed to show that at the moment at least she was not worrying about being an old maid.

She acknowledged his bow with a smile.

'It is heavenly to be at sea again, Captain,' she said. 'You have given me no opportunity so far to tell you how grateful I am to you for taking me away from Panama. To be a prisoner was bad enough, but to be free and yet to be confined there by force of circumstances would have driven me out of my mind. Believe me, Captain, you have won my eternal gratitude.'

Hornblower bowed again.

'I trust the Dons treated your ladyship with all respect?'

She shrugged her shoulders.

'Well enough. But Spanish manners can grow trying. I was in the charge of Her Excellency – an admirable woman, but insupportably dull. In Spanish America women are treated like Mohammedans. And Spanish-American food—'

The words recalled to Hornblower the banquet he had just endured, and the expression on his face made Lady Barbara break off her sentence to laugh so infectiously that Hornblower could not help but join in.

'Will you not sit down, Captain?'

Hornblower resented the suggestion. He had never once during this commission sat in a chair on his own deck, and he disliked innovations in his habits.

'Thank you, your ladyship, but I prefer to stand if I may. I came to give you good news.'

'Indeed? Then your company is doubly pleasant. I am all eagerness to hear.'

'Your brother, Sir Arthur, has won a great victory in Portugal over the French. Under the terms of a convention the French are evacuating the country and are handing over Lisbon to the English army.'

'That is very good news. I have always been proud of Arthur – this makes me prouder still.'

'It gives me great pleasure to be the first to congratulate his sister.'

Lady Barbara contrived miraculously to bow although seated in her hammock chair – Hornblower was conscious of the difficulty of the feat and grudgingly admitted to himself that it was well done.

'How did the news come?'

'It was announced to the Viceroy while I was at dinner with him. A ship had reached Porto Bello from Cadiz, and a messenger rode express by the waggon road. There was other news as well – how true is more than I can say.'

'To what effect, Captain?'

'The Spaniards claim a victory, too. They say a whole army of Bonaparte's has surrendered to them in Andalusia. They are already looking forward to an invasion of France in company with the English army.'

'And how true do you think it is?'

'I distrust it. They may have cut off a detachment by good luck. But it will need more than a Spanish army to beat Bonaparte. I can foresee no speedy end to the war.'

Lady Barbara nodded a grave approval. She looked out to where the sun was sinking into the sea, and Hornblower looked with her. To him, the disappearance of the sun each evening into those placid waters was a daily miracle of beauty. The line of the horizon cut the disc now. They watched silently as the sun sank farther and farther. Soon only a tiny edge was left; it vanished, reappeared for a second like a glint of gold as the *Lydia* heaved up over the swell, and then faded once more. The sky glowed red in the west, but overhead it grew perceptibly darker with the approach of night.

'Beautiful! Exquisite!' said Lady Barbara; her hands were tightly clasped together. She was silent for a moment before she spoke again, returning to the last subject of conversation. 'Yes. One gleam of success and the Spaniards will look on the war as good as over. And in England the herd will be expecting my brother to lead the army into Paris by Christmas. And if he does not they will forget his victories and clamour for his head.'

Hornblower resented the word 'herd' – by birth and by blood he was one of the herd himself – but he was aware of the profound truth of Lady Barbara's remarks. She had summed up for him his opinion both of the Spanish national temperament and of the British mob. Along with that went her appreciation of the sunset and her opinion of Spanish-American food. He actually felt well disposed towards her.

'I hope,' he said, ponderously, 'that your ladyship was provided today during my absence with everything necessary? A ship is poorly provided with comforts for women, but I hope that my officers did their best for your ladyship.'

'Thank you, Captain, they did indeed. There is only one more thing that I wish for, which I should like to ask as a favour.'

'Yes, your ladyship?'

'And that is that you do not call me "your ladyship". Call me Lady Barbara, if you will.'

'Certainly, your – Lady Barbara. Ha – h'm.'

Ghosts of dimples appeared in the thin cheeks, and the bright eyes sparkled.

'And if "Lady Barbara" does not come easily to you, Captain, and you wish to attract my attention, you can always say "ha – h'm."'

Hornblower stiffened with anger at this impertinence. He was about to turn on his heel, drawing a deep breath as he did so, and he was about to exhale that breath and clear this throat when he realised that he would never again, or at least until he had reached some port where he could get rid of this woman, be able to make use of that useful and non-committal sound. But Lady Barbara checked him with outstretched hand; even at that moment he noticed her long slender fingers.

'I am sorry, Captain,' she said, all contrition, 'please accept my apologies, although I know now that it was quite unforgivable.'

She looked positively pretty as she pleaded. Hornblower stood hesitating, looking down at her. He realised that why he was angry was not because of the impertinence, but because this sharp-witted woman had already guessed at the use he made of this sound to hide his feelings, and with that realisation his anger changed into his usual contempt for himself.

'There is nothing to forgive, ma'am,' he said, heavily. 'And now, if you will forgive me in your turn, I will attend to my duties in the ship.'

He left her there in the fast-falling night. A ship's boy had just come aft and lighted the binnacle lamps, and he stopped and read on the slate and traverse board the record of the afternoon's run. He wrote in his painstaking hand the instructions with regard to calling him – because some time that night they would round Cape Mala and have to change course to the northward – and then he went below again to his cabin.

He felt oddly disturbed and ill at ease and not merely because of the upsetting of all his habits. It was annoying that his own private water closet was barred to him now so that he had to use the wardroom one, but it was not just because of this. Not even was it merely because he was on his way to fight the *Natividad* again in the certain knowledge that with Vice-Admiral Cristobal de Crespo in command it would be a hard battle. That was part of what was troubling him – and then he realised with a shock that his disquiet was due to the added responsibility of Lady Barbara's presence on board.

He knew quite well what would be the fate of himself and his crew if the *Lydia* were beaten by the *Natividad*. They would be hanged or drowned or tortured to death – el Supremo would show no mercy to the Englishman who had turned against him. That possibility left him unmoved at present, because it was so entirely inevitable that he should fight the *Natividad*. But it was far different in Lady Barbara's case. He would have to see that she did not fall alive into Crespo's hands.

This brief wording of his difficulty brought him a sudden spasm of irritation. He cursed the yellow fever which had driven her on board; he cursed his own slavish obedience to orders which had resulted in the *Natividad*'s fighting on the rebels' side. He found himself clenching his hands and gritting his teeth with rage. If he won his fight, public opinion would censure him (with all public opinion's usual ignorance of circumstances) for risking the life of a lady – of a Wellesley. If he lost it – but he could not bear to think about that. He cursed his own weakness for allowing her to come on board; for a moment he even dallied with the notion of putting back to Panama and setting her on shore. But he put that notion aside. The *Natividad* might take the Manila galleon. His crew, already discomposed by all the recent changes of plan, would fret still more if he went back and then went to sea again. And Lady Barbara might refuse – and with yellow fever raging in Panama she would be justified in refusing. He could not exercise his authority so brutally as to force a woman to land in a fever-stricken town. He swore to himself again, senselessly, making use of all the filthy oaths and frantic blasphemies acquired during his sea experience.

From the deck came a shrilling of pipes and a shouting of orders and a clatter of feet; apparently the wind had backed round now with the fall of night. As the sound died away, the feeling of oppression in the tiny cabin overcame him. It was hot and stuffy; the oil lamp swinging over his head stank horribly. He plunged up on deck again. Aft from the taffrail he heard a merry laugh from Lady Barbara, instantly followed by a chorus of guffaws. The dark mass there must be at least half a dozen officers, all grouped round Lady Barbara's chair. It was only to be expected that after seven months – eight, nearly, now – without seeing an English woman they would cluster round her like bees round a hive.

His first instinct was to drive them away, but he checked himself. He could not dictate to his officers how they spent their watch below, and they would attribute his action to his desire to monopolise her society to himself – and that was not in the least the case. He went down again, unobserved by the group, to a stuffy cabin and the stinking lamp. It was the beginning of a sleepless and restless night.

CHAPTER XII

Morning found the *Lydia* heaving and swooping lightly over a quartering sea. On the starboard beam, just jutting over the horizon, were the greyish-pink summits of the volcanoes of that tormented country; by ranging along, just in sight of the coast, the *Lydia* stood her best chance of discovering the *Natividad*. The captain was already afoot – indeed, his coxswain, Brown, had had apologetically to sand the captain's portion of the quarter-deck while he paced up and down it.

Far away on the port side the black shape of a whale broke the surface in a flurry of foam – dazzling white against the blue sea – and a thin plume of white smoke was visible as the whale emptied its lungs. Hornblower liked whales for some reason or other; the sight of this one, in fact, led him on his first step back towards good temper. With the imminent prospect of his cold shower bath before him, the prickle of sweat under his shirt was gratifying now instead of irritating. Two hours ago he had been telling himself that he loathed this Pacific coast, its blue sea and its hideous volcanoes – even its freedom from navigational difficulties. He had felt himself homesick for the rocks and shoals and fogs and tides of the Channel, but now, bathed in sunshine, his opinion changed once more. There was something to be said in favour of the Pacific after all. Perhaps this new alliance between Spain and England would induce the Dons to relax some of their selfish laws prohibiting trade with America; they might even go so far as to try to exploit the possibility of that canal across Nicaragua which the British Admiralty had in mind, and in that case this blue Pacific could come into its own. El Supremo would have to be suppressed first, of course, but on this pleasant morning Hornblower foresaw less difficulty in that.

Gray, the master's mate, had come aft to heave the log. Hornblower checked in his walk to watch the operation. Gray tossed the little triangle of wood over the stern, and, log line in hand, he gazed fixedly with his boyish blue eyes at the dancing bit of wood.

'Turn!' he cried sharply to the hand with the sand glass, while the line ran out freely over the rail.

'Stop!' called the man with the glass.

Gray nipped the line with his fingers and checked its progress, and then read off the length run out. A sharp jerk at the thin cord, which had run out with the line, freed the peg so that the log now floated with its edge towards the ship, enabling Gray to pull the log in hand over hand.

'How much?' called Hornblower to Gray.

'Seven an' nigh on a half, sir.'

The *Lydia* was a good ship to reel off seven and a half knots in that breeze, even though her best point of sailing was with the wind on her quarter. It would not take long if the wind held to reach waters where the *Natividad* might be expected to be found. The *Natividad* was a slow sailer, as nearly all those two-decker fifty-gun ships were, and as Hornblower had noticed when he had sailed in her company ten days back – it might as well be ten years, so long did it seem – from the Gulf of Fonseca to La Libertad.

If he met her in the open sea he could trust to the handiness of his ship and the experience of his crew to outmanoeuvre her and discount her superior weight of metal. If the ships once closed, and the rebels boarded, their superior numbers would overwhelm his crew. He must keep clear, slip across her stern and rake her half a dozen times. Hornblower's busy mind, as he paced up and down the deck, began to visualise the battle, and to make plans for the possible eventualities – whether or not he might hold the weather gauge, whether or not there might be a high sea running, whether or not the battle began close inshore.

The little negress Hebe came picking her way across the deck, her red handkerchief brilliant in the sunshine, and before the scandalised crew could prevent her she had interrupted the captain in his sacred morning walk.

'Milady says would the captain breakfast with her,' she lisped.

'Eh – what's that?' asked Hornblower, taken by surprise and coming out of his daydream with a jerk, and then, as he realised the triviality for which he had been interrupted 'No no no! Tell her ladyship I will *not* breakfast with her. Tell her that I will *never* breakfast with her. Tell her that on *no* account am I to be sent messages during the morning. Tell her you are *not* allowed and neither is she on this deck before eight bells. *Get below!*'

Even then the little negress did not seem to realise how enormous had been her offence. She nodded and smiled as she backed away without a sign of contrition. Apparently she was used to white gentlemen who were irascible before breakfast and attributed little importance to the symptoms. The open skylight of the after-cabin was close beside him as he walked, and through it he could hear, now that his reverie had been broken into, the clatter of crockery, and then first Hebe's and then Lady Barbara's voice.

The sound of the men scrubbing the decks, the harping of the rigging and the creaking of the timbers were noises to which he was used. From forward came the thunderous beat of a sledge-hammer as the armourer and his mate worked upon the fluke of the anchor which had been bent in yesterday's misadventure. He could tolerate all the ship's noises, but this clack-clack-clack of women's tongues through the open skylight would drive him mad. He stamped off the deck in a rage again. He did not enjoy his bath after all, and he cursed Polwheal for clumsiness in handing him his dressing gown, and he tore the threadbare suit which Polwheal had put out for him and cursed again. It was intolerable that he should be driven in this fashion off his own deck. Even the excellent coffee, sweetened (as he liked it) to a syrup with sugar, did not relieve his fresh ill-temper. Nor, most assuredly, did the necessity of having to explain to Bush that the *Lydia* was now sailing to seek out and to capture the *Natividad*, having already been to enormous pains to capture her and hand her over to the rebels who were now their foes.

'Aye aye, sir,' said Bush gravely, having heard the new development. He was being so obviously tactful, and he so pointedly refrained from comment, that Hornblower swore at him.

'Aye aye, sir,' said Bush again, knowing perfectly well why he was being sworn at, and also knowing that he would be sworn at far worse if he said anything beyond 'aye aye, sir'. Really what he wanted to say was some expression of sympathy for Hornblower in his present situation, but he knew he dared not sympathise with his queer-tempered captain.

As the day wore on Hornblower came to repent of his ill-humour. The saw-edged volcanic coast was slipping past them steadily, and ahead of them somewhere lay the *Natividad*. There was a desperate battle awaiting them, and, before they should fight it, it would be tactful for him to entertain his officers to dinner. And he knew that any captain with an eye to his professional advancement would be careful not to treat a Wellesley in the cavalier fashion he had employed up to the present. And ordinary politeness dictated that he should at this, the earliest opportunity, arrange that his guest should meet his officers formally at dinner, even though he knew full well that she had already, in her emancipated manner, conversed with half of them in the darkness of the quarterdeck.

He sent Polwheal across to Lady Barbara with a politely worded request that Lady Barbara would be so kind as to allow Captain Hornblower and his officers to dine with her in the after-cabin and Polwheal returned with a politely worded message to the effect that Lady Barbara would be delighted. Six was the maximum number that could sit round the after cabin table; and superstitiously Hornblower remembered that on the eve of his last encounter with the *Natividad* Galbraith, Clay and Savage had been his guests. He would never have admitted to himself that it was for this reason that he invited them again in the hope of encountering similar good fortune, but it was the case nevertheless. He invited Bush as the sixth – the other possible choice was Gerard, and Gerard was so handsome and had acquired somehow such a knowledge of the world that Hornblower did not want to bring him into too frequent contact with Lady Barbara – solely, he hastened to assure himself, for the sake of peace and quiet in his ship. And when that was all settled he could go on deck again to take his noon sights and pace his quarterdeck in his consuming restlessness, feeling that he could (after this exchange of polite messages) meet Lady Barbara's eyes without the embarrassment that would previously have prevented him, unreasoningly.

The dinner at three o'clock was a success. Clay and Savage passed through the stages of behaviour that might have been expected of boys their age. At first they were brusque and shy in Lady Barbara's presence, and then, when the novelty had worn off and they had a glass of wine inside them they moved towards the other extreme of over-familiarity. Even the hard-bitten Bush, surprisingly, showed the same symptoms in the same order, while poor Galbraith was, of course, shy all the time.

But Hornblower was astonished at the ease with which Lady Barbara handled them. His own Maria would have been too gauche ever to have pulled that party together, and in a world where he knew few women, Hornblower was prone to measure the ones he met by Maria's standard. Lady Barbara laughed away Clay's bumptiousness, listened appreciatively to Bush's account of Trafalgar (when he had been a junior lieutenant on the *Temeraire*) and then won Galbraith's heart completely by displaying a close knowledge of a remarkable poem called 'The Lay of the Last Minstrel' by an Edinburgh lawyer – every line of which Galbraith knew by heart, and which Galbraith thought was the greatest poem in the English language. His cheeks glowed with pleasure as they discussed it.

Hornblower kept his opinion of the work to himself. His model author was Gibbon, whose *Decline and Fall of the Roman Empire* was to be found in the very locker on which he sat, and he was surprised that a woman who could quote Juvenal with ease should be so interested in a barbaric romantic poem with no polish about it whatever. He contented himself with sitting back and watching the faces round the table – Galbraith tense and pleased, Clay and Savage and Bush a little out of their depth but interested in spite of themselves, and Lady Barbara completely at ease, conversing with a fearless self-confidence which nevertheless (as Hornblower grudgingly admitted to himself) seemed to owe nothing to her great position.

She made no use of her sex, either, Hornblower realised, and yet she was, marvellously, neither cold nor masculine. She might have been Savage's aunt, or Galbraith's sister. She could talk to men as an equal, and yet could keep from her manner both invitation and hostility. She was very different from Maria. And when dinner was over and the officers rose to drink the health of the King, stooping under the deck beams (not until twenty-five more years had passed would a King who had been a sailor himself give permission to the Navy to drink his health sitting) she echoed 'God bless him!' and finished her single glass of wine with exactly the right touch of light-hearted solemnity which befitted the occasion. Hornblower suddenly realised that he was passionately anxious for the evening not to end.

'Do you play whist, Lady Barbara?' he asked.

'Why, yes,' she said, 'are there whist players on board this ship?'

'There are some who are not too enthusiastic,' replied Hornblower, grinning at his juniors.

But nobody had nearly as much objection to playing in a four with Lady Barbara, the more so as her presence might moderate the captain's dry strictness. The cut allotted Lady Barbara as the captain's partner against Clay and Galbraith. Clay dealt and turned up a heart as trump; it was Lady Barbara's lead. She led the king of hearts, and Hornblower writhed uneasily in his seat. This might well be the play of a mere tyro, and somehow it hurt him to think that Lady Barbara was a bad whist player. But the king of hearts was followed by the king of diamonds, which also took the trick, and that by the ace of hearts, followed by the seven. Hornblower took the trick with the queen – his last heart, making a total of eleven played, and returned a diamond. Down came Lady Barbara's queen. Next came the ace of diamonds, and then two small ones to follow. At his first discard Hornblower dropped the seven from his suit of four clubs headed by king and knave. His opponents each discarded small spades on that remorseless string of diamonds. From doubt Hornblower changed instantly to complete confidence in his partner, which was entirely justified. She led the ace of clubs followed by the three, Hornblower finessed his knave, played his king, on which his partner discarded her singleton spade and then claimed the last two tricks with her remaining trumps. They had made a slam even though their opponents held every trick in spades.

Lady Barbara had shown that she could play a good hand well; later she proved that she could fight out a losing hand with equal brilliance. She watched every discard, noted every signal, finessed boldly when there was a chance of profit, returned her partner's leads and yet resolutely ignored them if her hand justified the risk; she played low from a sequence and led high. Not since the *Lydia* left England had Hornblower had such a good partner. In his pleasure at this discovery Hornblower quite forgot to have any qualms at the fact that here was a woman who could do something well.

And the next evening she displayed another accomplishment, when she brought out a guitar on to the quarterdeck and accompanied herself in the songs which she sang in a sweet soprano – so sweet that the crew came creeping aft and crouched to listen under the gangways and coughed and fidgeted sentimentally at the close of each song. Galbraith was her slave, and she could play on his musical heartstrings as on her guitar. The midshipmen loved her. Even the barnacle-encrusted officers like Bush and Crystal softened towards her, and Gerard flashed his brilliant smile at her and made play with his good looks and told her

stories of his privateering days and of his slaving adventures up
the African rivers. Hornblower watched Gerard anxiously during
that voyage up the Nicaraguan coast, and cursed his own tone
deafness which made Lady Barbara's singing not merely indifferent to him but almost painful.

CHAPTER XIII

The long volcanic coastline slid past them day after day. Every day brought its eternal panorama of blue sea and blue sky, of slaty-pink volcanic peaks and a fringing coastline of vivid green. With decks cleared for action, and every man at his post, they ran once more into the Gulf of Fonseca and sailed round the island of Manguera in search of the *Natividad*, but they did not find her. They saw no sign of life on the shores of the bay, either. Someone fired a musket at the ship from the cliffs of Manguera – the spent bullet thudded into the mainchains – but they did not see the man who fired it. Bush steered the *Lydia* out of the gulf again and north-eastward in his search for the *Natividad*.

The *Natividad* was not to be found in the roadstead of La Libertad, nor in any of the little ports farther along. There was much smoke to be seen at Champerico, and Hornblower, training his glass upon it, could see that for once it was not volcanic. Champerico was in flames, so that presumably el Supremo's men had come there spreading enlightenment, but there was no sign of the *Natividad*.

Storms awaited them in the Gulf of Tehuantepec, for that corner of the Pacific is always stormy, lashed by the wind which blows hither from the Gulf of Mexico through a gap in the sierras. Hornblower was made aware of the change by an increase in the motion of the ship. She was rising and swooping more violently than usual and a gusty wind was heeling her sharply over. It was just eight bells, and the watch was being called; he could hear the bellowings of the master's mates – 'Show a leg! Show a leg! Lash up and stow! Lash up and stow!' – as he ran up to the quarterdeck. The sky was still blue overhead and the sun was hot, but the sea was grey, now, and running high, and the *Lydia* was beginning to labour under her press of sail.

'I was just sending down to you, sir, for permission to shorten sail,' said Bush.

Hornblower glanced up at the canvas, and over towards the clouds towards the coast.

'Yes. Get the courses and t'gallants off her,' he said.

The *Lydia* plunged heavily as he spoke, and then rose again, labouring, the water creaming under her bows. The whole ship was alive with the creaking of timber and the harping of the rigging. Under shortened sail she rode more easily, but the wind of her beam was growing stronger, and she was bowing down to it as she crashed over the waves. Looking round, Hornblower saw Lady Barbara standing with one hand on the taffrail. The wind was whipping her skirts about her, and with her other hand she was trying to restrain the curls that streamed round her head. Her cheeks were pink under their tan, and her eyes sparkled.

'You ought to be below, Lady Barbara,' he said.

'Oh no, Captain. This is too delicious after the heat we have been enduring.'

A shower of spray came rattling over the bulwarks and wetted them both.

'It is your health, ma'am, about which I am anxious.'

'If salt water was harmful sailors would die young.'

Her cheeks were bright as if she had been using cosmetics. Hornblower could refuse her nothing, even though he bitterly remembered how last evening she had sat in the shadow of the mizzen rigging talking so animatedly to Gerard that no one else had been able to profit by her society.

'Then you can stay on deck, ma'am, since you wish it, unless this gale increases – and I fancy it will.'

'Thank you, Captain,' she replied. There was a look in her eye which seemed to indicate that the question as to what would happen if the gale increased was not nearly as decided as the captain appeared to think – but like her great brother she crossed no bridges until she came to them.

Hornblower turned away; he would clearly have liked to have stayed there talking, with the spray pattering about them, but his duty was with his ship. As he reached the wheel there came a hail from the masthead.

'Sail ho! Deck, there, a sail right ahead. Looks like *Natividad*, sir.'

Hornblower glanced up at the canvas, and over towards the clouds towards the coast.

'Up you go, Knyvett,' he snapped to the midshipman beside him. 'Take a glass with you and tell me what you can see.' He knew that he himself would be of no use as a lookout in that wild weather – he was ashamed of it, but he had to admit it to himself. Soon Knyvett's boyish voice came calling down to him through the gale.

'She's the *Natividad*, sir. I can see the cut of her tops'ls.'

'How's she heading?'

'On the starboard tack, sir, same course as us. Her masts are in one line. Now she's altering course, sir. She's wearing round. She must have seen us, sir. Now she's on the port tack, sir, heading up to wind'ard of us, close hauled, sir.'

'Oh, is she,' said Hornblower to himself, grimly. It was an unusual experience to have a Spanish ship face about and challenge action – but he remembered that she was a Spanish ship no longer. He would not allow her to get the weather gauge of him, come what might.

'Man the braces, there!' he shouted, and then to the man at the wheel: 'Port your helm. And mark ye, fellow, keep her as near the wind as she'll lie. Mr Bush, beat to quarters, if you please, and clear for action.'

As the drum rolled and the hands came pouring up he remembered the woman aft by the taffrail, and his stolid fatalism changed to anxiety.

'Your place is below, Lady Barbara,' he said. 'Take your maid with you. You must stay in the cockpit until the action is over – no, not the cockpit. Go to the cable tier.'

'Captain—,' she began, but Hornblower was not in the mood
for argument – if indeed she had argument in mind.

'Mr Clay!' he rasped. 'Conduct her ladyship and her maid to
the cable tier. See that she is safe before you leave her. Those
are my *orders*, Mr Clay. Ha – h'm.'

A cowardly way out, perhaps, to throw on Clay the responsibility of seeing his orders carried out. He knew it, but he was
angry with the woman because of the sick feeling of worry which
she was occasioning him. She left him, nevertheless, with a smile
and a wave of the hand, Clay trotting before her.

For several minutes the ship was a turmoil of industry as the
men went through the well-learned drill. The guns were run out,
the decks sanded, the horses rigged to the pumps, the fires extinguished, the bulkheads torn down. The *Natividad* could be seen
from the deck now, sailing on the opposite tack towards her,
obviously clawing her hardest up to windward to get the weather
gauge. Hornblower looked up at the sails to mark the least shiver.

'Steer small, blast you,' he growled at the quartermaster.

The *Lydia* lay over before the gale, the waves crashing and
hissing overside, the rigging playing a wild symphony. Last night
she had been stealing peacefully over a calm and moonlit sea,
and now here she was, twelve hours later, thrashing through a
storm with a battle awaiting her. The wind was undoubtedly
increasing – a wilder puff almost took her aback – and she stag-
gered and rolled until the helmsman allowed her to pay off.

'*Natividad* won't be able to open her lower deck ports!' gloated
Bush beside him. Hornblower stared across the grey sea at the
enemy. He saw a cloud of spray break over her bows.

'No,' he said heavily. He would not discuss the possibilities
of the approaching action for fear lest he might be too talkative.
'I'll trouble you, Mr Bush, to have two reefs taken in those tops'ls.'

On opposite tacks, the ships were nearing each other along
the sides of an obtuse angle. Look as closely as he would, he
could not decide which ship would be to windward when they
met at the apex.

'Mr Gerard,' he called down to the lieutenant in charge of the port side main-deck battery. 'See that the matches in your tubs are alight.'

'Aye aye, sir.'

With all this spray breaking aboard, the flintlock trigger mechanism could not be relied upon until the guns grew hot and the old-fashioned method of ignition might have to be used – in the tubs on deck were coils of slow-match to meet this emergency. He stared across again at the *Natividad*. She, too, had reefed her topsail now, and was staggering along, close-hauled, under storm canvas. She was flying the blue flag with the yellow star; Hornblower glanced up overhead to where the dingy white ensign fluttered from the peak.

'She's opened fire, sir,' said Bush beside him.

Hornblower looked back at the *Natividad* just in time to see the last of a puff of smoke blown to shreds by the wind. The sound of the shot did not reach them, and where the ball went no one could say – the jet of water which it struck up somewhere was hidden in the tossing waves.

'Ha – h'm,' said Hornblower.

It was bad policy, even with a well-drilled crew, to open fire at long range. That first broadside, discharged from guns loaded carefully and at leisure, and aimed by crews with time to think, was too precious a thing to be dissipated lightly. It should be saved up for use at the moment when it would do maximum harm, however great might be the strain of waiting inactive.

'We'll be passing mighty close, sir,' said Bush.

'Ha – h'm,' said Hornblower.

Still there was no means of telling which ship would hold the weather gauge when they met. It appeared as if they would meet bow to bow in collision if both captains held rigidly to their present courses. Hornblower had to exert all his willpower to keep himself standing still and apparently unemotional as the tension increased.

Another puff of smoke from the *Natividad*'s starboard bow, and this time they heard the sound of the shot as it passed overhead between the masts.

'Closer!' said Bush.

Another puff, and simultaneously a crash from the waist told where the shot had struck.

'Two men down at number four gun,' said Bush, stooping to look forward under the gangway, and then, eyeing the distance between the two ships: 'Christ! It's going to be a near thing.'

It was a situation which Hornblower had visualised several times in his solitary walks on the quarterdeck. He took a last glance up at the weathervane, and at the topsails on the point of shivering as the ship tossed on the heaving sea.

'Stand by, Mr Rayner. Fire as your guns bear,' he called. Rayner was in command of the starboard-side main-deck battery. Then, from the corner of his mouth to the men at the wheel – 'Put your helm a-weather. Catch her! Hold her so!'

The *Lydia* spun round and shot down the lee side of the *Natividad* and her starboard side guns went off almost simultaneously in a rolling crash that shook the ship to her keel. The billow of smoke that enveloped her momentarily was blown away instantly by the gale. Every shot crashed into the *Natividad*'s side; the wind brought to their ears the screams of the wounded. So unexpected had the manoeuvre been that only one single shot was fired from the *Natividad*, and that did no damage – her lower deck ports on this, her lee side, were closed because of the high sea.

'Grand!' Oh, grand!' said Bush. He sniffed at the bitter powder smoke eddying round him as if it had been sweet incense.

'Stand by to go about,' rasped Hornblower.

A well-drilled crew, trained in months of storms under Bush's eagle eye, was ready at sheets and braces. The *Lydia* tacked about, turning like a machine, before *Natividad* could offer any counter to this unexpected attack, and Gerard fired his battery into her helpless stern. The ship's boys were cheering aimlessly in high piping trebles as they came running up from below with new charges for the guns. On the starboard side the guns were already loaded; on the port side the guns' crews were thrusting wet swabs down the bore to extinguish any residual fragments of smouldering cartridge, ramming in the charges and shot, and heaving the guns up into firing position again. Hornblower stared across the tossing water at the *Natividad*. He could see Crespo up on her poop; the fellow actually had the insolence to wave his hand to him, airily, while in the midst of bellowing orders at his unhandy crew.

The *Lydia* had wrung the utmost advantage out of her manoeuvre; she had fired her two broadsides at close range and had only received a single shot in reply, but now she had to pay for it. By her possession of the weather gauge the *Natividad* could force close action for a space if resolutely handled. Hornblower could just see her rudder from where he stood. He saw it kick over, and next moment the two-decker had swung round and was hurtling down upon them. Gerard stood in the midst of his battery gazing with narrowed eyes into the wind at the impressive bulk close overside. His swarthy beauty was accentuated by the tenseness of the moment and the fierce concentration of his expression, but for once he was quite unconscious of his good looks.

'Cock your locks!' he ordered. 'Take your aim! Fire!'

The roar of the broadside coincided exactly with that of the *Natividad*'s. The ship was enveloped in smoke, through which could be heard the rattling of splinters, the sound of cut rigging tumbling to the deck, and through it all Gerard's voice continuing with his drill – 'Stop your vents!' The quicker the touch holes of the muzzle loaders were plugged after firing the less would be the wear caused by the rush of the acid gases through them.

The guns' crews strained at the tackles as the heave of the ship bade fair to send them surging back against the ship's sides. They sponged and they rammed.

'Fire as you will, boys!' shouted Gerard. He was up on the hammock-netting now, gazing through the smoke wreaths at the *Natividad* rising and swooping alongside. The next broadside crashed out raggedly, and the next more raggedly still, as the more expert gun crews got off their shots more quickly than the others; soon the sound of firing was continuous, and the *Lydia* was constantly a-tremble. At intervals through the roar of her cannon came the thunderous crash of the *Natividad*'s broadside – Crespo evidently could not trust his crew to fire independently with efficiency, and was working them to the word of command. He was doing it well, too; at intervals as the sea permitted, her lower deck ports were opening like clockwork and the big twenty-four pounders were vomiting flame and smoke.

'Hot work, this, sir,' said Bush.

The iron hail was sweeping the *Lydia*'s decks. There were dead men piled round the masts, whither they had been hastily dragged so as not to encumber the guns' crews. Wounded men were being dragged along the deck and down the hatchways to where the horrors of the cockpit awaited them. As Hornblower looked he saw a powder boy flung across the deck, dissolved into a red inhuman mass as a twenty-four pounder ball hit him.

'Ha – h'm,' said Hornblower, but the sound was drowned in the roar of the quarterdeck carronade beside him. It was hot work indeed, too hot. This five minutes of close firing was sufficient to convince him that the *Natividad*'s guns were too well worked for the *Lydia* to have any chance against her overpowering strength broadside to broadside, despite the damage done in the first few minutes of the action. He would have to win by craft if he was to win at all.

'Hands to the braces!' he yelled, his voice, high-pitched, cutting through the din of the guns. He stared narrow-eyed at the *Natividad* with the smoke pouring from her sides, he estimated the force of the wind and the speeds of the ships. His mind was making calculations with delirious rapidity, keyed up by the excitement, as he began the new manoeuvre. Throwing the main topsail aback a trifle allowed the *Natividad* to shoot ahead without taking so much way off the *Lydia* as to make her unhandy, and then the next moment Hornblower tacked his ship about so that the waiting starboard battery was able to fire into the *Natividad*'s stern. The *Natividad* came up into the wind in the endeavour to follow her opponent round and keep broadside to broadside with her, but the frigate was far quicker in stays than the clumsy, stumpy two-decker. Hornblower, watching his enemy with his keen gaze, tacked once more, instantly, and shot past the *Natividad*'s stern on the opposite tack while Gerard, running from gun to gun, sent every shot crashing into the shattered timbers.

'Glorious! Damme! Damn my eyes! Damn my soul! Glorious!' spluttered Bush, thumping his right fist into his left hand and leaping up and down on the quarterdeck.

Hornblower had no attention to spare for Bush nor for Bush's good opinion, although later he was to remember hearing the words and find warm comfort in them. As the ships diverged he shouted for the *Lydia* to go about again, but, even as the sheets were handed and the helm put over, the *Natividad* wore round to pass her to leeward. So much the better. At the cost of a single exchange of broadsides he would be able to assail that vulnerable stern again, and if the *Natividad* attempted to circle, his was the handier ship and he could rely on getting in at least two effective shots to his opponent's one. He watched the *Natividad* come foaming up; her bulwarks were riddled with shot and there was a trickle of blood from her scuppers. He caught a glimpse of Crespo on the poop – he had hoped that he might have been killed in the last two broadsides, for that would mean, almost for certain, a slackening in the attack. But her guns were run out ready, and on this, her weather side, her lower deck ports were open.

'For what we are about to receive—,' said Bush, repeating the hackneyed old blasphemy quoted in every ship awaiting a broadside.

Seconds seemed as long as minutes as the two ships neared. They were passing within a dozen yards of each other. Bow overlapped bow, foremast passed foremast and then foremast passed mainmast. Rayner was looking aft, and as soon as he saw that the aftermost gun bore on the target he shouted the order to fire. The *Lydia* lifted to the recoil of the guns, ears were split with the sound of the discharge, and then, even before the gale had time to blow away the smoke, came the *Natividad*'s crashing reply.

It seemed to Hornblower as if the heavens were falling round him. The wind of a shot made him reel; he found at his feet a palpitating red mass which represented half the starboard side carronade's crew, and then with a thunderous crackling the mizzen mast gave way beside him. The weather mizzen rigging entangled him and flung him down into the blood on the deck, and while he struggled to free himself he felt the *Lydia* swing round as she paid off despite the efforts of the men at the wheel.

He got to his feet, dizzy and shaken, to find ruin all round him. The mizzen mast was gone, snapped off nine feet from the deck, taking the main topgallant mast with it, and masts and yards and sails and rigging trailed alongside and astern by the unparted shrouds. With the loss of the balancing pressure of the mizzen topsail the *Lydia* had been unable to keep her course on the wind and was now drifting helplessly dead before the gale. And at that very moment he saw the *Natividad* going about to cross his stern and repay, with a crushing broadside, the several unanswered salvoes to which earlier she had been forced to submit. His whole world seemed to be shattered. He gulped convulsively, with a sudden sick fear of defeat at the pit of his stomach.

CHAPTER XIV

But he knew, and he told himself, at the moment of his getting to his feet, that he must not delay an instant in making the *Lydia* ready for action again.

'Afterguard!' he roared – his voice sounding unnatural to himself as he spoke – 'Mr Clay! Benskin! Axes here! Cut that wreckage away!'

Clay came pounding aft at the head of a rush of men with axes and cutlasses. As they were chopping at the mizzen shrouds he noticed Bush sitting up on the deck with his face in his hands – apparently a falling block had struck him down but there was no time to spare for Bush. The *Natividad* was coming down remorselessly on them; he could see exultant figures on her deck waving their hats in triumph. To his strained senses it seemed to him that even through the din on board the *Lydia* he could hear the creaking of *Natividad*'s rigging and the rumble of her reloaded guns being run out. She was steering to pass as close as possible. Hornblower saw her bowsprit go by, felt her reefed fore topsail loom over him, and then her broadside crashed out as gun after gun bore on the *Lydia*'s stern. The wind caught the smoke and whipped it round Hornblower, blinding him. He felt the deck leap as the shots struck home, heard a scream from Clay's party beside him, felt a splinter scream past his cheek, and then, just as annihilation seemed about to engulf him, the frightful succession of shots ended, the smoke was borne away, the *Natividad* had gone by, and he was still alive and could look round him. The slide of the aftermost carronade had been smashed, and one of Clay's men was lying screaming on the deck with the gun across his thighs and two or three of his mates striving futilely to prise it off them.

'Stop that!' screamed Hornblower – the necessity of having to give such an order sent his voice up to the same pitch as that of the miserable wretch in his agony – 'Cut that bloody wreckage away! Mr Clay, keep them at work!'

A cable's length away, over the grey-topped waves, the *Natividad* was slowly wearing round to return and deal a fresh blow at her helpless opponent. It was lucky that the *Natividad* was an unhandy ship, like all those stumpy fourth rates – it gave Hornblower more time between the broadsides to try and get the *Lydia* into a condition so that she could face her enemy again.

'Foretop, there! Mr Galbraith! Get the headsails in.'

'Aye aye, sir.'

The absence of the fore topmast staysail and storm jib would balance to some extent the loss of the mizzen topsail and driver. He might, by juggling with the helm, get the *Lydia* to lie to the wind a trifle then, and hit back at his big opponent. But there was no hope of doing so while all this wreckage was trailing astern like a vast sea anchor. Until that was cut away she could only lie helpless, dead before the wind, suffering her enemy's blows in silence. A glance showed him that the *Natividad* had worn round now, and was heading to cross their stern again.

'Hurry up!' he screamed to the axe men. 'You, there, Holroyd, Tooms, get down into the mizzen chains.'

He suddenly realised how high-pitched and hysterical his voice had become. At all costs he must preserve before Clay and the men his reputation for imperturbability. He forced himself convulsively, to look casually at the *Natividad* as she came plunging down on them again, wicked with menace; he made himself grin, and shrug his shoulders, and speak in his normal voice.

'Don't mind about her, my lads. One thing at a time. Cut this wreckage away first, and we'll give the Dagoes their bellyful after.'

The men hacked with renewed force at the tough tangles of cordage. Something gave way, and a new extravagant plunge on the part of the *Lydia* as a huge wave lifted her stern caused the wreckage to run out a little farther before catching again, this time on the mizzen stay, which, sweeping the deck, tumbled three men off their feet. Hornblower seized one of the fallen axes, and fell desperately on the rope as it sawed back and forth with the roll of the ship. From the tail of his eye he saw the *Natividad* looming up, but he could spare no attention for her. For the moment she represented merely a tiresome interruption to his work, not a menace to his life.

Then once more he was engulfed in the smoke and din of the *Natividad*'s broadside. He felt the wind of shot round him, and heard the scream of splinters. The cries of the man under the carronade ceased abruptly, and beneath his feet he could feel the crash as the shot struck home in the *Lydia*'s vitals. But he was mesmerised by the necessity of completing his task. The mizzen stay parted under his axe; he saw another rope draw up taut, and cut that as well – the pattern of the seams of the deck planking at that point caught his notice – felt another severed and flick past him, and then knew that the *Lydia* was free from the wreckage. Almost at his feet lay young Clay, sprawled upon the deck, but Clay had no head. He noted that as an interesting phenomenon, like the pattern of the deck seams.

A sudden breaking wave drenched him with spray; he swept the water from his eyes and looked about him. Most of the men who had been on the quarterdeck with him were dead: marines, seamen, officers. Simmonds had what was left of the marines lined up against the taffrail, ready to reply with musketry to the *Natividad*'s twenty-four pounders. Bush was in the main top, and Hornblower suddenly realised that to him was due the cutting of the mizzen top mast stay which had finally freed the ship. At the wheel stood the two quartermasters, rigid, unmoving, gazing straight ahead; they were not the same as the men who had stood there when the action began, but the iron discipline of the Navy and its unbending routine had kept the wheel manned through the vicissitudes of the battle.

Out on the starboard quarter, the *Natividad* was wearing round again. Hornblower realised with a little thrill that this time he need not submit meekly to the punishment she was determined to adminster. It called for an effort to make himself work out the problem of how to work the ship round, but he forced his mind to concentrate on it, comparing the proportional leverages of the fore and main topsails, and visualising in his mind the relative positions of the centre of the ship and the mainmast – luckily this latter was stepped a little aft.

'Man the braces, there!' he called. 'Mr Bush, we'll try and bring her to the wind.'

'Aye aye, sir.'

He looked back at the *Natividad*, plunging and heaving towards them.

'Hard-a-starboard!' he snapped at the quartermaster. 'Stand to your guns, men.'

The crew of the *Natividad*, looking along their guns, suddenly saw the *Lydia*'s battered stern slowly turn from them. For a fleeting half minute, while the English frigate held her way, the quartermasters straining at her wheel were able to bring the wind abeam of her as the *Natividad* swept by.

'Fire!' yelled Gerard – his voice, too, was cracking with excitement.

The *Lydia* heaved again with the recoil of the guns, and the smoke billowed over her deck, and through the smoke came the iron hail of the *Natividad*'s broadside.

'Give it her again, lads!' screamed Gerard. 'There goes her foremast! Well done, lads.'

The guns' crews cheered madly, even though their two hundred voices sounded feeble against the gale. In that sudden flurry of action the enemy had been hard hit. Through the smoke Hornblower saw the *Natividad*'s foremast shrouds suddenly slacken, tauten again, slacken once more, and then her whole foremast bowed forward; her main topmast whipped and then followed it, and the whole vanished over the side. The *Natividad* turned instantly up into the wind, while at the same time the *Lydia*'s head fell off as she turned downwind despite the efforts of the men at the wheel. The gale screamed past Hornblower's ears as the strip of grey sea which divided the ships widened more and more. One last gun went off on the main deck, and then the two ships lay pitching upon the turbulent sea, each unable to harm the other.

Hornblower wiped the spray slowly from his eyes again. This battle was like some long drawn nightmare, where one situation of fantastic unreality merged into the next. He felt as if he were in a nightmare, too – he could think clearly, but only by compelling himself to do so, as though it was unnatural to him.

The gap between the ships had widened to a full half mile, and was widening further. Through his glass he could see the *Natividad*'s forecastle black with men struggling with the wreck of the foremast. The ship which was first ready for action again would win. He snapped the glass shut and turned to face all the problems which he knew were awaiting his immediate solution.

CHAPTER XV

The captain of the *Lydia* stood on his quarterdeck while his ship, hove to under the main staysail and three-reefed main topsail, pitched and wallowed in the fantastic sea. It was raining now, with such violence that nothing could be seen a hundred yards away, and there were deluges of spray sweeping the deck, too, so that he and his clothes were as wet as if he had been swimming in the sea, but he was not aware of it. Everyone was appealing to him for orders – first lieutenant, gunner, boatswain, carpenter, surgeon, purser. The ship had to be made fit to fight again, even though there was every doubt as to whether she would even live through the storm which shrieked round her. It was the acting-surgeon who was appealing to him at the moment.

'But what am I to *do*, sir?' he said pathetically, white faced, wringing his hands. This was Laurie, the purser's steward, who had been appointed acting-surgeon when Hankey the surgeon died. He had fifty wounded down in the grim dark cockpit, maddened with pain, some with limbs torn off, and all of them begging for the assistance which he had no idea of how to give.

'What are you to *do*, sir?' mimicked Hornblower scornfully, beside himself with exasperation at this incompetence. 'After two months in which to study your duties you have to ask what to do!'

Laurie only blenched a little more at this, and Hornblower had to make himself be a little helpful and put some heart in this lily-livered incompetent.

'See here, Laurie,' he said, in more kindly fashion. 'Nobody expects miracles of you. Do what you can. Those who are going to die you must make easy. You have my orders to reckon every man who has lost a limb as one of those. Give them laudanum – twenty-five drops a man, or more if that won't ease them. Pretend to bandage 'em. Tell 'em they're certain to get better and draw a pension for the next fifty years. As for the others, surely your mother wit can guide you. Bandage 'em until the bleeding stops. You have rags enough to bandage the whole ship's crew. Put splints on the broken bones. Don't move any man more than is necessary. Keep every man quiet. A tot of rum to every wounded man, and promise 'em another at eight bells if they lie still. I never knew a Jack yet who wouldn't go through hell fire for a tot of rum. Get below, man, and see to it.'

'Aye aye, sir.'

Laurie could only think of his own responsibility and duty; he scuttled away below without a thought for the hell-turned-loose on the main deck. Here, one of the twelve-pounders had come adrift, its breechings shot away by the *Natividad*'s last broadside. With every roll of the ship it was rumbling back and forth across the deck, a ton and a half of insensate weight, threatening at any moment to burst through the ship's side. Galbraith, with twenty men trailing ropes, and fifty men carrying mats and hammocks, was trailing it cautiously from point to point in the hope of tying it or smothering it into helplessness. As Hornblower watched them, a fresh heave of the ship canted it round and sent it thundering in a mad charge straight at them. They parted wildly before it, and it charged through them, its trucks squealing like a forest of pigs, and brought up with a shattering crash against the mainmast.

'Now's your chance, lads! Jump to it!' yelled Hornblower.

Galbraith, running forward, risked limb and life to pass a rope's end through an eye tackle. Yet he had no sooner done it than a new movement of the ship swung the gun round and threatened to waste his effort.

'Hammocks, there!' shouted Hornblower. 'Pile them quick! Mr Galbraith, take a turn with that line round the mainmast. Whipple, put your rope through the breeching ring. Quick, man! Now take a turn!'

Hornblower had accomplished what Galbraith had failed to do – had correlated the efforts of the men in the nick of time so that now the gun was bound and helpless. There only remained the ticklish job of manoeuvring it back to its gun port and securing it with fresh breechings. Howell the carpenter was at his elbow now, waiting until he could spare a moment's attention from this business with the gun.

'Four feet an' more in the well, sir,' said Howell, knuckling his forehead. 'Nearer five, an' making fast as well as I could tell. Can I have some more men for the pumps, sir?'

'Not until that gun's in place,' said Hornblower, grimly. 'What damage have you found?'

'Seven shot holes, sir, below water line. There's no pluggin' of 'em not with this sea runnin', sir.'

'I know that,' snapped Hornblower. 'Where are they?'

'All of 'em for'ard, somehow, sir. One clean through the third frame timber, starboard side. Two more—'

'I'll have a sail forthered under the bottom as soon as there are enough men to spare. Your men at the pumps will have to continue pumping. Report to the first lieutenant's party with your mates now.'

The first lieutenant and the boatswain were busily engaged upon the duty of erecting a jury mizzen mast. Already the boatswain had come ruefully to the captain with the information that half the spare spars secured between the gangways had been damaged by shot, but there was a main topsail yard left which would serve. But to sway up its fifty-five-foot length into a vertical position was going to be a tricky business – hard enough in a smooth sea, dangerous and prolonged out here with the Pacific running mad. In harbour an old ship – a sheer hulk – would be brought alongside, and would employ the two immense spars which constituted her sheers as a crane in which to lift the new mast vertically into the ship. Here there was nothing of the sort available, and the problem of raising the spar might seem insoluble, but Bush and Harrison between them were tackling it with all the resource and energy the navy could display.

Happily there was that stump of the old mizzenmast left – its nine feet of length relieved them of the tiresome complication of steeping the new mast, which they proposed instead merely to fish to the stump. The after-part of the ship was alive with working parties, each intent on its own contribution to the work in hand. With tackles and rollers, the spar had been eased aft until its butt was solidly against the stump of the mizzenmast. Harrison was now supervising the task of noosing shrouds to the new masthead; after that he would have to prepare the masthead to receive the cap and the trussel trees which the carpenter and his mates would now have to make.

In the mizzen chains on either side, Harrison's mates were supervising the efforts of two other parties engaged upon attaching the other ends of the shrouds to the channels, where with dead eyes and lanyards the shrouds could be kept taut as the mast rose. Bush was attending to the preparation of the jears and tackle at the mainmast which would help to accomplish a great part of the lift; the sailmaker and his mates were rousing out and adapting sails to fit the new mast, gaff and yards. Another party of men under the gunner was engaged on the difficult task of remounting the dismounted quarterdeck carronade, while Gerard was aloft with the topmen attending to the repair of the damage done to the standing and running rigging of the remaining masts. All this was in the rain, with the wind shrieking round them; and yet the rain and the wind seemed warm to the touch, so oppressively hot was it. The half-naked seamen, slaving at their task, were running wet with sweat as well as with rainwater and spray. The ship was a nightmare of insane yet ordered activity.

A sudden flurry of rain heralded the arrival of a clear spell. Braced upon the heaving deck, Hornblower set his glass to his eye; the *Natividad* was visible again, hull down now, across the tossing grey-flecked sea. She was hove-to as well, looking queerly lopsided in her partially dismasted condition. Hornblower's glass could discover no sign of any immediate replacement of the missing spars; he thought it extremely probable that there was nothing left in the ship to serve as jury masts. In that case as soon as the *Lydia* could carry enough sail aft to enable her to beat to windward he would have the *Natividad* at his mercy – as long as the sea was not running high enough to make gunnery impossible.

He glowered round the horizon; at present there was no sign of the storm abating, and it was long past noon. With the coming of night he might lose the *Natividad* altogether, and nightfall would give his enemy a further respite in which to achieve repairs.

'How much longer, Mr Harrison?' he rasped.

'Not long now, sir. Nearly ready, sir.'

'You've had long enough and to spare for a simple piece of work like that. Keep the men moving, there.'

'Aye aye, sir.'

Hornblower knew that the men were cursing him under their breath; he did not know they admired him as well, as men will admire a hard master despite themselves.

Now it was the cook come to report to him – the cook and his mates had been the only men in the ship who could be spared for the grisly work allotted to them.

'All ready, sir,' he said.

Without a word Hornblower strode forward down the starboard side gangway, taking his prayer book from his pocket. The fourteen dead were there, shrouded in their hammocks, two to a grating, a roundshot sewn into the foot of each hammock. Hornblower blew a long blast upon his silver whistle, and activity ceased on board while he read, compromising between haste and solemnity, the office for the burial of the dead at sea.

'We therefore commit their bodies to the deep—'

The cook and his mates tilted each grating in turn, and the bodies fell with sullen splashes overside while Hornblower read the concluding words of the service. As soon as the last words were said he blew his whistle again and all the bustle and activity recommenced. He grudged those few minutes taken from the work bitterly, but he knew that any unceremonious pitching overboard of the dead would be resented by his men, who set all the store by forms and ceremonies to be expected of the uneducated.

And now there was something else to plague him. Picking her way across the main deck below him came Lady Barbara, the little negress clinging to her skirts.

'My orders were for you to stay below, ma'am,' he shouted to her.

'This deck is no place for you.'

Lady Barbara looked round the seething deck and then tilted her chin to answer him.

'I can see that without having it pointed out to me,' she said, and then, softening her manner: 'I have no intention of obstructing, Captain. I was going to shut myself in my cabin.'

'Your cabin?'

Hornblower laughed. Four broadsides from the *Natividad* had blasted their way through that cabin. The idea of Lady Barbara shutting herself up there struck him as being intensely funny. He laughed again, and then again, before checking himself in hurried mistrust as an abyss of hysteria opened itself before him. He controlled himself.

'There is no cabin left for you, ma'am. I regret that the only course open to you is to go back whence you have come. There is no other place in the ship that can accommodate you at present.'

Lady Barbara, looking up at him, thought of the cable tier she had just left. Pitch dark, with only room to sit hunched up on the slimy cable, rats squeaking and scampering over her legs; the ship pitching and rolling madly, and Hebe howling with fright beside her; the tremendous din of the guns, and the thunderous rumble of the gun trucks immediately over her head as the guns were run in and out; the tearing crash which had echoed through the ship when the mizzenmast fell; the ignorance of how the battle was progressing – at this very moment she was still unaware whether it had been lost or won or merely suspended; the stench of the bilge, the hunger and the thirst.

The thought of going back there appalled her. But she saw the captain's face, white with fatigue and strain under its tan, and she had noted that laugh with its hysterical pitch, abruptly cut off, and the grim effort that had been made to speak to her reasonably. The captain's coat was torn across the breast, and his white trousers were stained – with blood, she suddenly realised. She felt pity for him, then. She knew now that to speak to him of rats and stinks and baseless fears would be ridiculous.

'Very good, Captain,' she said quietly, and turned to retrace her steps.

The little negress set up a howl, and was promptly shaken into silence as Lady Barbara dragged her along.

CHAPTER XVI

'Ready now, sir,' said Bush.

The crew of the *Lydia* had worked marvellously. The guns were all secured now, and the main deck cleared of most of the traces of the fight. A sail stretched over the bottom of the ship had done much to check the inflow of water, so that now only twenty men were at work upon the pumps and the level in the well was measurably sinking. The sailmaster had his new sails ready, the boatswain his rigging, the carpenter his accessories. Already Harrison had his men at the windlass, and the mast lay ready for hoisting.

Hornblower looked round him. All the mad effort put into the work to get it done speedily was wasted, for the gale still showed no signs of abating and with this present wind blowing it would be hopeless to try to beat over to the *Natividad*. He had driven his men hard – overdriven them – to lose no time, and now it was obvious that they might have done it all at their leisure. But the work might as well be completed now. He ran his eye over the waiting groups of men; each knew their duty, and there was an officer at each strategic point to see that orders were carried out.

'Very good, Mr Bush,' he said.

'Hoist away, there!' yelled Bush to the windlass crew.

The windlass began to tum, the rope began to groan through the jears, and the mast rose, little by little, watched by every eye. The mad plunges of the ship threatened to ruin everything. There was danger of the masthead escaping from the ropes that held it; there was danger of the butt slipping away from the stump of the mizzen mast against which it rested. Everything had to be watched, every precaution taken, to see that neither of these possibilities developed. Bush watched the jears, while Gerard at the main masthead attended to the slings. Galbraith was in the mizzen chains on one side, Rayner on the other. Boatswain and carpenter stood with ropes and spars at the butt end of the mast, but it was the captain, leaning on the quarterdeck rail, whose duty it was to see that every part of the cumbrous machine did its work in its proper relation to the others. It was he whom the crew would blame for failure.

He knew it, too. He watched the dizzy heave and pitch of the ship, and the masthead wavering in the slings, and he heard the butt end grinding upon the deck as it moved uneasily between the two spars lashed as buttresses against the stump of the mizzen mast. It was an effort to think clearly, and he could only compel his mind to it by an exertion of all his will. He was sick and tired and nervous.

It was of vital importance that the hands at the shrouds and back stays only took up as much slack as was won for them by the jears, and refrained from tightening up when a roll of the ship swung the mast over on their side a trifle. Yet this was just what they persisted in doing, maddeningly, so obsessed were they with the necessity of keeping all taut to prevent the swaying mast from taking charge. Twice the grip of the slings on the masthead was imperilled in this way, and Hornblower had to key himself up to his highest pitch for several seconds, watching the roll of the ship, so as to time precisely the next heave which would obviate the danger. His voice was hoarse with shouting.

Slowly the mast left the horizontal and swayed up towards the perpendicular. Hornblower's calculating eye, measuring stresses and reactions, saw that the crisis was now come – the moment when the jears could raise the masthead no more and the final lifting must be accomplished by the pull of the backstays aft. The next few moments were tricky ones, because the mast-head would not be deprived of the positive support of the slings. The jears had to be disconnected from the windlass and their work done by the backstays. Two lengths of cable had to be passed round the sloping jury mast and the vertical stump, with gangs of men ready to tighten them, tourniquet fashion, with capstan bars as each gain was made. Yet in these first seconds the backstays were at a mechanical disadvantage and would certainly not bear the strain which would be imposed on them if the windlass were employed in an endeavour to drag the mast upright by brute force.

The motion of the ship must be utilised to help. Hornblower had to watch the motion carefully, calling to the men to wait as the ship rolled and plunged, and then, as the bow slowly emerged from the creaming sea and climbed steadily skywards, he had to set windlass men and tourniquet men and lanyard men all in action at once, and then check them all instantly as the bow began to sink again and full strain came on to the rigging. Twice he managed it successfully, and then three times – although the third time an unexpected wave lifted the *Lydia*'s stern at the wrong moment and nearly wrecked everything.

Then the fourth heave settled it all. The mast was now so nearly vertical that shrouds and backstays were at a mechanical advantage, and everything could be hove taut regardless of the ship's motion. Shrouds and backstays could be set up now in normal fashion, the jury mast adequately fished to the stump – in fact all the difficult part of the work was completed. Hornblower leaned against the rail, sick with weariness, wondering dully how these iron-framed men of his could find the strength to cheer as they put the finishing touches to their work.

He found Bush beside him – Bush had a rag round his head, bloodstained because of the cut in his forehead inflicted by the falling block.

'A magnificent piece of work, if I may say so, sir,' he said.

Hornblower eyed him sharply, suspicious as ever of congratulation, knowing his own weakness so well. But Bush, surprisingly, seemed to mean in all sincerity what he said.

'Thank you,' said Hornblower, grudgingly.

'Shall I send up the topmast and yards, sir?'

Hornblower looked round the horizon once more. The gale was blowing as madly as ever, and only a grey smudge on the distant horizon marked where the *Natividad* was battling with it. Hornblower could see that there was no chance of showing any more canvas at present, no chance of renewing the fight while the *Natividad* was still unprepared. It was a bitter pill to swallow. He could imagine what would be said in service circles when he sent in his report to the Admiralty. His statement that the weather was too bad to renew the action, after having received such a severe handling, would be received with pitying smiles and knowing wags of the head. It was a hackneyed excuse, like the uncharted rock which explained faulty navigation. Cowardice, moral or even perhaps physical, would be the unspoken comment on every side – at ten thousand miles distance no one could judge of the strength of a storm. He could divest himself of some of his responsibility by asking Bush his opinion, and requesting him to go through the formality of putting it in writing; but he turned irritably from the thought of displaying weakness before his inferior.

'No,' he said, without expression. 'We shall stay hove-to until the weather moderates.'

There was a gleam of admiration in Bush's bloodshot eyes – Bush could well admire a captain who could make with such small debate a decision so nearly touching his professional reputation. Hornblower noticed it, but his cursed temperament forbade him to interpret it correctly.

'Aye aye, sir,' said Bush, warned by the scowl on his captain's forehead not to enlarge on the subject. But his affection for his captain compelled him to open a fresh one. 'If that's the case, sir, why not take a rest? You look mortally tired, sir, indeed you do. Let me send and have a berth screened off for you in the ward room.'

Bush found his hand twitching – he had been about to commit the enormity of patting his captain's shoulder, and restrained himself just in time.

'Fiddlesticks!' snapped Hornblower. As if a captain of a frigate could publicly admit that he was tired! And Hornblower could not trust himself to show any weakness at all – he always remembered how on his first commisson his second-in-command had taken advantages of lapses on his part.

'It is rather you who need a rest,' said Hornblower. 'Dismiss the starboard watch, and go below and turn in. Have someone attend to that forehead of yours, first. With the enemy in sight I shall stay on deck.'

After that it was Polwheal who came to plague him – Hornblower wondered ineffectively whether he came of his own initiative or whether Bush sent him up.

'I've been to attend to the lady, sir,' said Polwheal; Hornblower's tired mind was just beginning to grapple with the problem of what to do with Lady Barbara in a damaged ship cleared for action. 'I've screened off a bit of the orlop for her, sir. The wounded's mostly quiet by now, sir. I slung a 'ammock for her – nipped into it like a bird, she did, sir. She's taken food, too, sir – what was left of that cold chicken an' a glass of wine. Not that she wanted to, sir, but I persuaded her, like.'

'Very good, Polwheal,' said Hornblower. It was an enormous relief to hear that one responsibility at least was lifted from his shoulders.

'An' now about you, sir,' went on Polwheal. 'I've got you up some dry clothes from your chest in your storeroom, sir – I'm afraid that last broadside spoilt everything in your cabin, sir. An' I've got your boat cloak, sir, all warm an' dry. Do you care to shift your clothes up here or down below, sir?'

Polwheal could take much for granted and could wheedle the rest. Hornblower had anticipated dragging his weary form in his waterlogged clothes up and down the quarterdeck all through the night, his nervous irritation not permitting him to contemplate any other course. Polwheal unearthed Lady Barbara's hammock chair from somewhere and lashed it to the rail and persuaded Hornblower to sit in it and consume a supper of biscuit and rum. Polwheal draped the boat cloak about him and airily took it for granted that he would continue to sit there, since his determination was fixed not to turn in while the enemy was still close at hand.

And marvellously, as he sat there, with the spray wetting his face and the ship leaping and rolling under him, his head drooped upon his breast and he slept. It was only a broken and fitful sleep, but astonishingly restorative. He awoke every few minutes. Twice it was the sound of his own snores which roused him. At other times he woke with a start to see whether the weather was moderating; at other times still the thoughts which went running on through his mind despite his dozing called him out of his unconsciousness when they reached some fresh startling conclusion regarding what opinion England and his crew would hold of him after this battle.

Soon after midnight his sailor's instinct called him definitely into complete wakefulness. Something was happening to the weather. He scrambled stiffly to his feet. The ship was rolling more wildly than ever, but as he sniffed round him he knew that there was an improvement. He walked across to the binnacle, and Bush looked vastly out of the darkness beside him.

'Wind's shifting southerly an' moderating, sir,' said Bush.

The shift of the wind was breaking up the long Pacific waves into steeper seas, as the *Lydia*'s antics displayed well enough.

'Black as the Earl of Hell's riding boots, all the same, sir,' grumbled Bush, peering into the darkness.

Somewhere, perhaps twenty miles from them, perhaps only two hundred yards, the *Natividad* was combating the same gale. If the moon were to break through the scurrying clouds they might be at grips with her at any moment, yet while they were talking it was so dark that they could hardly make out the loom of the main topsail from the quarterdeck.

'She was going away to leeward much faster than us when we saw her last,' said Bush meditatively.

'I happened to notice that myself,' snapped Hornblower.

In this present darkness, however much the gale might moderate, there was nothing they could do. Hornblower could foresee, awaiting them, another of those long intervals of time with nothing to do and everything ready which punctuate the life of a naval officer and which were so liable to irritate him if he allowed them to. He realised that here was another opportunity to show himself as an iron-nerved man whom no tension could disturb. He yawned elaborately.

'I think I shall got to sleep again,' he said, speaking with the utmost unconcern. 'See that the lookouts keep awake, if you please, Mr Bush. And have me called as soon as it grows lighter.'

'Aye aye, sir,' said Bush, and Hornblower went back to his boat cloak and his hammock chair.

He lay there for the rest of the night, unsleeping, and yet staying rigidly still so that the quarterdeck officers might think him asleep and admire the steadiness of his nerves. His mind was busy on the task of guessing what Crespo might be planning in the *Natividad*.

The latter was so badly crippled that probably he would be able to make no effective repairs while at sea. It would be much to his advantage to make for the Gulf of Fonseca again. There he could step a foremast and send up a new main topmast. If the *Lydia* tried to interfere with her there she could overwhelm her by her superior weight in those confined waters; and besides, she would have the assistance of shore boats and possibly even of shore batteries. Moreover he could land his wounded and refill the gaps in his crew caused by the recent action – even landsmen would be of use in a fight to a finish. Crespo was a man of sufficient flexibility of mind not to scorn a retreat if it were to his advantage. The doubtful point was whether Crespo would dare to face el Supremo after an unsuccessful action.

Hornblower lay considering the matter, balancing his estimate of Crespo's character against what he knew of el Supremo. He remembered Crespo's glibness of tongue; that man would be able to convince even el Supremo that his return to his base with the *Lydia* undefeated was all part of a cunning plan for the

more certain destruction of the enemy. Certainly his best course
would be to return, and probably that would be the course he
would adopt, and that course implied an attempted evasion of
the *Lydia*. In that case he would – Hornblower's mind began
feverish calculations of the *Natividad*'s present position and
future course. In consequence of her bigger bulk, and her two
decks, she would have made far more leeway during the night
– she was far to leeward at nightfall, for that matter. With the
wind shifting and moderating as it was doing at present she
would soon be able to make what sail her crippled condition
would permit. The wind would be nearly foul for a run to the
Gulf of Fonseca. Making for the mainland would be dangerous
in Crespo's opinion, for the *Lydia* could hem her in between sea
and shore and compel her to fight. Most likely he would reach
far out to sea, clawing southward at the same time as much as
he could, and make for the Gulf of Fonseca by a long detour
out of sight of land. In that case Hornblower must guess at what
would be his position at dawn. He plunged into further tortuous
mental calculations.

Eight bells sounded; the watch was called; he heard Gerard
come to take over the deck from Bush. The wind was dropping
fast, although the sea showed no sign of moderating as yet. The
sky as he looked up at it was perceptibly lighter – here and there
he could see stars between the clouds. Crespo would certainly
be able to make sail now and attempt his escape. It was time for
Hornblower to come to a decision. He climbed out of the
hammock chair and walked across to the wheel.

'We will make sail, if you please, Mr Bush.'

'Aye aye, sir.'

Hornblower gave the course, and he knew as he gave it that
it might be quite the wrong one. He might have completely
miscalculated. Every yard that the *Lydia* was sailing now might
be in a direction away from the *Natividad*. Crespo might, at this
very moment, be heading past him to safety. He might never
destroy the *Natividad* at all if she fortified herself in the Gulf of

Fonseca. There would be some who would attribute his failure to incompetence, and there would be not a few who would call it cowardice.

CHAPTER XVII

From the *Lydia*'s masthead, in the clear daylight of the Pacific, a ship might be seen at a distance of as much as twenty miles, perhaps. A circle of twenty miles' radius, therefore, covered the extent of sea over which she had observation. It kept Hornblower occupied, during the remaining hours of darkness, to calculate the size of the circle in which the *Natividad* would necessarily be found next morning. She might be close at hand; she might be as much as a hundred and fifty miles away. That meant that if pure chance dictated the positions of the ships at dawn, it was almost exactly fifty to one against the *Natividad* being in sight; fifty to one on the ruin of Hornblower's professional reputation and only his professional abilities to counterbalance those odds. Only if he had guessed his enemy's plans correctly would he stand justified, and his officers knew it as well as he. Hornblower was conscious that Gerard was looking at him with interest through the darkness, and the consciousness caused him to hold himself rigid and immobile on the deck, neither walking up and down nor fidgeting, even though he could feel his heart beating faster each time he realised that dawn was approaching.

The blackness turned to grey. Now the outlines of the ship could be ascertained. The main topsail could be seen clearly. So could the fore topsail. Astern of them now the faintest hint of pink began to show in the greyness of the sky. Now the bulk of the grey waves overside could be seen as well as their white edges. Overhead by now the stars were invisible. The accustomed eye could pierce the greyness for a mile about the ship. And then astern, to the eastward, as the *Lydia* lifted on a wave, a grain of gold showed over the horizon, vanished, returned, and grew. Soon it became a great slice of the sun, sucking up greedily the faint mist which hung over the sea. Then the whole disk lifted clear, and the miracle of the dawn was accomplished.

'Sail ho!' came pealing down from the masthead; Hornblower had calculated aright.

Dead ahead, and ten miles distant, she was wallowing along, her appearance oddly at contrast with the one she had presented yesterday morning. Something had been done to give her a jury rig. A stumpy topmast had been erected where her foremast had stood, raked far back in clumsy fashion; her main topmast had been replaced by a slight spar – a royal mast, presumably – and on this jury rig she carried a queer collection of jibs and foresails and spritsails all badly set – 'Like old Mother Brown's washing on the line,' said Bush – to enable her to keep away from the wind with main course and mizzen topsail and driver set.

At sight of the *Lydia* she put her helm over and came round until her masts were in line, heading away from the frigate.

'Making a stern chase of it,' said Gerard, his glass to his eye. 'He had enough yesterday, I fancy.'

Hornblower heard the remark. He could understand Crespo's psychology better than that. If it were profitable to him to post-pone action, and it undoubtably was, he was quite right to continue doing so, even at the eleventh hour. At sea nothing was certain. Something might prevent the *Lydia*'s coming into action; a squall of wind, the accidental carrying away of a spar, an opportune descent of mist – any one of the myriad things which might happen at sea. There was still a chance that the *Natividad* might get clear away, and Crespo was exploiting that chance to the last of his ability. That was logical though unheroic, exactly as one might expect of Crespo.

It was Hornblower's duty to see that the chance did not occur. He examined the *Natividad* closely, ran his eyes over the *Lydia*'s sails to see that every one was drawing, and bethought himself of his crew.

'Send the hands to breakfast,' he said – every captain of a king's ship took his men into action with full bellies if possible.

He remained, pacing up and down the quarterdeck, unable to keep himself still any longer. The *Natividad* might be running away, but he knew well that she would fight hard enough when he caught her up. Those smashing twenty-four pounders which she carried on her lower deck were heavy metal against which to oppose the frail timbers of a frigate. They had wrought enough damage yesterday – he could hear the melancholy clanking of the pumps keeping down the water which leaked through the holes they had made; that clinking sound had continued without a break since yesterday. With a jury mizzenmast, and leaking like a sieve despite the sail under her bottom, with sixty-four of her attenuated crew *hors de combat*, the *Lydia* was in no condition to fight a severe battle. Defeat for her and death for him might be awaiting them across the strip of blue sea.

Polwheal suddenly appeared beside him on the quarterdeck, a tray in his hand.

'Your breakfast, sir,' he said, 'seeing as how we'll be in action when your usual time comes.'

As he proffered the tray Hornblower suddenly realised how much he wanted that steaming cup of coffee. He took it eagerly and drank thirstily before he remembered that he must not display human weakness of appetite before his servant.

'Thank you, Polwheal,' he said, sipping discreetly.

'An' 'er la'ships's compliments, sir, an' please may she stay where she is in the orlop when the action is renooed.'

'Ha – h'm,' said Hornblower, staring at him, thrown out of his stride by this unexpected question. All through the night he had been trying to forget the problem of Lady Barbara, as a man tries to forget an aching tooth. The orlop meant that Lady Barbara would be next to the wounded, separated from them only by a canvas screen – no place for a woman. But for that matter neither was the cable tier. The obvious truth was that there was no place for a woman in a frigate about to fight a battle.

'Put her wherever you like as long as she is not in reach of shot,' he said, irritably.

'Aye aye, sir. An' 'er la'ship told me to say that she wished you the best of good fortune today, sir, an' – an' – she was confident that you would meet with the success you – you deserve, sir.' Polwheal stumbled over this long speech in a manner which revealed that he had not been quite as successful in learning it fluently as he wished.

'Thank you, Polwheal,' said Hornblower, gravely. He remembered Lady Barbara's face as she looked up at him from the main deck yesterday. It was clean cut and eager – like a sword, was the absurd simile which came up in his mind.

'Ha – h'm,' said Hornblower angrily. He was aware that his expression had softened, and he feared lest Polwheal should have noticed it, at a moment when he knew about whom he was thinking. 'Get below and see that her ladyship is comfortable.'

The hands were pouring up from breakfast now; the pumps were clanking with a faster rhythm now that a fresh crew was at work upon them. The guns' crews were gathered about their guns, and the few idlers were crowded on the forecastle eagerly watching the progress of the chase.

'Do you think the wind's going to hold, sir?' asked Bush, coming on to the quarterdeck like a bird of ill omen. 'Seems to me as if the sun's swallowing it.'

There was no doubting the fact that as the sun climbed higher in the sky the wind was diminishing in force. The sea was still short, steep and rough, but the *Lydia*'s motion over it was no longer light and graceful. She was pitching and jerking inelegantly, deprived of the steady pressure of a good sailing wind. The sky overhead was fast becoming of a hard metallic blue.

'We're overhauling 'em fast,' said Hornblower, staring fixedly at the chase so as to ignore these portents of the elements.

'Three hours and we're up to 'em,' said Bush. 'If the wind only holds.'

It was fast growing hot. The heat which the sun was pouring down on them was intensified by its contrast with the comparative coolness of the night before. The crew had begun to seek

the strips of shade under the gangways, and were lying there
wearily. The steady clanking of the pumps seemed to sound
louder now that the wind was losing its force. Hornblower
suddenly realised that he would feel intensely weary if he
permitted himself to think about it. He stood stubborn on the
quarterdeck with the sun beating on his back, every few moments
raising his telescope to stare at the *Natividad* while Bush fussed
about the trimming of the sails as the breeze began to waver.

'Steer small, blast you,' he growled at the quartermaster at
the wheel as the ship's head fell away in the trough of a wave.

'I can't, sir, begging your pardon,' was the reply. 'There aren't
enough wind.'

It was true enough. The wind had died away so that the *Lydia*
could not maintain the two-knot speed which was sufficient to
give her rudder power to act.

'We'll have to wet the sails. Mr Bush, see to it, if you please,'
said Hornblower.

One division of one watch was roused up to this duty. A
soaking wet sail will hold air which would escape if it were
dry. Whips were rove through the blocks on the yards, and sea
water hoisted up and poured over the canvas. So hot was the
sun and so rapid the evaporation that the buckets had to be
kept continually in action. To the clanging of the pumps was
now added the shrilling of the sheaves in the blocks. The *Lydia*
crept, still plunging madly, over the tossing sea and under the
glaring sky.

'She's boxing the compass now,' said Bush with a jerk of his
thumb at the distant *Natividad*. 'She can't compare with this
beauty. She won't find the new rig of hers any help, neither.'

The *Natividad* was turning idly backwards and forwards on
the waves, showing sometimes her broadside and sometimes her
three masts in line, unable to steer any course in the light air
prevailing. Bush looked complacently up at his new mizzen mast,
a pyramid of canvas, and then across at the swaying *Natividad*,
less than five miles away. The minutes crept by, their passage

marked only by the monotonous noises of the ship. Hornblower stood in the scorching sunlight, fingering his telescope.

'Here comes the wind again, by God!' said Bush, suddenly. It was sufficient wind to make the ship heel a little, and to summon a faint harping from the rigging. ''Vast heaving with those buckets, there.'

The *Lydia* crept steadily forward, heaving and plunging to the music of the water under her bows, while the *Natividad* grew perceptibly nearer.

'It will reach him quickly enough. There! What did I say?'

The *Natividad*'s sails filled as the breeze came down to her. She straightened upon her course.

''Twon't help him as much as it helps us. God, if it only holds,' commented Bush.

The breeze wavered and then renewed itself. The *Natividad* was hull-up now across the water when a wave lifted her. Another hour – less than an hour – and she would be in range.

'We'll be trying long shots at her soon,' said Bush.

'Mr Bush,' said Hornblower, spitefully, 'I can judge of the situation without the assistance of your comments, profound though they be.'

'I beg your pardon, sir,' said Bush, hurt. He flushed angrily for a moment until he noticed the anxiety in Hornblower's tired eyes, and then stumped away to the opposite rail to forget his rage.

As if by way of comment, the big main-course flapped loudly, once, like a gun. The breeze was dying away as motivelessly as it had begun. And the *Natividad* still held it; she was holding her course steadily, drawing away once more, helped by the fluky wind. Here in the tropical Pacific one ship can have a fair wind while another two miles away lies becalmed, just as the heavy sea in which they were rolling indicated that last night's gale was still blowing, over the horizon, at the farther side of the Gulf of Tehuantepec. Hornblower stirred uneasily in the blazing sun. He feared lest he should see the *Natividad* sail clean away from him; the wind had died away so much that there was no point in wetting the sails, and the *Lydia* was rolling and sagging about aimlessly now to the send of the waves. Ten minutes passed before he was reassured by the sight of the *Natividad*'s similar behaviour.

There was not a breath of wind now. The *Lydia* rolled wildly, to the accompaniment of a spasmodic creaking of woodwork, flapping of sails, and clattering of blocks. Only the clangour of the pumps sounded steadily through the hot air. The *Natividad* was four miles away now – a mile and a half beyond the farthest range of any of the *Lydia*'s guns.

'Mr Bush,' said Hornblower. 'We will tow with the boats. Have the launch and the cutter hoisted out.'

Bush looked doubtful for a moment. He feared that two could play at that game. But he realised – as Hornblower had realised before him – that the *Lydia*'s graceful hull would be more amenable to towing than the *Natividad*'s ungainly bulk, even without counting the possibility that yesterday's action might have left her with no boat left that would swim. It was Hornblower's duty to try every course that might bring his ship into action with the enemy.

'Boats away!' roared Harrison. 'Cutter's crew, launch's crew.'

The pipes of his mates endorsed the orders. The hands tailed on to the tackles, and each boat in turn was swayed up into the air, and lowered outboard, the boats' crews fending off as the *Lydia* rolled in the swell.

There began for the boats' crews a period of the most exhausting and exasperating labour. They would tug and strain at the oars, moving the ponderous boats over the heaving waves, until the tow ropes tightened with a jerk as the strain came upon them. Then, tug as they would, they would seem to make no progress at all, the oar blades foaming impotently through the blue water, until the *Lydia* consented to crawl forward a little and the whole operation could be repeated. The heaving waves were a hindrance to them – sometimes every man on one side of a boat would catch a simultaneous crab so that the boat would spin round and become a nuisance to the other one – and the *Lydia*, so graceful and willing when under sail, was a perfect bitch when being towed.

She yawed and she sagged, falling away in the trough on occasions so much that the launch and the cutter were dragged, with much splashing from the oars, stern first after her wavering bows, and then changing her mind and heaving forward so fast after the two ropes that the men, flinging their weight upon the oar looms in expectation of a profitless pull, were precipitated backwards with the ease of progression while in imminent danger of being run down.

They sat naked on the thwarts while the sweat ran in streams down their faces and chests, unable – unlike their comrades at the pumps – to forget their fatigues in the numbness of monotonous work when every moment called for vigilance and attention, tugging painfully away, their agonies of thirst hardly relieved by the allowance of water doled out to them by the petty officers in the sternsheets, tugging away until even hands calloused by years of pulling and hauling cracked and blistered so that the oars were agony to touch.

Hornblower knew well enough the hardship they were undergoing. He went forward and looked down at the toiling seamen, knowing perfectly well that his own body would not be able to endure that labour for more than half an hour at most. He gave orders for an hourly relief at the oars, and he did his best to cheer the men on. He felt an uneasy sympathy for them – three-quarters of them had never been sailors until this commission, and had no desire to be sailors either, but had been swept up by the all-embracing press seven months ago. Hornblower was always able (rather against his will) to do what most of his officers failed to do – he saw his crew not as topmen or hands, but as what they had been before the press caught them: stevedores, wherry men, porters.

He had waggoners and potters – he had even two draper's assistants and a printer among his crew; men snatched without notice from their families and their employment and forced into this sort of labour, on wretched food, in hideous working conditions, haunted always by the fear of the cat or of Harrison's rattan, and with the chance of death by drowning or by hostile action to seal the bargain. So imaginative an individualist as Hornblower was bound to feel sympathy with them even when he felt he ought not, especially as he (in common with a few other liberals) found himself growing more and more liberal-minded with the progress of years. But to counterbalance this weakness of his there was his restless nervous anxiety to finish off well any task he had set himself to do. With the *Natividad* in sight he could not rest until he had engaged her, and when a captain of a ship cannot rest, his crew certainly cannot – aching backs or bleeding hands notwithstanding.

By careful measurement with his sextant of the subtended angles he was able to say with certainty at the end of an hour that the efforts of the boats' crews had dragged the *Lydia* a little nearer to the *Natividad*, and Bush, who had taken the same measurements, was in agreement. The sun rose higher and the *Lydia* crept inch by inch towards the enemy.

'*Natividad*'s hoisting out a boat, sir,' hailed Knyvett from the foretop.

'How many oars?'

'Twelve, sir, I think. They're taking the ship in tow.'

'And they're welcome,' scoffed Bush. 'Twelve oars won't move that old tub of a *Natividad* very far.'

Hornblower glared at him and Bush retired to his own side of the quarterdeck again; he had forgotten his captain was in this unconversational mood. Hornblower was fretting himself into a fever. He stood in the glaring sun while the heat was reflected up into his face from the deck under his feet. His shirt chaffed him where he sweated. He felt caged, like a captive beast, within the limitations of practical details. The endless clanking of the pumps, the rolling of the ship, the rattle of the rigging, the noise of the oars in the rowlocks, were driving him mad, as though he could scream (or weep) at the slightest additional provocation.

At noon he changed the men at the oars and pumps, and sent the crew to dinner – he remembered bitterly that he had already made them breakfast in anticipation of immediate action. At two bells he began to wonder whether the *Natividad* might be within extreme long range, but the mere fact of wondering told him that it was not the case – he knew his own sanguine temperament too well, and he fought down the temptation to waste powder and shot. And then, as he looked for the thousandth time through his telescope, he suddenly saw a disk of white appear on the high stern of the *Natividad*. The disk spread and expanded into a thin cloud, and six seconds after its first appearance the dull thud of the shot reached his ears. The *Natividad* was evidently willing to try the range.

'*Natividad* carries two long eighteens aft on the quarterdeck,' said Gerard to Bush in Hornblower's hearing. 'Heavy metal for stern-chasers.'

Hornblower knew it already. He would have to run the gauntlet of those two guns for an hour, possibly, before he could bring the brass nine pounder on his forecastle into action. Another puff of smoke from the *Natividad*, and this time Hornblower saw a spout of water rise from the breast of a wave half a mile ahead. But at that long range and on that tossing sea it did not mean that the *Lydia* was still half a mile beyond the *Natividad*'s reach. Hornblower heard the next shot arrive, and saw a brief fountain of water rise no more than fifty yards from the *Lydia*'s starboard quarter.

'Mr Gerard,' said Hornblower. 'Send for Mr Marsh and see what he can do with the long nine forward.'

It would cheer the men up to have a gun banging away occasionally instead of being merely shot at without making any reply. Marsh came waddling up from the darkness of the magazine, and blinked in the blinding sunshine. He shook his head doubtfully as he eyed the distance between the ships, but he had the gun cleared away, and he loaded it with his own hands, lovingly. He measured out the powder charge on the fullest scale, and he

spent several seconds selecting the roundest and truest shot from
the locker. He trained the gun with care, and then stood aside,
lanyard in hand, watching the heave of the ship and the send of
the bows, while a dozen telescopes were trained on the *Natividad*
and every eye watched for the fall of the shot. Suddenly he jerked
the lanyard and the cannon roared out, its report sounding flat in
the heated motionless air.

'Two cables' lengths astern of her!' yelled Knyvett from the
foretop. Hornblower had missed the splash – another proof, to
his mind, of his own incompetence, but he concealed the fact
under a mask of imperturbability.

'Try again, Mr Marsh,' he said.

The *Natividad* was firing both stern-chasers together now. As
Hornblower spoke there came a crash forward as one of the
eighteen-pounder balls struck home close above the water line.
Hornblower could hear young Savage, down in the launch hurling
shrill blasphemies at the men at the oars to urge them on – that
shot must have passed just over his head. Marsh stroked his beard
and addressed himself to the task of reloading the long nine
pounder. While he was so engaged, Hornblower was deep in the
calculation of the chances of battle.

That long nine, although of smaller calibre, was of longer
range than his shorter main-deck guns, while the carronades,
which comprised half of the *Lydia*'s armament, were useless at
anything longer than close range. The *Lydia* would have to draw
up close to her enemy before she could attack her with effect.
There would be a long and damaging interval between the moment
when the *Natividad* should be able to bring all her guns into
action and the moment when the *Lydia* could hit back at her.
There would be casualties, guns dismounted perhaps, serious
losses. Hornblower balanced the arguments for and against continuing to try and close with the enemy while Mr Marsh was
squinting along the sights of the nine pounder. Then Hornblower
scowled to himself, and ceased tugging at his chin, his mind
made up. He had started the action; he would go through with

it to the end, cost what it might. His flexibility of mind could crystallise into sullen obstinacy.

The nine pounder went off as though to signal this decision. 'Just alongside her!' screamed Knyvett triumphantly from the foretop.

'Well done, Mr Marsh,' said Hornblower, and Marsh wagged his beard complacently.

The *Natividad* was firing faster now. Three times a splintering crash told of a shot which had been aimed true. Then suddenly a thrust as if from an invisible hand made Hornblower reel on the quarterdeck, and his ears were filled with a brief rending noise. A skimming shot had ploughed a channel along the planking of the quarterdeck. A marine was sitting near the taffrail stupidly contemplating his left leg, which no longer had a foot on the end of it; another marine dropped his musket with a clatter and clapped his hands to his face, which a splinter had torn open, with the blood spouting between his fingers.

'Are you hurt, sir?' cried Bush, leaping across to Hornblower. 'No.'

Hornblower turned back to stare through his glass at the *Natividad* while the wounded were being dragged away. He saw a dark dot appear alongside the *Natividad*, and lengthen and diverge. It was the boat with which they had been trying to row – perhaps they were giving up the attempt. But the boat was not being hoisted in. For a second Hornblower was puzzled. The *Natividad*'s stumpy fore mast and main mast came into view. The boat was pulling the ship laboriously round so that her whole broadside would bear. Not two, but twenty-five guns would soon be opening their fire on the *Lydia*.

Hornblower felt his breath come a little quicker, unexpectedly, so that he had to swallow in order to regulate things again. His pulse was faster, too. He made himself keep the glass to his eye until he was certain of the enemy's manoeuvre, and then walked forward leisurely to the gangway. He was compelling himself to appear lighthearted and carefree; he knew that the fools of men whom he commanded would fight more diligently for a captain like that.

'They're waiting for us now, lads,' he said. 'We shall have some pebbles about our ears before long. Let's show 'em that Englishmen don't care.'

They cheered him for that, as he expected and hoped they would do. He looked through his glass again at the *Natividad*. She was still turning, very slowly – it was a lengthy process to turn a clumsy two-decker in a dead calm. But he could see a hint of the broad white stripes which ornamented her side.

'Ha – h'm,' he said.

Forward he could hear the oars grinding away as the men in the boats laboured to drag the *Lydia* to grips with her enemy. Across the deck a little group of officers – Bush and Crystal among them – were academically discussing what percentage of hits might be expected from a Spanish broadside at a range of a mile. They were cold-blooded about it in a fashion he could never hope to imitate with sincerity. He did not fear death so much – nor nearly as much – as defeat and the pitying contempt of his colleagues. The chiefest dread at the back of his mind was the fear of mutilation. An ex-naval officer stumping about on two wooden legs might be an object of condolence, might receive lip service as one of Britain's heroic defenders, but he was a figure of fun, nevertheless. Hornblower dreaded the thought of being a figure of fun. He might lose his nose or his cheek and be so mutilated that people would not be able to bear to look at him. It was a horrible thought which set him shuddering while he looked through the telescope, so horrible that he did not stop to think of the associated details, of the agonies he would have to bear down there in the dark cockpit at the mercy of Laurie's incompetence.

The *Natividad* was suddenly engulfed in smoke, and some seconds later the air and the water around the *Lydia* and the ship herself, were torn by the hurtling broadside.

'Not more than two hits,' said Bush, gleefully.

'Just what I said,' said Crystal. 'That captain of theirs ought to go round and train every gun himself.'

'How do you know he did not?' argued Bush.

As punctuation the nine pounder forward banged out its defiance. Hornblower fancied that his straining eyes saw splinters fly amidships of the *Natividad*, unlikely though it was at that distance.

'Well aimed, Mr Marsh!' he called. 'You hit him squarely.'

Another broadside came from the *Natividad*, and another followed it, and another after that. Time after time the *Lydia*'s decks were swept from end to end with shot. There were dead men laid out again on the deck, and the groaning wounded were dragged below.

'It is obvious to anyone of a mathematical turn of mind,' said Crystal, 'that those guns are all laid by different hands. The shots are too scattered for it to be otherwise.'

'Nonsense!' maintained Bush sturdily. 'See how long it is between broadsides. Time enough for one man to train each gun. What would they be doing in that time otherwise?'

'A Dago crew —,' began Crystal, but a sudden shriek of cannon balls over his head silenced him for a moment.

'Mr Galbraith!' shouted Bush. 'Have that main t'gallant stay spliced directly.' Then he turned triumphantly on Crystal. 'Did you notice,' he asked, 'how every shot from that broadside went high? How does the mathematical mind explain that?'

'They fired on the upward roll, Mr Bush. Really, Mr Bush, I think that after Trafalgar —'

Hornblower longed to order them to cease the argument which was lacerating his nerves, but he could not be such a tyrant as that.

In the still air the smoke from the *Natividad*'s firing had banked up around about her so that she showed ghostly through the cloud, her solitary mizzen topmast protruding above it into the clear air.

'Mr Bush,' he asked, 'at what distance do you think she is now?'

Bush gauged the distance carefully.

'Three parts of a mile, I should say, sir!'

'Two-thirds, more likely, sir,' said Crystal.

'Your opinion was not asked for, Mr Crystal,' snapped Hornblower.

At three-quarters of a mile, even at two-thirds, the *Lydia*'s carronades would be ineffective. She must continue running the gauntlet. Bush was evidently of the same opinion, to judge by his next orders.

'Time for the men at the oars to be relieved,' he said, and went forward to attend it. Hornblower heard him bustling the new crews down into the boats, anxious that the pulling should be resumed before the *Lydia* had time to lose what little way she carried.

It was terribly hot under the blazing sun, even though it was now long past noon. The smell of the blood which had been spilt on the decks mingled with the smell of the hot deck seams and of the powder smoke from the nine pounder with which Marsh was still steadily bombarding the enemy. Hornblower felt sick – so sick that he began to fear lest he should disgrace himself eternally by vomiting in full view of his men. When fatigue and anxiety had weakened him thus he was far more conscious of the pitching and rolling of the ship under his feet. The men at the guns were silent now, he noticed – for long they had laughed and joked at their posts, but now they were beginning to sulk under the punishment. That was a bad sign.

'Pass the word for Sullivan and his fiddle,' he ordered.

The red-haired Irish madman came aft, and knuckled his forehead, his fiddle and bow under his arm.

'Give us a tune, Sullivan,' he ordered. 'Hey there, men, who is there among you who dances the best hornpipe?'

There was a difference of opinion about that, apparently.

'Benskin, sir,' said some voices.

'Hall, sir,' said others.

'No, MacEvoy, sir.'

'Then we'll have a tournament,' said Hornblower. 'Here, Benskin, Hall, MacEvoy. A hornpipe from each of you, and a guinea for the man who does it best.'

In later years it was a tale told and retold, how the *Lydia* was towed into action with hornpipes being danced on her main deck. It was quoted as an example of Hornblower's cool courage, and only Hornblower knew how little truth there was in the attribution. It kept the men happy, which was why he did it. No one guessed how nearly he came to vomiting when a shot came in through a forward gunport and spattered Hall with a seaman's brains without causing him to miss a step.

Then later in that dreadful afternoon there came a crash from forward, followed by a chorus of shouts and screams overside.

'Launch sunk, sir!' hailed Galbraith from the forecastle, but Hornblower was there as soon as he had uttered the words.

A round shot had dashed the launch practically into its component planks, and the men were scrambling in the water, leaping up for the babstay or struggling to climb into the cutter, all of them who survived wild with fear of sharks.

'The Dagoes have saved us the trouble of hoisting her in,' he said, loudly. 'We're close enough now for them to feel our teeth.'

The men who heard him cheered.

'Mr Hooker!' he called to the midshipman in the cutter. 'When you have picked up those men, kindly starboard your helm. We are going to open fire.'

He came aft to the quarterdeck again.

'Hard a-starboard,' he growled at the quartermaster. 'Mr Gerard, you may open first when your guns bear.'

Very slowly the *Lydia* swung round. Another broadside from the *Natividad* came crashing into her before she had completed the turn, but Hornblower actually did not notice it. The period of inaction was now over. He had brought his ship within four hundred yards of the enemy, and all his duty now was to walk the deck as an example to his men. There were no more decisions to make.

'Cock your locks!' shouted Gerard in the waist.

'Easy, Mr Hooker. Way enough!' roared Hornblower.

The *Lydia* turned inch by inch, with Gerard squinting along one of the starboard guns to judge of the moment when it would first bear. 'Take your aim!' he yelled, and stood back, timing the roll of the ship in the heavy swell. 'Fire!'

The smoke billowed out amid the thunder of the discharge, and the *Lydia* heaved to the recoil of the guns.

'Give him another, lads!' shouted Hornblower through the din. Now that action was joined he found himself exalted and happy, the dreadful fears of mutilation forgotten. In thirty seconds the guns were reloaded, run out, and fired. Again and again and again, with Gerard watching the roll of the ship and giving the word. Counting back in his mind, Hornblower reckoned five broadsides from the *Lydia*, and he could only remember two from the *Natividad* in that time. At that rate of firing the *Natividad*'s superiority in numbers of guns and weight of metal would be more than counterbalanced. At the sixth broadside a gun went off prematurely, a second before Gerard gave the word. Hornblower sprang forward to detect the guilty crew – it was easy enough from their furtive look and suspicious appearance of busyness. He shook his finger at them.

'Steady, there!' he shouted. 'I'll flog the next man who fires out of turn.'

It was very necessary to keep the men in hand while the range was as long as at present, because in the heat and excitement of the action the gun captains could not be trusted to judge the motion of the ship while preoccupied with loading and laying.

'Good old Horny!' piped up some unknown voice forward, and there was a burst of laughing and cheering, cut short by Gerard's next order to fire.

The smoke was banked thick about the ship already – as thick as a London fog so that from the quarterdeck it was impossible to see individuals on the forecastle, and in the unnatural darkness which it brought with it one could see the long orange flashes of the guns despite the vivid sunshine outside. Of the *Natividad* all that could be seen was her high smoke cloud and the single topmast jutting out from it. The thick smoke, trailing about the ship in greasy wreaths, made the eyes smart and irritated the lungs, and affected the skin like thundery weather until it pricked uncomfortably.

Hornblower found Bush beside him.

'*Natividad*'s feeling our fire, sir,' he roared through the racket. 'She's firing very wild. Look at that, sir.'

Of the broadside fired only one or two shots struck home. Half a dozen plunged together into the sea astern of the *Lydia* so that the spray from the fountains which they struck up splashed round them on the quarterdeck. Hornblower nodded happily. This was his justification for closing to that range and for running the risks involved in the approach. To maintain a rapid fire, well aimed, amid the din and the smoke and the losses and the confusion of a naval battle called for discipline and practice of a sort that he knew the *Natividad*'s crew could not boast.

He looked down through the smoke at the *Lydia*'s main deck. The inexperienced eye, observing the hurry and bustle of the boys with the cartridge buckets, the mad efforts of the gun crews, the dead and the wounded, the darkness and the din, might well think it a scene of confusion, but Hornblower knew better. Everything that was being done there, every single action, was part of the scheme worked out by Hornblower seven months before when he commissioned the *Lydia*, and grained into the minds of all on board during the long and painful drills since. He could see Gerard standing by the mainmast, looking almost saintly in his ecstasy – gunnery was as much Gerard's ruling passion as women; he could see the midshipmen and other warrant officers each by his subdivision of guns, each looking to Gerard for his orders and keeping his guns working rhythmically, the loaders with their rammers, the cleaners with their sponges, the gun captains crouching over the breeches, right hands raised.

The port-side battery was already depleted of most of its men; there were only two men to a gun there, standing idle yet ready to spring into action if a shift of the fight should bring their guns to bear. The remainder were on duty round the ship – replacing casualties on the starboard side, manning the pumps, whose doleful clanking continued steadily through the fearful din, resting on their oars in the cutter, hard at work aloft repairing damages. Hornblower found time to be thankful that he had been granted seven months in which to bring his crew into its present state of training and discipline.

Something – the concussion of the guns, a faint breath of air, or the send of the sea – was causing the *Lydia* to turn away a trifle from her enemy. Hornblower could see that the guns were having to be trained round farther and farther so that the rate of firing was being slowed down. He raced forward, running out along the bowsprit until he was over the cutter where Hooker and his men sat staring at the fight.

'Mr Hooker, bring her head round two points to starboard.'

'Aye aye, sir.'

The men bent to their oars and headed their boat towards the *Natividad*; the tow-rope tightened while another badly aimed broadside tore the water all round them into foam. Tugging and straining at the oars they would work the ship round in time. Hornblower left them and ran back to the quarterdeck. There was a white-faced ship's boy seeking him there.

'Mr Howell sent me, sir. Starboard-side chain pump's knocked all to pieces.'

'Yes?' Hornblower knew that Howell, the ship's carpenter, would not merely send a message of despair.

'He's rigging another one, sir, but it will be an hour before it works, sir. He told me to tell you the water's gaining a little, sir.'

'Ha – h'm,' said Hornblower. The infant addressing him grew round-eyed and confidential now that the first strangeness of speaking to his captain had worn off.

'There was fourteen men all knocked into smash at the pump, sir. 'Orrible, sir.'

'Very good. Run back to Mr Howell and tell him the captain is sure he will do his best to get the new pump rigged.'

'Aye aye, sir.'

The boy dived down to the main deck, and Hornblower watched him running forward, dodging the hurrying individuals in the crowded space there. He had to explain himself to the marine sentry at the fore hatchway – no one could go below without being able to show that it was his duty which was calling him there. Hornblower felt as if the message Howell had sent did not matter at all. It called for no decision on his part. All there was to do was to go on fighting, whether the ship was sinking under their feet or not. There was a comfort in being free of all responsibility in this way.

'One hour and a half already,' said Bush, coming up rubbing his hands. 'Glorious, sir. Glorious.'

It might have been no more than ten minutes for all Hornblower could tell, but Bush had in duty bound been watching the sand glass by the binnacle.

'I've never known Dagoes stick to their guns like this before,' commented Bush. 'Their aim's poor, but they're firing as fast as ever. And it's my belief we've hit them hard, sir.'

He tried to look through the eddying smoke, even fanning ridiculously with his hands in the attempt – a gesture which, by showing that he was not quite as calm as he appeared to be, gave Hornblower an absurd pleasure. Crystal came up as well as he spoke.

'The smoke's thinning a little, sir. It's my belief that there's a light air of wind blowing.'

He held up a wetted finger.

'There is indeed, sir. A trifle of breeze over the port quarter. Ah!'

There came a stronger puff as he spoke, which rolled away the smoke in a solid mass over the starboard bow and revealed the scene as if a theatre curtain had been raised. There was the *Natividad*, looking like a wreck. Her jury foremast had gone the way of its predecessor, and her mainmast has followed it. Only her mizzen mast stood now, and she was rolling wildly in the swell with a huge tangle of rigging trailing over her disengaged side. Abreast her foremast three ports had been battered into one; the gap looked like a missing tooth.

'She's low in the water,' said Bush, but on the instant a fresh broadside vomited smoke from her battered side, and this time by some chance every shot told in the *Lydia*, as the crash below well indicated. The smoke billowed round the *Natividad*, and as it cleared the watchers saw her swinging round head to the wind, helpless in the light air. The *Lydia* had felt the breeze. Hornblower could tell by the feel of her that she had steerage way again; the quartermaster at the wheel was twirling the spokes to hold her steady. He saw his chance on the instant.

'Starboard a point,' he ordered. 'Forward, there! Cast off the cutter.'

The *Lydia* steadied across her enemy's bows and raked her with thunder and flame.

'Back the main tops'l!' ordered Hornblower.

The men were cheering again on the main deck through the roar of the guns. Astern the red sun was dipping to the water's edge in a glory of scarlet and gold. Soon it would be night.

'She must strike soon. Christ! Why don't she strike?' Bush was saying, as at close range the broadsides tore into the helpless enemy, raking her from bow to stern. Hornblower knew better. No ship under Crespo's command and flying el Supremo's flag would strike her colours. He could see the golden star on a blue ground fluttering through the smoke.

'Pound him, lads, pound him!' shouted Gerard.

With the shortening range he could rely on his gun captains to fire independently now. Every gun's crew was loading and firing as rapidly as possible. So hot were the guns that at each discharge they leaped high in their carriages, and the dripping

sponges thrust down their bores sizzled and steamed at the touch
of the scorching hot metal. It was growing darker, too. The flashes
of the guns could be seen again now, leaping in long orange
tongues from the gun muzzles. High above the fast-fading sunset
could be seen the first star, shining out brilliantly.

The *Natividad*'s bowsprit was gone, splintered and broken and
hanging under her forefoot, and then in the dwindling light the
mizzenmast fell as well, cut through by shots which had ripped
their way down the whole length of the ship.

'She must strike now, by God!' said Bush.

At Trafalgar Bush had been sent as prize master into a captured
Spanish ship, and his mind was full of busy memories of what
a beaten ship looked like – the dismounted guns, the dead and
wounded heaped on the deck and rolling back and forth as the
dismasted ship rolled on the swell, the misery, the pain, the
helplessness. As if in reply to him there came a sudden flash and
report from the *Natividad*'s bows. Some devoted souls with
tackles and hand-spikes had contrived to slew a gun round so
that it would bear right forward, and were firing into the looming
bulk of the *Lydia*.

'Pound him, lads, pound him!' screamed Gerard, half mad
with fatigue and strain.

The *Lydia* by virtue of her top hamper was going down to
leeward fast upon the rolling hulk. At every second the range
was shortening. Through the darkness, when their eyes were not
blinded with gun flashes, Hornblower and Bush could see figures
moving about on the *Natividad*'s deck. They were firing muskets
now, as well. The flashes pricked the darkness and Hornblower
heard a bullet thud into the rail beside him. He did not care. He
was conscious now of his overmastering weariness.

The wind was fluky, coming in sudden puffs and veering
unexpectedly. It was hard, especially in the darkness, to judge
exactly how the two ships were nearing each other.

'The closer we are, the quicker we'll finish it,' said Bush.

'Yes, but we'll run on board of her soon,' said Hornblower.

He roused himself for a further effort.

'Call the hands to stand by to repel boarders,' he said, and he walked across to where the two starboard side quarterdeck carronades were thundering away. So intent were their crews on their work, so hypnotised by the monotony of loading and firing, that it took him several seconds to attract their notice. Then they stood still, sweating, while Hornblower gave his orders. The two carronades were loaded with canister brought from the reserve locker beside the taffrail. They waited, crouching beside the guns, while the two ships drifted closer and closer together, the *Lydia*'s main deck guns still blazing away. There were shouts and yells of defiance from the *Natividad*, and the musket flashes from her bows showed a dark mass of men crowding there waiting for the ships to come together. Yet the actual contact was unexpected, as a sudden combination of wind and sea closed the gap with a rush. The *Natividad*'s bow hit the *Lydia* amidships, just forward of the mizzenmast, with a jarring crash. There was a pandemonium of yells from the *Natividad* as they swarmed forward to board, and the captains of the carronades sprang to their lanyards.

'Wait!' shouted Hornblower.

His mind was like a calculating machine, judging wind and sea, time and distance, as the *Lydia* slowly swung round. With hand spikes and the brute strength of the men he trained one carronade round and the other followed his example, while the mob on the *Natividad*'s forecastle surged along the bulwarks waiting for the moment to board. The two carronades came right up against them.

'Fire!'

A thousand musket balls were vomited from the carronades straight into the packed crowd. There was a moment of silence, and then the pandemonium of shouts and cheers was replaced by a thin chorus of screams and cries – the blast of musket balls had swept the *Natividad*'s forecastle clear from side to side.

For a space the two ships clung together in this position; the *Lydia* still had a dozen guns that would bear, and these pounded away with their muzzles almost touching the *Natividad*'s bow. Then wind and sea parted them again, the *Lydia* to leeward now, drifting away from the rolling hulk; in the English ship every gun was in action, while from the *Natividad* came not a gun, not even a musket shot.

Hornblower fought off his weariness again.

'Cease firing,' he shouted to Gerard on the main deck, and the guns fell silent.

Hornblower stared through the darkness at the vague mass of the *Natividad*, wallowing in the waves.

'Surrender!' he shouted.

'Never!' came the reply – Crespo's voice, he could have sworn to it, thin and high pitched. It added two or three words of obscene insult.

Hornblower could afford to smile at that, even through his weariness. He had fought his battle and won it.

'You have done all that brave men could do,' he shouted.

'Not all, yet, Captain,' wailed the voice in the darkness.

Then something caught Hornblower's eyes – a wavering glow of red about the *Natividad*'s vague bows.

'Crespo, you fool!' he shouted. 'Your ship's on fire! Surrender, while you can.'

'Never!'

The *Lydia*'s guns, hard against the *Natividad*'s side, had flung their flaming wads in amongst the splintered timbers. The tinder-dry wood of the old ship had taken fire from them, and the fire was spreading fast. It was brighter already than when Hornblower had noticed it; the ship would be a mass of flames soon. Hornblower's first duty was to his own ship – when the fire should reach the powder charges on the *Natividad*'s decks, or when it should attain the magazine, the ship would become a volcano of flaming fragments, imperilling the *Lydia*.

'We must haul off from her, Mr Bush,' said Hornblower, speaking formally to conceal the tremor in his voice. 'Man the braces, there.'

The *Lydia* swung away, close hauled, clawing her way up to windward of the flaming wreck. Bush and Hornblower gazed back at her. There were bright flames now to be seen, spouting from the shattered bows – the red glow was reflected in the heaving sea around her. And then, as they looked, they saw the flames vanish abruptly, like an extinguished candle. There was nothing to be seen at all, nothing save darkness and the faint glimmer of the wave crests. The sea had swallowed the *Natividad* before the flames could destroy her.

'Sunk, by God!' exclaimed Bush, leaning out over the rail.

Hornblower still seemed to hear that last wailing 'Never!' during the seconds of silence that followed. Yet he was perhaps the first of all his ship's company to recover from the shock. He put his ship about and ran down to the scene of the *Natividad*'s sinking. He sent off Hooker and the cutter to search for survivors – the cutter was the only boat left, for gig and jolly boat had been shattered by the *Natividad*'s fire, and the planks of the launch were floating five miles away. They picked up a few men – two were hauled out of the water by men in the *Lydia*'s chains, and the cutter found half a dozen swimmers; that was all. The *Lydia*'s crew tried to be kind to them, as they stood on her deck in the lantern light with the water streaming from their ragged clothes and their lank black hair, but they were sullen and silent; there was even one who struggled for a moment, as if to continue the battle which the *Natividad* had fought so desperately.

'Never mind, we'll make topmen of them yet,' said Hornblower, trying to speak lightly.

Fatigue had reached such a pitch now that he was speaking as if out of a dream, as if all these solid surroundings of his, the ship, her guns and masts and sails, Bush's burly figure, were unreal and ghostlike, and only his weariness and the ache inside his skull were existing things. He heard his voice as though he were speaking from a yard away.

'Aye aye, sir,' said the boatswain.

Anything was grist that came to the Royal Navy's mill – Harrison was prepared to make seamen out of the strangest human material; he had done so all his life, for that matter.

'What course shall I set, sir?' asked Bush, as Hornblower turned back to the quarterdeck.

'Course?' said Hornblower, vaguely. 'Course?'

It was terribly hard to realise that the battle was over, the *Natividad* sunk, that there was no enemy afloat within thousands of miles of sea. It was hard to realise that the *Lydia* was in acute danger, too; that the pumps, clanking away monotonously, were not quite able to keep the leaks under, that the *Lydia* still had a sail stretched under her bottom, and stood in the acutest need of a complete refit.

Hornblower came by degrees to realise that now he had to start a new chapter in the history of the *Lydia*, to make fresh plans. And there was a long line of people waiting for immediate orders, too – Bush, here, and the boatswain and the carpenter and the gunner and that fool Laurie. He had to force his tired brain to think again. He estimated the wind's force and direction, as though it were an academic exercise and not a mental process which for twenty years had been second nature to him. He went wearily down to his cabin and found the shattered chart cases amid the indescribable wreckage, and he pored over the torn chart.

He must report his success at Panama as soon as he could; that was obvious to him now. Perhaps he could refit there, although he saw small chance of it in that inhospitable roadstead, especially with yellow fever in the town. So he must carry the shattered *Lydia* to Panama. He laid off a course for Cape Mala, by a supreme effort compelled his mind to realise that he had a fair wind, and came up again with his orders to find that the mass of people who were clamouring for his attention had miraculously vanished. Bush had chased them all away, although he never discovered it. He gave the course to Bush, and then Polwheal materialised himself at his elbow, with boat cloak and hammock chair. Hornblower had no protest left in him. He allowed himself to be wrapped in the cloak, and he fell, half fainting, into the chair. It was twenty-one hours since he had last sat down. Polwheal had brought food, too, but he merely ignored that. He wanted no food! All he wanted was rest.

Then for a second he was wide awake again. He had remembered Lady Barbara, battened down below with the wounded in the dark and stifling bowels of the ship. But he relaxed at once. The blasted woman could look after herself – she was quite capable of doing so. Nothing mattered now. His head sank on his breast again. The next thing to disturb him was the sound of his own snores, and that did not disturb him long. He slept and he snored through all the din which the crew made in their endeavour to get the *Lydia* shipshape again.

CHAPTER XVIII

What awoke Hornblower was the sun, which lifted itself over the horizon and shone straight into his eyes. He stirred and blinked, and for a space he tried, like a child, to shield his eyes with his hands and return to sleep. He did not know where he was, and for that time he did not care. Then he began to remember the events of yesterday, and he ceased trying to sleep and instead tried to wake up. Oddly, at first he remembered the details of the fighting and could not recall the sinking of the *Natividad*. When that recollection shot into his brain he was fully awake.

He rose from his chair, stretching himself painfully, for all his joints ached with the fatigues of yesterday. Bush was standing by the wheel, his face grey and lined and strangely old in the hard light. Hornblower nodded to him and received his salute in return; Bush was wearing his cocked hat over the dirty white bandage round his forehead. Hornblower would have spoken to him, but all his attention was caught up immediately in looking round the ship. There was a good breeze blowing which must have backed round during the night, for the *Lydia* could only just hold her course close hauled. She was under all plain sail; Hornblower's rapid inspection revealed to him innumerable splices both in standing and running rigging; the jury mizzenmast seemed to be standing up well to its work, but every sail that was spread seemed to have at least one shot hole in it – some of them a dozen or more. They gave the ship a little of the appearance of a tattered vagabond. The first part of today's work would be spreading a new suit of sails; new rigging could wait for a space.

It was only then, after weather and course and sail set had been noted, that Hornblower's sailor's eye came down to the decks. From forward came the monotonous clangour of the pumps; the clear white water which was gushing from them was the surest indication that the ship was making so much water that it could only just be kept in check. On the lee-side gangway was a long, long row of corpses, each in its hammock. Hornblower flinched when he saw the length of the row, and it called for all his will to count them. There were twenty-four dead men along the gangway; and fourteen had been buried yesterday. Some of these dead might be – probably were – the mortally wounded of yesterday, but thirty-eight dead seemed certainly to indicate at least seventy wounded down below. Rather more than one third of the *Lydia*'s company were casualties, then. He wondered who they were, wondered whose distorted faces were concealed beneath those hammocks.

The dead on deck outnumbered the living. Bush seemed to have sent below every man save for a dozen men to hand and steer, which was sensible of him, seeing that everyone must be worn out with yesterday's toil while one man out of every seven on board would have to be employed at the pumps until the shot holes could be got at and plugged. The rest of the crew, at first glance, were all asleep, sprawled on the main deck under the gangways. Hardly anyone had had the strength to sling a hammock (if their hammocks had survived the battle); all the rest lay as they had dropped, lying tangled here and there, heads pillowed on each other or on more unsympathetic objects like ring bolts and the hind axletrees of the guns.

There were still evident many signs of yesterday's battle, quite apart from the sheeted corpses and the dark stains, not thoroughly swabbed, which disfigured the white planking. The decks were furrowed and grooved in all directions, with jagged splinters still standing up here and there. There were shot holes in the ship's sides with canvas roughly stretched over them. The port sills were stained black with powder; on one of them an eighteen-pounder shot stood out, half buried in the tough oak. But on the other hand an immense amount of work had been done, from laying out the dead to securing the guns and frapping the breechings. Apart from the weariness of her crew, the *Lydia* was ready to fight another battle at two minutes' notice.

Hornblower felt a prick of shame that so much should have been done while he slept lazily in his hammock chair. He forced himself to feel no ill will on that account. Although to praise Bush's work was to admit his own deficiencies he felt that he must be generous.

'Very good indeed, Mr Bush,' he said, walking over to him; yet his natural shyness combined with his feeling of shame to make his speech stilted. 'I am both astonished and pleased at the work you have accomplished.'

'Today is Sunday, sir,' said Bush, simply.

So it was. Sunday was the day of the captain's inspection, when he went round every part of the ship examining everything, to see that the first lieutenant was doing his duty in keeping the ship efficient. On Sunday the ship had to be swept and garnished, all the falls of rope flemished down, the hands fallen in by divisions in their best clothes, divine service held, the Articles of War read – Sunday was the day when the professional ability of every first lieutenant in His Britannic Majesty's Navy was tried in the balance. Hornblower could not fight down a smile at this ingenious explanation.

'Sunday or no Sunday,' he said, 'you have done magnificently, Mr Bush.'

'Thank you, sir.'

'And I shall remember to say so in my report to the Admiralty.'

'I know you'll do that, sir.'

Bush's weary face was illuminated by a gleam of pleasure. A successful single-ship action was usually rewarded by promotion to Commander of the first lieutenant, and for a man like Bush, with no family and no connections, it was his only hope of making that vitally important step. But a captain who was anxious to enhance his own glory could word his report so that it appeared that he had won his victory despite of, instead of by the aid of, his first lieutenant – instances were known.

'They may make much of this in England, when eventually they hear about it,' said Hornblower.

'I'm certain of it, sir. It isn't every day of the week that a frigate sinks a ship of the line.' It was stretching a point to call the *Natividad* that – sixty years ago when she was built she may have been considered just fit to lie in the line, but times had changed since then. But it was a very notable feat that the *Lydia* had accomplished, all the same. It was only now that Hornblower began to appreciate how notable it was, and his spirit rose in proportion.

There was another criterion which the British public was prone to apply in estimating the merit of a naval action, and the Board of Admiralty itself not infrequently used the same standard.

'What's the butcher's bill?' demanded Hornblower, brutally, voicing the thoughts of both of them – brutally because otherwise he might be thought guilty of sentiment.

'Thirty-eight killed, sir,' said Bush, taking a dirty scrap of paper from his pocket. 'Seventy-five wounded. Four missing. The missing are Harper, Dawson, North and Chump the negro, sir – they were lost when the launch was sunk. Clay was killed in the first day's action—'

Hornblower nodded; he remembered Clay's headless body sprawled on the quarterdeck.

'—and John Summers, master's mate, Henry Vincent and James Clifton, boatswain's mates, killed yesterday, and Donald Scott Galbraith, third lieutenant, Lieutenant Samuel Simmonds of the Marines, Midshipman Howard Savage and four other warrant officers wounded.'

'Galbraith?' said Hornblower. That piece of news prevented him from beginning to wonder what would be the reward of a casualty list of a hundred and seventeen, when frigate captains had been knighted before this for a total of eighty killed and wounded.

'Badly, sir. Both legs smashed below the knees.'

Galbraith had met the fate which Hornblower had dreaded for himself. The shock recalled Hornblower to his duty.

'I shall go down and visit the wounded at once,' he said, and checked himself and looked searchingly at his first lieutenant. 'What about you, Bush? You don't look fit for duty.'

'I am perfectly fit, sir,' protested Bush. 'I shall take an hour's rest when Gerard comes up to take over the deck from me.'

'As you will, then.'

Down below decks in the orlop it was like some canto in the *Inferno*. It was dark; the four oil lamps whose flickering, reddish yellow glimmer wavered from the deck beams above seemed to serve only to cast shadows. The atmosphere was stifling. To the normal stenches of bilge and a ship's stores were added the stinks of sick men crowded together, of the sooty lamps, of the bitter powder smell which had drifted in yesterday and had not yet succeeded in making its way out again. It was appallingly hot; the heat and the stink hit Hornblower in the face as he entered, and within five seconds of his entry his face was as wet as if it had been dipped in water, so hot was it and so laden was the atmosphere with moisture.

As complex as the air was the noise. There were the ordinary ship noises – the creaking and groaning of timber, the vibration of the rigging transmitted downward from the chains, the sound of the sea outside, the wash of the bilge below, and the monotonous clangour of the pumps forward intensified by the ship-timbers acting as sounding boards. But all the noises acted only as accompaniment to the din in the cockpit, where seventy-five wounded men, crammed together, were groaning and sobbing and screaming, blaspheming and vomiting. Lost souls in hell could hardly have had a more hideous environment, or be suffering more.

Hornblower found Laurie, standing aimlessly in the gloom.

'Thank God you've come, sir,' he said. His tone implied that he cast all responsibility, gladly, from that moment on the shoulders of his captain.

'Come round with me and make your report,' snapped Hornblower. He hated this business, and yet, although he was completely omnipotent on board, he could not turn and fly as his instincts told him to do. The work had to be done, and Hornblower knew that now Laurie had proved his incompetence he himself was the best man to deal with it. He approached the last man in the row, and drew back with a start of surprise. Lady Barbara was there; the wavering light caught her classic features as she knelt beside the wounded man. She was sponging his face and his throat as he writhed on the deck.

It was a shock to Hornblower to see her engaged thus. The day was yet to come when Florence Nightingale was to make nursing a profession in which women could engage. No man of taste could bear the thought of a woman occupied with the filthy work of a hospital. Sisters of Mercy might labour there for the good of their souls; boozy old women might attend to women in labour and occasionally take a hand at sick nursing, but to look after wounded men was entirely men's work – the work of men who deserved nothing better, either, and who were ordered to it on account of their incapacity or their bad record like men ordered to clean out latrines. Hornblower's stomach revolted at the sight of Lady Barbara here in contact with dirty bodies, with blood and pus and vomit.

'Don't do that!' he said, hoarsely. 'Go away from here. Go on deck.'

'I have begun this work now,' said Lady Barbara indifferently. 'I am not going to leave it unfinished.'

Her tone admitted no possibility of argument; she was apparently talking of the inevitable – much as she might say that she had caught cold and would have to bear with it until it had run its course.

'The gentleman in charge here,' she went on, 'knows nothing of his duties.'

Lady Barbara had no belief in the nobility of nursing, to her mind it was a more degrading occupation than cooking or mending clothes (work which had only occasionally, when the exigencies of travel demanded it, engaged her capable fingers) but she had found a job which was being inefficiently done when there was no one save herself to do it better, at a time when the King's service depended in part on its being done well. She had set herself to work with the same wholehearted attention to detail and neglect of personal comfort with which one of her brothers had governed India and another had fought the Mahrattas.

'This man,' went on Lady Barbara, 'has a splinter of wood under his skin here. It ought to be extracted at once.'

She displayed the man's bare chest, hairy and tattooed. Under the tattooing there was a horrible black bruise, stretching from the breast bone to the right armpit, and in the muscles of the armpit was a jagged projection under the skin; when Lady Barbara laid her fingers on it the man writhed and groaned with pain. In fighting between wooden ships, splinter wounds constituted a high proportion of the casualties, and the hurtling pieces of wood could never be extracted by the route by which they entered, because their shape gave them natural barbs. In this case the splinter had been deflected by the ribs so as to pass round under the skin, bruising and lacerating, to its present place in the armpit.

'Are you ready to do it now?' asked Lady Barbara of the unhappy Laurie.

'Well, madam—'

'If you will not, then I will. Don't be a fool, man.'

'I will see that it is done, Lady Barbara,' interposed Hornblower. He would promise anything to get this finished and done with.

'Very well, then, Captain.'

Lady Barbara rose from her knees, but she showed no sign of any intention of retiring in a decent female fashion. Hornblower and Laurie looked at each other.

'Now, Laurie,' said Hornblower, harshly. 'Where are your instruments? Here, you, Wilcox, Hudson. Bring him a good stiff tot of rum. Now, Williams, we're going to get that splinter out of you. It is going to hurt you.'

Hornblower had to struggle hard to keep his face from writhing in disgust and fear of the task before him. He spoke harshly to stop his voice from trembling; he hated the whole business. And it was a painful and bloody business, too. Although Williams tried hard to show no weakness, he writhed as the incision was made, and Wilcox and Hudson had to catch his hands and force his shoulders back. He gave a horrible cry as the long dark strip of wood was dragged out, and then fell limp, fainting, so that he uttered no protest at the prick of the needle as the edges of the wound were clumsily sewn together.

Lady Barbara's lips were firmly compressed. She watched Laurie's muddled attempts at bandaging, and then she stooped without a word and took the rags from him. The men watched her fascinated as with one hand firmly behind Williams' spine she passed the roll dexterously round his body and bound the fast-reddening waste firmly to the wound.

'He will do now,' said Lady Barbara, rising.

Hornblower spent two stifling hours down there in the cockpit going the round with Laurie and Lady Barbara, but they were not nearly such agonising hours as they might have been. One of the main reasons for his feeling so unhappy regarding the care of the wounded had been his consciousness of his own incompetence. Insensibly he came to shift some of his responsibility on to Lady Barbara's shoulders; she was so obviously capable and so unintimidated that she was the person most fitted of all in the ship to be given the supervision of the wounded. When Hornblower had gone round every bed, when the five newly dead men had been dragged out, he faced her under the wavering light of the last lamp in the row.

'I don't know how I can thank you, ma'am,' he said. 'I am as grateful to you as any of these wounded men.'

'There is no gratitude needed,' said Lady Barbara, shrugging her slim shoulders, 'for work which had to be done.' A good many years later her ducal brother was to say 'The King's government must be carried on,' in exactly the same tone.

The man in the bed beside them waved a bandaged arm.

'Three cheers for her leddyship,' he croaked. 'Hip hip, hurrah!'

Some of the shattered invalids joined him in his cheers – a melancholy chorus, blended with the wheezing and groaning of the delirious men around them. Lady Barbara waved a deprecating hand and turned back to the captain.

'We must have air down here,' she said. 'Can that be arranged? I remember my brother telling me how the mortality in the hospital at Bombay declined as soon as they began to give the patients air. Perhaps those men who can be moved can be brought on deck?'

'I will arrange it, ma'am,' said Hornblower.

Lady Barbara's request was strongly accented by the contrast which Hornblower noticed when he went on deck – the fresh Pacific air, despite the scorching sunshine, was like champagne after the solid stink of the orlop. He gave orders for the immediate re-establishment of the canvas ventilating shafts which had been removed when the decks were cleared for action.

'And there are certain of the wounded, Mr Rayner,' he went on, 'who would do better if brought up on deck. You must find Lady Barbara Wellesley and ask her which men are to be moved.'

'Lady Barbara Wellesley, sir?' said Rayner, surprised and tactless, because he knew nothing of the last development.

'You heard what I said,' snapped Hornblower.

'Aye aye, sir,' said Rayner hurriedly, and dived away below in fear lest he should say anything further to annoy his captain.

So that on board HMS *Lydia* that morning divisions were held and divine service conducted a little late, after the burial of the dead, with a row of wounded swaying in hammocks on each side of the main deck, and with the faint echo of the horrible sounds below floating up through the air shafts.

CHAPTER XIX

Once more the *Lydia* held her course along the Pacific coast of Central America. The grey volcanic peaks, tinged with pink, slid past her to the eastward, with the lush green of the coastal strip sometimes just visible at their feet. The sea was blue and the sky was blue; the flying-fish skimmed the surface, leaving their fleeting furrows behind them. But every minute of the day and night twenty men toiled at the pumps to keep her from sinking, and the rest of the able-bodied crew worked all their waking hours at the task of refitting.

The fortnight which elapsed before she rounded Cape Mala went far to reduce her list of wounded. Some of the men were by then already convalescent – the hard physical condition which they had enjoyed, thanks to months of heavy work at sea, enabled them to make light of wounds which would have been fatal to men of soft physique. Shock and exhaustion had relieved the ship of others, and now gangrene, the grim Nemesis which awaited so many men with open wounds in those pre-antiseptic days, was relieving her of still more. Every morning there was the same ceremony at the ship's side, when two or three or six hammock-wrapped bundles were slid over into the blue Pacific.

Galbraith went that way. He had borne the shock of his wound, he had even survived the torture to which Laurie submitted him when, goaded by Lady Barbara's urgent representations, he had set to work with knife and saw upon the smashed tangle of flesh and bone which had been his legs. He had bade fair to make a good recovery, lying blanched and feeble in his cot, so that Laurie had been heard to boast of his surgical skill and of the fine stumps he had made and of the neatness with which he had tied the arteries. Then, suddenly, the fatal symptoms had shown themselves, and Galbraith had died five days later after a fortunate delirium.

Hornblower and Lady Barbara drew nearer to each other during those days. Lady Barbara had fought a losing battle for Galbraith's life to the very end, had fought hard and without sparing herself, and yet seemingly without emotion as if she were merely applying herself to a job which had to be done. Hornblower would have thought this was the case if had not seen her face on the occasion when Galbraith was holding her hands and talking to her under the impression that she was his mother. The dying boy was babbling feverishly in the broad Scots into which he had lapsed as soon as delirium overcame him, clutching her hands and refusing to let her go, while she sat with him talking calmly and quietly in an effort to soothe him. So still was her voice, so calm and unmoved was her attitude, that Hornblower would have been deceived had he not seen the torment in her face.

And for Hornblower it was unexpectedly painful when Galbraith died. Hornblower always looked upon himself as a man content to make use of others, pleasingly devoid of human weaknesses. It was a surprise to him to find how hurt and sorry he was at Galbraith's death, and to find his voice trembling and tears in his eyes as he read the service, and to feel a shudder of distress at the thought of what the sharks were doing to Galbraith's body, down there below the blue surface of the Pacific. He told himself that he was being weak, and then hastened to assure himself that he was merely annoyed at the loss of a useful subordinate, but he could not convince himself. In a fury of reaction he flung himself into the business of driving his men harder in their task of refitting the *Lydia*, and yet now when his eyes met Lady Barbara's on deck or across the dinner table, it was not with the complete lack of sympathy which had previously prevailed. There was a hint of understanding between them now.

Hornblower saw little enough of Lady Barbara. They dined together on some occasions, always with at least one other officer present, but for the most part he was busy with his professional duties and she with her care of the sick. They neither of them had the time, and he at least had not the superfluous energy to spare for the flirtations that those mild tropic nights should have brought in their train. And Hornblower, as soon as they entered the Gulf of Panama, had sufficient additional worries for the moment to drive away all possibility of a flirtation.

The Pearl Islands were just in view over the port bow, and the *Lydia*, close-hauled, was heading for Panama one day's sail ahead when the *guarda-costa* lugger which had encountered them before hove up over the horizon to windward. At sight of the *Lydia* she altered course and came running downwind towards her, while Hornblower kept steadily on his course. He was a little elated with the prospect of making even such a fever-ridden port as badly equipped as Panama, because the strain of keeping the *Lydia* afloat was beginning to tell on him.

The lugger hove-to a couple of cables' lengths away, and a few minutes later the same smart officer in the brilliant uniform came clambering on to the *Lydia*'s deck as had boarded from her once before.

'Good morning, Captain,' he said, bowing profoundly. 'I trust Your Excellency is enjoying the best of health?'

'Thank you,' said Hornblower.

The Spanish officer was looking curiously about him; the *Lydia* still bore many marks of her recent battle – the row of wounded in hammocks told a good part of the story. Hornblower saw that the Spaniard seemed to be on his guard, as though determined to be noncommittal at present until something unknown had revealed itself.

'I see,' said the Spaniard, 'that your fine ship has been recently in action. I hope that Your Excellency had good fortune in the encounter?'

'We sank the *Natividad* if that is what you mean,' said Hornblower brutally.

'You sank her, Captain?'

'I did.'

'She is destroyed?'

'She is.'

The Spaniard's expression hardened – Hornblower was led for a moment to think that it was a bitter blow to him to hear that for a second time the Spanish ship had been beaten by an English ship of half her force.

'Then, sir,' said the Spaniard, 'I have a letter to give you.'

He felt in his breast pocket, but with a curious gesture of hesitation – Hornblower realised later that he must have had two letters, one in one pocket and one in another, of different import, one to be delivered if the *Natividad* were destroyed and the other if she were still able to do damage. The letter which he handed over when he was quite certain which was which was not very brief, but was worded with a terseness that implied (having regard to the ornateness of the Spanish official style) absolute rudeness, as Hornblower was quick to realise when he tore open the wrapper and read the contents. It was a formal prohibition from the Viceroy of Peru for the *Lydia* to drop anchor in, or to enter into, any port of Spanish America, in the Viceroyalty of Peru, of the Viceroyalty of Mexico, or the Captain-Generalcy of New Granada.

Hornblower re-read the letter, and while he did so the dismal clangour of the pumps, drifting aft to his ears, made more acute the worries which instantly leaped upon him. He thought of his battered, leaking ship, his sick and wounded, his weary crew and attenuated stores, of the rounding of the Horn and the four thousand miles of Atlantic which lay between him and England. And more than that; he remembered the supplementary orders which had been given him when he left England, regarding the effort he was to make to open Spanish America to British trade and to establish an Isthmian canal.

'You are aware of the contents of this letter, sir?' he asked.

'Yes, sir.'

The Spaniard was haughty, even brazen about it.

'Can you explain this most unfriendly behaviour on the part of the Viceroy?'

'I would not presume to explain my master's actions, sir.'

'And yet they are in sore need of explanation. I cannot understand how any civilised man could abandon an ally who has fought his battles for him and is in need of help solely because of those battles.'

'You came unasked into these seas, sir. There would have been no battle for you to fight if you had stayed in those parts of the world where your King rules. The South Sea is the property of His Most Catholic Majesty, who will tolerate no intruder upon it.'

'I understand,' said Hornblower.

He guessed that new orders had come out to Spanish America now that the government of Spain had heard of the presence of an English frigate in the Pacific. The retention of the American monopoly was to the Spanish mind as dear as life itself. There was no length to which the Spanish government would not go to retain it, even though it meant offending an ally while in the midst of a life-and-death struggle with the most powerful despot in Europe. To the Spaniards in Madrid, the *Lydia*'s presence in the Pacific hinted at the coming of a flood of British traders, at the drying up of the constant stream of gold and silver on which the Spanish government depended, at – worse still – the introduction of heresy into a part of the world which had been kept faithful to the Pope through three centuries. It did not matter if Spanish America were poor, misgoverned, disease-ridden, nor if the rest of the world felt the pinch of being shut out at a time when the Continental System had ruined European trade.

In a clear-sighted moment Hornblower foresaw that the world could not long tolerate selfishness carried to these lengths, and that soon, amid general approval, Spanish America would throw off the Spanish yoke. Later, if neither Spain nor New Granada would cut that canal, someone else would step in and do it for them. He was minded to say so, but his innate caution restrained him. However badly he had been treated, there was nothing to be gained by causing an open breach. There was a sweeter revenge in keeping his thoughts to himself.

'Very good, sir,' he said. 'My compliments to your master. I will call at no port on the Spanish Main. Please convey to His Excellency my lively sense of gratitude at the courtesy with which I have been treated, and my pleasure at this further proof of the good relations between the governments of which we have the good fortune to be subjects.'

The Spanish officer looked at him sharply, but Hornblower kept his face immobile while bending his spine with studied courtesy.

'And now, sir,' went on Hornblower drily, 'I must, much to my regret, wish you good day and a pleasant journey. I have much to attend to.'

It was irksome to the Spaniard to be dismissed in this cavalier fashion, but he could take no open exception to anything Hornblower had said. He could only return Hornblower's bow and walk back to the ship's side. No sooner was he back in his boat than Hornblower turned to Bush.

'Keep the ship hove-to, if you please, Mr Bush,' he said.

The *Lydia* rolled heavily, hove-to, on the swell, while her captain resumed his uninterrupted pacing of the quarterdeck, eyed furtively by those officers and men who had guessed at the bad news this latest despatch contained. Up and down, up and down, walked Hornblower, between the carronade slides on the one hand and the ring bolts on the other, while the clanking of the pumps, floating drearily on the heavy air, told him at every second how urgent it was that he should form some new decision.

First of all, however, before even the question of the condition of the ship arose, he must decide about stores and water – every ship's captain had to consider that problem first. Six weeks back he had filled his storerooms and his water barrels. But since that time he had lost a quarter of his crew. At a pinch, even allowing for a long time to refit, there was enough food to last them back to England, therefore; especially as the easterly rounding of the Horn was never as prolonged as the westerly one, and (now that all need of secrecy had disappeared) if necessary St Helena or Sierra Leone or Gibraltar would be open to him to replenish.

That was intensely satisfactory. He could devote his whole
mind now to his ship. Refit he must. The *Lydia* could not hope
to survive the storms of Cape Horn in her present condition,
leaking like a sieve, jury rigged, and with a sail fothered under
her bottom. The work could not be done at sea, and the harbours
were barred to him. He must do as old buccaneers did – as Drake
and Anson and Dampier had done in these very waters – find
some secluded cove where he could careen his ship. It would
not be easy on the mainland, for the Spaniards had settled round
every navigable bay. It would have to be an island, therefore.

Those Pearl Islands on the horizon would not be suitable, for
Hornblower knew them to be inhabited and to be frequently
visited from Panama – besides, the lugger was still in sight and
watching his movements. Hornblower went down below and got
out his charts; there was the island of Coiba which the *Lydia* had
passed yesterday. His charts told him nothing of it save its position, but it was clearly the place to investigate first. Hornblower
laid off his course and then went on deck again.

'We will put the ship about, if you please, Mr Bush,' he said.

CHAPTER XX

Inch by inch, His Britannic Majesty's frigate *Lydia* crept into the bay. The cutter was out ahead, with Rayner sounding industriously, while, with a dying breath of air behind her and a shred of sail set, the *Lydia* felt her way between the two headlands into the tortuous channel. Those capes, one each side of the entrance, were steep rocky cliffs, and the one overlapped the other a trifle so that only an eye sharpened by necessity, and which had made the most of its recent opportunities of learning the typical rock formations of that coast could have guessed at the possibility of an expanse of water behind them.

Hornblower took his eye from the ship's course as she crawled round the corner to study the bay before him. There were mountains all round it, but on the farther side the slope down to the water was not nearly as steep, and on the water's edge there, at the foot of the dazzling green which clothed the banks all round, there was a hint of golden sand which told of the sort of bottom which he sought. It would be shelving there, without a doubt, and free from rock.

'This seems very suitable,' said Hornblower to Bush.

'Aye aye, sir. Made for the job,' said Bush.

'Then you may drop anchor. We shall start work at once.'

It was terribly hot in that little bay in the island of Coiba. The lofty mountains all about cut off any wind that might be blowing, and at the same time reflected the heat to a focus in the bay. As the cable rasped out through the hawsehole, Hornblower felt the heat descend upon him. He was wet with sweat even while he stood still on the quarterdeck; he longed for a bath and for a little leisure, to rest until the cool of the evening, but he could not allow himself any such luxury. Time was, as ever, of vital importance. He must make himself secure before the Spaniards could discover where he had hidden himself.

'Call back the cutter,' he said.

On land it was even hotter than on the water. Hornblower had himself rowed to the sandy beach, sounding as he went, and examining with care the sample of the bottom which the tallow on the bottom of the lead brought up for his inspection. It was sand without a doubt – he could beach the *Lydia* safely there. He landed in the breathless jungle; there was clearly no human life here, to judge by the pathlessness of the close-packed vegetation. Tall trees and scrub, creepers and parasites, were all tangled together in their silent struggle for life. Strange birds with strange cries flitted through the twilight of the branches; Hornblower's nostrils were assailed by the reek of the decaying matter beneath his feet. With a sweating escort, musket in hand, about him, he cut his way through the forest. He emerged where the rock was too steep for vegetation ever to have gained a foothold, into the blinding sunlight at the mouth of the bay. He climbed, sweating and exhausted, up the steep ledges. The *Lydia* floated idly on the dazzling blue of the little bay. The opposite headland frowned down upon him across the mouth, and he studied its soaring ledges through his glass. Then he went back to his ship, to goad his men into frantic activity.

Before she could be beached, before the carpenter and his men could set to work upon her bottom, the *Lydia* must be lightened. And also, before she could be laid defenceless on her side, this bay must be made secure from all aggressors. Tackles were rigged, and the two-ton eighteen-pounders were swayed up from the main deck. With careful management and exact balancing the cutter could just carry one of these monsters. One at a time they were ferried to the headlands, where Rayner and Gerard were ready at work with parties preparing emplacements. Toiling gangs were set to work preparing rough paths up the faces of the cliffs, and no sooner were these complete than the men were turned on with tackles and ropes to drag the guns up the paths. Powder and shot for the guns followed them, and then food and water for the garrisons. At the end of thirty-six hours of exacting labour the *Lydia* was a hundred tons lighter, and the entrance to the bay was so defended that any vessel attempting it would have to brave the plunging fire of twenty guns.

In the meanwhile, another party had been working like furies on shore above the sandy beach. Here they cleared away a section of forest, and dragged the fallen trees into a rough breastwork, and into the rude fort so delimited, among the tree stumps, another party brought up beef barrels, and flour bags, and spars, and guns, and shot, and powder barrels, until the *Lydia* was a mere empty shell rolling in the tiny waves of the bay. The men stretched canvas shelters for themselves as protection against the frequent tropical showers which deluged on them, and for their officers they built rude timber huts – and one for the women as well.

In giving that order Hornblower made his sole acknowledge-ment of the women's existence. During this flurry of work, and under the strain of the responsibility which he bore, he had neither the time nor the surplus energy to spare for conversation with Lady Barbara. He was tired, and the steamy heat drained his energies, but his natural reaction to these conditions, having in mind the need for haste, was to flog himself into working harder and harder, obstinately and unreasonably, so that the days passed in a nightmare of fatigue, during which the minutes he passed with Lady Barbara were like the glimpses a man has of a beau-tiful woman during delirium.

He drove his men hard from earliest dawn as long as daylight lasted, keeping them slaving away in the crushing heat until they shook their heads over him in rueful admiration. They did not grudge him the efforts he called for; that would have been impossible for British sailors led by a man who was so little prepared to spare himself. And besides, the men displayed the constant characteristics of British crews of working the more cheerfully the more unusual the conditions. Sleeping on beds of sand instead of in their far more comfortable hammocks, working on solid earth instead of on board ship, hemmed in by dense forest instead of engirdled by a distant horizon – all this was stimulating and cheering.

The fireflies in the forest, the strange fruits which were found for them by their impressed prisoners from the *Natividad*, the very mosquitoes which plagued them, helped at the same time to keep them happy. Down the cliff face, beside one of the entrance batteries there tumbled a constant stream of clear water, so that for once in their lives the men were allowed as much fresh water as they could use, and to men who for months at a time had to submit to having a sentry standing guard over their drinking water this was an inexpressible luxury.

Soon, on the sandy shore, and as far as possible from the stored powder barrels, canvas-covered and sentry-guarded, there were fires lit over which was melted the pitch brought from the boatswain's store. There had not been enough defaulters during those days to pick all the oakum required – some of the ship's company had to work at oakum picking while the *Lydia* was hove over and the carpenter applied himself to the task of settling her bottom to rights. The shot holes were plugged, and strained seams caulked and pitched, the missing sheets of copper were replaced by the last few sheets which the *Lydia* carried in reserve. For four days the tiny bay was filled with the sound of the caulking hammers at work, and the reek of melting pitch drifted over the still water as the smoking cauldrons were carried across to the working parties.

At the end of that time the carpenter expressed himself as satisfied, and Hornblower, anxiously going over every foot of the ship's bottom, grudgingly agreed with him. The *Lydia* was hove off, and still empty, was kedged and towed across the bay until she lay at the foot of the high cliff where one of the batteries was established – the shore was steep enough at this point to allow her to lie close in here when empty of guns and stores. At this point Lieutenant Bush had been busy setting up a projecting gallows, a hundred feet above, and vertically over, the ship's deck. Painfully, and after many trials, the *Lydia* was manoeuvred until she could be moored so that the stump of her mizzen mast stood against the plumb line which Bush dropped from the tackles high above. Then the wedges were knocked out, the tackles set to work, and the stump was drawn out of her like a decayed tooth.

That part of the work was easy compared with the next step. The seventy-five foot main yard had to be swayed up to the gallows, and then hung vertically down from them; if it had slipped it would have shot down like some monstrous arrow and would have sunk her for certain. When the yard was exactly vertical and exactly above the mizzenmast step it was lowered down, inch by inch, until its solid butt could be coaxed by anxious gangs through the main deck and through the orlop until it came at last solidly to rest in its step upon the kelson. It only remained then to wedge it firmly in, to set up new shrouds, and the *Lydia* had once more a mizzen mast which could face the gales of the Horn.

Back at her anchorage, the *Lydia* could be ballasted once more, with her beef barrels and water barrels, her guns and her shot, save what was left in the entrance batteries. Ballasted and steady upon her keel, she could be re-rigged and her topmasts set up again. Every rope was re-rove, her standing rigging newly set up and replacements affected until she was as efficient a ship as when she had left Portsmouth newly commissioned.

It was then that Hornblower could allow himself time to draw breath and relax. The captain of a ship that is no ship, but only a mere hulk helpless in a landlocked inlet, cannot feel a moment's peace. A heretic in an Inquisitor's dungeon is happy compared with him. There is the menacing land all about him, the torment of helplessness as a perpetual goad, the fear of an ignominious siege to wake him in the night. Hornblower was like a man released from a sentence of death when he trod the *Lydia*'s deck once more and allowed his eye to rove contentedly upward and ever upward through the aspiring rigging, with the clangour of the pumps which had echoed in his ears during the last fortnight's cruise completely stilled, happy in the consciousness of a staunch ship under his feet, comfortable in the knowledge that there would be no more campaigns to plan until he reached England.

At this very moment they were dismantling one of the entrance batteries, and the guns were being ferried out to the *Lydia* one by one. Already he had a broadside battery which could fire, a ship which could manoeuvre, and he could snap his fingers at every Spaniard in the Pacific. It was a glorious sensation. He turned and found Lady Barbara on the quarterdeck beside him, and he smiled at her dazzlingly.

'Good morning, ma'am,' he said. 'I trust you found your cabin comfortable again?'

Lady Barbara smiled back at him – in fact she almost laughed, so comical was the contrast between this greeting and the scowls she had encountered from him during the last eleven days.

'Thank you, Captain,' she said. 'It is marvellously comfortable. Your crew has worked wonders to have done so much in so little time.'

Quite unconsciously, he had reached out and taken both her hands in his, and was standing there holding them, smiling all over his face in the sunshine. Lady Barbara felt that it would only need a word from her to set him dancing.

'We shall be at sea before nightfall,' he said, ecstatically.

She could not be dignified with him, any more than she could have been dignified with a baby; she knew enough of men and affairs not to resent his previous preoccupation. Truth to tell, she was a trifle fond of him because of it.

'You are a very fine sailor, sir,' she said to him suddenly. 'I doubt if there is another officer in the King's service who could have done all you have done on this voyage.'

'I am glad you think so, ma'am,' he said, but the spell was broken. He had been reminded of himself, and his cursed self-consciousness closed in upon him again. He dropped her hands, awkwardly, and there was a hint of a blush in his tanned cheeks.

'I have only done my duty,' he mumbled, looking away.

'Many men can do that,' said Lady Barbara, 'but few can do it well. The country is your debtor – my sincerest hope is that England will acknowledge the debt.'

The words started a sudden train of thought in Hornblower's mind; it was a train he had followed up often before. England would only remember that his battle with the *Natividad* had been unnecessary; that a more fortunate captain would have heard of the new alliance between Spain and England before he had handed the *Natividad* over to the rebels, and would have saved all the trouble and friction and loss which had resulted. A frigate action with a hundred casualties might be glorious, but an unnecessary action with a hundred casualties was quite inglorious. No one would stop to think that it was his careful obedience to orders and skill in carrying them out which had been the reason of it. He would be blamed for his own merits, and life was suddenly full of bitterness again.

'Your pardon, ma'am,' he said, and he turned away from her and walked forward to bawl orders at the men engaged in swaying an eighteen pounder up from the launch.

Lady Barbara shook her head at his back.

'Bless the man!' she said to herself, softly. 'He was almost human for a while.'

Lady Barbara was fast acquiring, in her forced loneliness, the habit of talking to herself like the sole inhabitant of a desert island. She checked herself as soon as she found herself doing so, and went below and rated Hebe soundly for some minor sin of omission in the unpacking of her wardrobe.

CHAPTER XXI

The rumour had gone round the crew that the *Lydia* was at last homeward bound. The men had fought and worked, first on the one side and then on the other, without understanding the trend of high politics which had decided whom they should fight and for whom they should work. That Spaniards should be first enemies, and then friends, and then almost hostile neutrals, had hardly caused one of them a single thought. They had been content to obey orders unthinkingly; but now, it seemed certain, so solidly based was the rumour, that the *Lydia* was on her way home. To the scatter-brained crew it seemed as if England was just over the horizon. They gave no thought to the five thousand stormy miles of sea that lay before them. Their heads were full of England. The pressed men thought of their wives; the volunteers thought of the women of the ports and of the joys of paying off. The sun of their rapture was not even overcast by any cloud of doubt as to the chances of their being turned over to another ship and sent off half round the world again before ever they could set foot on English soil.

They had flung themselves with a will into the labour of warping out of the bay, and not one of them looked back with regret to the refuge which alone had made their homeward voyage possible. They had chattered and played antics like a crew of monkeys when they dashed aloft to set sail, and the watch below had danced and set to partners through the warm evening while the *Lydia* bowled along with a favourable breeze over the blue Pacific. Then during the night the wind died away with its usual tropical freakishness, from a good breeze to a faint air, and from a faint air to a slow succession of fluky puffs which set the sails slatting and the rigging creaking and kept the watch continually at work at the braces trimming the sails.

Hornblower awoke in his cot in the cool hour before dawn. It was still too dark to see the telltale compass in the deck over his head, but he could guess from the long roll of the ship and the intermittent noises overhead that calm weather had overtaken them. It was almost time for him to start his morning walk on the quarterdeck, and he rested, blissfully free of all feeling of responsibility, until Polwheal came in to get out his clothes. He was putting on his trousers when a hail from the masthead lookout came echoing down through the scuttle.

'Sail ho! Broad on the larboard beam. It's that there lugger again, sir.'

That feeling of freedom from worry vanished on the instant. Twice had that ill-omened lugger been seen in this very Gulf of Panama, and twice she had been the bearer of bad news. Hornblower wondered, with a twinge of superstition, what this third encounter would bring forth. He snatched his coat from Polwheal's hands and put it on as he dashed up the companionway.

The lugger was there, sure enough, lying becalmed some two miles away; there were half a dozen glasses trained on her – apparently Hornblower's officers shared his superstition.

'There's something about that craft's rig which gives me the horrors,' grumbled Gerard.

'She's just a plain Spanish *guarda-costa*,' said Crystal. 'I've seen 'em in dozens. I remember off Havana—'

'Who hasn't seen 'em?' snapped Gerard. 'I was saying – hullo! There's a boat putting off.'

He glanced round and saw his captain appearing on the deck.

'Lugger's sending a boat, sir.'

Hornblower did his best to make his expression one of sturdy indifference. He told himself that commanding, as he did, the fastest and most powerful ship on the Pacific coast, he need fear nothing. He was equipped and ready to sail half round the world, to fight any ship up to fifty guns. The sight of the lugger ought to cause him no uneasiness, but it did.

For long minutes they watched the boat come bobbing towards
them over the swell. At first it was only a black speck showing
occasionally on the crests. Then the flash of the oar blades could
be seen, as they reflected the rays of the nearly level sun, and
then the oars themselves, as the boat grew like some great black
water beetle creeping over the surface, and at last she was within
hail, and a few minutes after for the third time the young Spanish
officer in his brilliant uniform mounted to the *Lydia*'s deck and
received Hornblower's bow.

He made no attempt to conceal his curiosity, nor the admiration which blended with it. He saw that the jury mizzen mast
had disappeared and had been replaced by a new spar as trim
and as efficient as any set up in a navy yard; he saw that the
shot holes had been expertly patched; he noticed that the pumps
were no longer at work – that in fact during the sixteen days
since he last saw her the ship had been entirely refitted, and, to
his certain knowledge, without any aid from the shore and in no
harbour save perhaps for some deserted inlet.

'It surprises me to see you here again, sir,' he said.

'To me,' said Hornblower, with perfect courtesy, 'it is a
pleasure as well as a surprise.'

'To me also it is a pleasure,' said the Spaniard quickly, 'but
I had thought you were far on your way home by now.'

'I am on my way home,' said Hornblower, determined to give
no cause for offence if possible, 'but as you see, sir, I have not
progressed far as yet. However, I have effected, as perhaps you
may notice, the repairs that were necessary, and now nothing will
delay me from proceeding to England with the utmost despatch
– unless, sir, there is some new development which makes it
advisable, for the sake of the common cause of our two countries,
for me to remain longer in these waters.'

Hornblower said these last words anxiously, and he was already
devising in his mind excuses to free himself from the conse-
quences of this offer if it were accepted. But the Spaniard's reply
reassured him.

'Thank you, sir,' he said, 'but there is no need for me to take advantage of your kindness. His Most Catholic Majesty's dominions are well able to guard themselves. I am sure that His Britannic Majesty will be glad to see such a fine frigate returning to forward his cause.'

The two captains bowed to each other profoundly at this exchange of compliments before the Spaniard resumed his speech.

'I was thinking, sir,' he went on, 'that perhaps if you would do me the great honour of visiting my ship for a moment, taking advantage of this prevailing calm, I should be able to show Your Excellency something which would be of interest and which would demonstrate our ability to continue without your kind assistance.'

'What is it?' asked Hornblower, suspiciously.

The Spaniard smiled.

'It would give me pleasure if I could show it to you as a surprise. Please, sir, would you not oblige me?'

Hornblower looked automatically round the horizon. He studied the Spaniard's face. The Spaniard was no fool; and only a fool could meditate treachery when almost within range of a frigate which could sink his ship in a single broadside. And mad though most Spaniards were, they were not mad enough to offer violence to a British captain. Besides, he was pleased with the thought of how his officers would receive his announcement that he was going on board the lugger.

'Thank you, sir,' he said. 'It will give me great pleasure to accompany you.'

The Spaniard bowed again, and Hornblower turned to his first lieutenant.

'I am going to visit the lugger, Mr Bush,' he said. 'I shall only be gone a short time. Call away the cutter and send her after me to bring me back.'

Hornblower was delighted to see how Bush struggled to conceal his consternation at the news.

'Aye aye, sir,' he said. He opened his mouth and shut it again; he wanted to expostulate and yet did not dare, and finally repeated feebly, 'Aye aye, sir.'

In the small boat rowing back to the lugger the Spaniard was the mirror of courtesy. He chatted politely about weather conditions. He mentioned the latest news of the war in Spain – it was quite undoubted that a French army had surrendered to the Spaniards in Andalusia, and that Spanish and British armies were assembling for a march into France. He described the ravages of yellow fever on the mainland. He contrived, all the same, to allow no single hint to drop as to the nature of the surprise which he was going to show Hornblower in the lugger.

The two captains were received with Spanish ceremony as they swung themselves up into the lugger's waist. There was a great deal of bustle and parade, and two bugles and two drums sounded a resounding march horribly out of tune.

'All in this ship is yours, sir,' said the Spaniard with Castilian courtesy, and seeing no incongruity in his next sentence. 'Your Excellency will take some refreshment? A cup of chocolate?'

'Thank you,' said Hornblower. He was not going to imperil his dignity by asking what was the nature of the surprise in store for him. He could wait – especially as he could see the launch already halfway towards the lugger.

The Spaniard was in no hurry to make the revelation. He was evidently savouring in anticipation the Englishman's certain astonishment. He pointed out certain peculiarities in the lugger's rig; he called up his officers to present to Hornblower; he discussed the merits of his crew – nearly all native Indians as on board the *Natividad*. In the end Hornblower won; the Spaniard could wait no longer to be asked.

'Would you please to come this way, sir?' he said. He led the way on to the foredeck, and there, chained by the waist to a ring bolt, with irons on his wrist and ankles, was el Supremo.

He was in rags – half naked in fact, and his beard and hair were matted and tangled, and his own filth lay on the deck about him.

'I think,' said the Spanish captain, 'that you have already had the pleasure, sir, of meeting His Excellency Don Julian Maria de Jesus de Alvarado y Moctezuma, who calls himself the Almighty?'

El Supremo showed no signs of being disconcerted by the gibe.

'Captain Hornblower has indeed been presented to me already,' he said loftily. 'He has worked for me long and devotedly. I trust you are enjoying the best of health, Captain?'

'Thank you, sir,' said Hornblower.

Despite his rags, and his filth, and his chains, el Supremo bore himself with the same elaborate dignity as Hornblower remembered so well those many weeks ago.

'I too,' he said, 'am as well as the world could desire. It is a source of continual satisfaction to me to see my affairs progressing so well.'

A negro servant appeared on the deck at that moment with a tray of chocolate; another followed him with a couple of chairs. Hornblower, at the invitation of his host, sat down. He was glad to do so, as his knees seemed suddenly weak under him, but he had no desire at all for his chocolate. The Spanish captain drank noisily, and el Supremo eyed him as he did so. There came a gleam of appetite in his face. His lips moistened and smacked softly together, his eyes brightened, his hand came out, and then next moment he was calm and indifferent again.

'I trust that the chocolate is to your liking, sirs,' he said. 'I ordered it specially for you. My own appetite for chocolate has long since disappeared.'

'That is just as well,' said the Spanish captain. He laughed loudly and drank again, smacking his lips.

El Supremo ignored him, and turned to Hornblower.

'You see I wear these chains,' he said. 'It is a strange whim on the part of myself and my servants that I should do so. I hope you agree with me that they set off my figure quite admirably?'

'Y-yes, sir,' stammered Hornblower.

'We are on our way to Panama, where I shall mount the throne of the world. They talk of hanging; these fellows here say that there is a gallows awaiting us on the bastion of the Citadel. That will be the framework of my golden throne. Golden, it will be, with diamond stars and a great turquoise moon. It will be from there that I shall issue my next decrees to the world.'

The Spanish captain guffawed again, but el Supremo still stood in quiet dignity, hugging his chains, with the sun blazing down on his tangled head.

'He will not last long in this mood,' said the Spanish captain to Hornblower behind his hand. 'I can see signs of the change coming. It gives me great felicity that you have had the opportunity of seeing him in both his moods.'

'The sun grows in his splendour every day,' said el Supremo. 'He is magnificent and terrible, as I am. He can kill – kill – kill, as he killed the men I exposed to him – when was it? And Moctezuma is dead, and all his line save me, in the hundreds of years ago. I alone remain. And Hernandez is dead, but it was not the sun that killed him. They hanged Hernandez even while the blood dripped from his wounds. They hanged him in my city of San Salvador, and as they hanged him he still called upon the name of el Supremo. They hanged the men and they hanged the women, in long rows at San Salvador. Only el Supremo is left, to govern from his golden throne. His throne! His throne!'

El Supremo was staring about him now. There was a hint of bewildered realisation in his face as he jangled his chains. He peered at them stupidly.

'Chains! These are chains!'

He was bawling and shouting. He laughed madly, and then he wept and he cursed, flinging himself about on the deck, biting at his chains. His words were no longer articulate as he slobbered and writhed.

'It is interesting, is it not?' said the Spanish captain. 'He will struggle and shout sometimes for twenty-four hours without a stop.'

'Bah!' said Hornblower, and his chair fell with a clatter to the deck as he got to his feet. He was on the verge of vomiting. The

Spaniard saw his white face and trembling lips, and was faintly amused, and made no attempt to conceal it.

But Hornblower could give no vent to the flood of protest which was welling up within him. His cautious mind told him that a madman in a ship as small as the lugger must of necessity be chained to the deck, and his conscience reminded him uneasily of the torments he had seen el Supremo inflict without expostulation. This Spanish way of making a show out of insanity and greatness was repulsive enough, but could be paralleled often enough in English history. One of the greatest writers of the English language, and a dignitary of the Church to boot, had once been shown in his dotage for a fee. There was only one line of argument which he could adopt.

'You are going to hang him, mad as he is?' he asked. 'With no chance of making his peace with God?'

The Spaniard shrugged.

'Mad or sane, rebels must hang. Your Excellency must know that as well as I do.'

Hornblower did know it. He was left without any argument at all, and was reduced to stammering inarticulation, even while he boiled with contempt for himself on that account. All that was left for him to do, having lost all his dignity in his own eyes, was to try and retain some few shreds of it in the eyes of his audience. He braced himself up, conscious of the hollowness of the fraud.

'I must thank you very much, sir,' he said, 'for having given me the opportunity of witnessing a most interesting spectacle. And now, repeating my thanks, I fear that I must regretfully take my departure. There seems to be a breath of wind blowing.'

He went down the side of the lugger as stiffly as he might, and took his seat in the sternsheets of the launch. He had to brace himself again to give the word to cast off, and then he sat silent and gloomy as he was rowed back to the *Lydia*. Bush and Gerard and Lady Barbara watched him as he came on deck. It was as if there was death in his face. He looked round him, unseeing and unhearing, and then hurried below to hide his misery. He even sobbed, with his face in his cot, for a second, before he was able to take hold of himself and curse himself for a weak fool. But it was days before he lost that deathly look, and during that time he kept himself solitary in his cabin, unable to bring himself to join the merry parties on the quarterdeck whose gay chatter drifted down to him through the skylight. To him it was a further proof of his weakness and folly that he should allow himself to be so upset by the sight of a criminal madman going to meet the fate he richly deserved.

CHAPTER XXII

Lady Barbara and Lieutenant Bush were sitting talking in the warm moonlit night beside the taffrail. It was the first time that Bush had happened to share a *tête-à-tête* with her, and he had only drifted into it by chance – presumably if he had foreseen it he would have avoided it, but now that he had drifted into conversation with her he was enjoying himself to the exclusion of any disquietude. He was sitting on a pile of the oakum-filled cushions which Harrison had had made for Lady Barbara, and he nursed his knees while Lady Barbara leaned back in her hammock chair. The *Lydia* was rising and falling softly to the gentle music of the waves and the harping of the rigging in the breeze. The white sails glimmered in the brilliant moonlight; overhead the stars shone with strange brightness. But Bush was not talking of himself, as any sensible man would do under a tropic moon with a young woman beside him.

'Aye, ma'am,' he was saying. 'He's like Nelson. He's nervous, just as Nelson was, and for the same reason. He's thinking all the time – you'd be surprised, ma'am, to know how much he thinks about.'

'I don't think it would surprise me,' said Lady Barbara.

'That's because you think, too, ma'am. It's us stupid ones who'd be surprised, I meant to say. He has more brains than all the rest of us in the ship put together, excepting you, ma'am. He's mighty clever, I do assure you.'

'I can well believe it.'

'And he's the best seaman of us all, and as for navigation – well, Crystal's a fool compared with him, ma'am.'

'Yes?'

'Of course, he's short with me sometimes, the same as he is with everyone else, but bless you, ma'am, that's only to be expected. I know how much he has to worry him, and he's not strong, the same as Nelson wasn't strong. I am concerned about him sometimes, ma'am.'

'You are fond of him.'

'Fond, ma'am?' Bush's sturdy English mind grappled with the word and its sentimental implications, and he laughed a trifle self-consciously. 'If you say so I suppose I must be. I hadn't ever thought of being fond of him before. I like him, ma'am, indeed I do.'

'That is what I meant.'

'The men worship him, ma'am. They would do anything for him. Look how much he has done this commission, and the lash not in use once in a week, ma'am. That is why he is like Nelson. They love him not for anything he does or says, but for what he is.'

'He's handsome, in a way,' said Barbara – she was woman enough to give that matter consideration.

'I suppose he is, ma'am, now you come to mention it. But it wouldn't matter if he were as ugly as sin as far as we was concerned.'

'Of course not.'

'But he's shy, ma'am. He never can guess how clever he is. It's that which always surprises me about him. You'd hardly believe it, ma'am, but he has no more faith in himself than – than I have in myself, ma'am, to put it that way. Less, ma'am, if anything.'

'How strange!' said Lady Barbara. She was accustomed to the sturdy self-reliance of her brothers, unloved and unlovable leaders of men, but her insight made her comment only one of politeness – it was not really strange to her.

'Look, ma'am,' said Bush, suddenly, dropping his voice.

Hornblower had come up on deck. They could see his face, white in the moonlight, as he looked round to assure himself that all was well with his ship, and they could read in it the torment which was obsessing him. He looked like a lost soul during the few seconds he was on deck.

'I wish to God I knew,' said Bush as Hornblower retreated again to the solitude of his cabin, 'what those devils did to him or said to him when he went on board the lugger. Hooker, who was in the cutter, said he heard someone on board howling like a madman. The torturing devils! It was some of their beastliness, I suppose. You could see how it has upset him, ma'am.'

'Yes,' said Lady Barbara softly.

'I should be grateful if you could try to take him out of himself a little, ma'am, begging your pardon. He is in need of distraction, I suspicion. Perhaps you could – if you'll forgive me, ma'am.'

'I'll try,' said Lady Barbara, 'but I don't think I shall succeed where you have failed. Captain Hornblower has never taken a great deal of notice of me, Mr Bush.'

Yet fortunately the formal invitation to dine with Lady Barbara, which Hebe conveyed to Polwheal and he to his captain, arrived at a moment when Hornblower was just trying to emerge from the black fit which had engulfed him. He read the words as carefully as Lady Barbara had written them – and she had devoted much care to the composition of the note. Hornblower read Lady Barbara's pretty little apology for breaking in upon him at a time when he was obviously engrossed in his work, and he went on to read how Lady Barbara had been informed by Mr Bush that the *Lydia* was about to cross the Equator, and that she thought such an occasion merited some mild celebration. If Captain Hornblower, therefore, would give Lady Barbara the pleasure of his company at dinner and would indicate to her which of his officers he considered should be invited at the same time, Lady Barbara would be delighted. Hornblower wrote back to say that Captain Hornblower had much pleasure in accepting Lady Barbara's kind invitation to dinner, and hoped that Lady Barbara would invite whomever she pleased in addition.

Yet even in the pleasure of returning to society there was some alloy. Hornblower had always been a poor man, and at the time when he commissioned the *Lydia* he had been at his wits' end about where to turn for money in the need for leaving Maria comfortably provided for. In consequence, he had not outfitted himself satisfactorily, and now, all these months later, his clothes were in the last stages of decay. The coats were all patched and darned; the epaulettes betrayed in their brassy sheen the fact that they had begun life merely coated with bullion; the cocked hats were all wrecks; he had neither breeches nor stockings fit to be seen; his once white scarves were all coarsened now, and could never be mistaken again for silk. Only the sword 'of fifty guineas' value' retained its good appearance, and he could not wear that at a dinner party.

He was conscious that his white duck trousers, made on board the *Lydia*, had none of the fashionable appearance to which Lady Barbara was accustomed. He looked shabby and he felt shabby, and as he peered at himself in his little mirror he was certain that Lady Barbara would sneer at him. There were grey hairs in his brown curls, too, and then, to his horror, as he straightened his parting, he caught a glimpse of pink scalp – his baldness had increased beyond all measure of late. He eyed himself with complete disgust, and yet he felt that he would gladly give a limb or his remaining hair in exchange for a ribbon and star with which to dazzle Lady Barbara; yet even that would be of no avail, for Lady Barbara had lived all her life in an atmosphere of Garters and Thistles, orders which he could never hope to wear.

He was on the verge of sending a message to Lady Barbara to say that he had changed his mind and would not dine with her that evening, until he thought that if he did so, after all these preparations, Polwheal would guess that it was the result of his realisation of his shabbiness and would laugh at him (and his shabbiness) in consequence. He went into dinner and had his revenge upon the world by sitting silent and preoccupied at the head of the table, blighting with his gloomy presence all attempts at conversation, so that the function began as a frigid failure. It was a poor sort of revenge, but there was a slight gratification to be found in observing Lady Barbara looking down the table at him in concern. In the end, he was deprived even of that, for Lady Barbara suddenly smiled and began talking lightly and captivatingly, and led Bush into describing his experiences at Trafalgar – a tale she had heard, to Hornblower's certain knowledge, twice at least already.

The conversation became general, and then animated, for Gerard could not bear to leave all the talking to Bush, and he had to break in with the story of his encounter with an Algerine corsair off Cape Spartel in his old slaving days. It was more than Hornblower's flesh and blood could stand, to stay silent with everyone talking in this fashion. Against his will, he found himself entering into the conversation, and an artless question from Lady Barbara about Sir Edward Pellew inveigled him still further in, for Hornblower had been both midshipman and lieutenant in Pellew's ship, and was proud of it. Not until the end of dinner was he able to steady himself, and decline, after the drinking of the King's health, Lady Barbara's invitation to a rubber of whist. That at least, he thought, would make an impression on her – it certainly did upon his officers, for he saw Bush and Gerard exchange startled glances on hearing their captain refuse to play whist. Back in his cabin again he listened through the bulkhead to the uproarious game of *vingt-et-un* which Lady Barbara had suggested instead. He almost wished he was playing, too, even though in his opinion *vingt-et-un* was a game for the feeble-minded.

The dinner had served its purpose, however, in making it possible to meet Lady Barbara's eye again on deck. He could converse with her, too, discussing with her the condition of the few wounded who remained upon the sick list, and after a few morning encounters it was easy to fall into conversation with her during the breathless afternoons and the magic tropical nights as the *Lydia* held her course over the calm Pacific. He had grown hardened again to his shabby coats and his shapeless trousers; he was forgetting the resentful plans he had once turned over in his mind to confine Lady Barbara to her cabin; and mercifully, his memory was no longer being so acutely troubled by the pictures of el Supremo chained to the

deck, of Galbraith dying, and of poor little Clay's body sprawled
headless on the bloody planks – and when those memories
lapsed he could no longer accuse himself of being a coward
for being worried by them.

Those were happy days indeed. The routine of the *Lydia*
progressed like clockwork. Almost every hour of every day
there was enough wind to give her steerage way, and sometimes
it blew just hard enough to relieve the monotony. There were
no storms during that endless succession of golden days, and
the mind could contemplate its endlessness with tranquillity,
for 50 degrees South Latitude seemed impossibly far away;
they could enjoy the blissfulness of eternity, disregarding the
constant warning conveyed to them as every noontide showed
the sun lower in the sky and every midnight showed the Southern
Cross higher.

They could be friends during those heavenly nights when the
ship's wake showed as a long trail or fire on the faintly luminous
water. They learned to talk together, endlessly. She could chatter
about the frivolities of the Vice-Regal court at Dublin, and of
the intrigues which could enmesh a Governor-General of India;
of penniless French émigrés putting purse-proud northern
iron-masters in their places; of Lord Byron's extravagancies and
of the Royal Dukes' stupidities; and Hornblower learned to listen
without a twinge of envy.

He could tell, in return, of months spent on blockade,
combating storms off the ironbound Biscay coast, of how Pellew
took his frigates into the very surf to sing the *Droits-de-l' homme*
with two thousand men on board, of hardship and cruelty and
privation – a monotonous toilsome life as fantastic to her as hers
appeared to him. He could even tell her, as his self-consciousness
dwindled, of the ambitions which he knew would seem to her
as trivial as those of a child yearning for a hobby horse; of the
two thousand pounds in prize money which he had decided would
be all that he would require to eke out his half-pay, the few acres
and the cottage and the shelves and shelves of books.

And yet she heard without a smile, with even a trace of envy in her calm face as the moon shone down on them; for her own ambitions were far more vague and far less likely to be realised. She hardly knew what it was that she wanted, and she knew that whatever it was, she could only hope to attain it by ensnaring a husband. That an earl's daughter could envy a penniless frigate captain moved Hornblower inexpressibly, as he watched her face in the moonlight; he was glad even while he was unhappy that Lady Barbara should have to envy anything of anyone.

They could talk of books and of poetry, and Hornblower championed the cause of the classical school who looked back to the days of Queen Anne against the barbarous leaders of the revolt who seemed to delight in setting every established rule at defiance. She heard him with patience, even with approval, as he talked of Gibbon (the object of his sincerest admiration) and Johnson and Swift, when he quoted from Pope and Gray, but she could approve of the barbarians as well. There was a madman called Wordsworth of whose revolutionary opinions in literature Hornblower had heard with vague horror; Lady Barbara thought there was something to be said for him. She turned the tables neatly on Hornblower by claiming Gray as a precursor of the same school; she quoted Campbell and that Gothic innovator, Scott, and she won Hornblower's grudging approval of an ungainly poem called 'The Rime of the Ancient Mariner,' although he maintained sturdily, in the last ditch, that its only merit lay in its content, and that it would have been infinitely better had Pope dealt with the theme in heroic couplets – especially if Pope had been assisted by someone who knew more about navigation and seamanship than did this Coleridge fellow.

Lady Barbara wondered vaguely, sometimes, whether it was not strange that a naval officer should be so earnest a student of literature, but she was learning rapidly. Sea captains were not all of a class, as the uninitiated might carelessly decide. From Bush and Gerard and Crystal, as well as from Hornblower, she had heard of captains who wrote Greek elegiacs, of captains who cluttered up their cabins with marbles looted from the Greek islands, captains who classified sea-urchins and corresponded with Cuvier – these on the one hand, just as there were captains who delighted in seeing human backs lacerated with the cat-o'-nine-tails, captains who drank themselves insensible every night and who raised hell in their ships during bouts of delirium tremens, captains who starved their crews and captains who turned up all hands at every bell, night and day. She found that she was sure, all the same, that Hornblower was an outstanding member of a class which people on shore tended not to credit with nearly as much ability as they actually possessed.

She had, from the time of her first arrival on board, found pleasure in Hornblower's society. Now they had formed a habit of each other, as though they were insidious drugs, and were vaguely uneasy when out of sight of each other. The voyage had been monotonous enough, as the *Lydia* held steadily southwards, for habits to be easily formed; it had become a habit to exchange a smile when they met on the quarterdeck in the morning – a smile illumined by secret memories of the intimacy of the conversation of the night before. It was a habit now for Hornblower to discuss the ship's progress with Lady Barbara after he had taken the noon sights, a habit now for him to drink coffee with her in the afternoons, and especially was it a habit for them to meet at sunset by the taffrail, although no appointment had been made and no hint of their meeting had ever been suggested, and to lounge in the warm darkness while conversation grew up, seemingly from no roots at all, and blossomed and flowered exotically, under the magic brilliance of the stars until, with a reluctance of which they were hardly conscious, they drifted off to bed, hours after midnight.

They could even sit silent together now, watching, wordlessly, the mastheads circling amid the stars with the rolling of the ship, listening to the faint orchestra of the ship's fabric, and their thoughts paralleling each other's so that when eventually one of them spoke it was to harmonise completely with what was in the other's mind. At those times Lady Barbara's hand, like a healthy young woman's, was at her side where it could be touched without too great effort. When she had not wanted them to do so men had taken her hand often before, at London balls and Governor-Generals' receptions, but now, conscious though she was of how reckless and imprudent it would be to encourage the slightest physical intimacy on this voyage with months more to last, she still was reckless and imprudent enough to risk it without attempting to analyse her motives. But Hornblower seemed unconscious of that hand. She would see his face lifted to the stars, peaceful and immobile, and she found pleasure in giving herself credit for the change in it from that evening when she had talked with Bush and seen Hornblower's torment.

For happy weeks that phase of the voyage lasted, while the *Lydia* ran steadily south and still more south, until the evenings grew chill and the mornings misty, until the blue sky changed to grey and the first rain they had known for three weeks wetted the *Lydia*'s decks, and the west wind blew more blustering and searching, so that Lady Barbara had to wrap herself in a boat cloak to be able to sit on deck at all. Those evenings by the taffrail came to an imperceptible end, and the *Lydia* thrashed along through half a gale, and it grew steadily colder, even though this was the Antipodean summer. For the first time in her life, Lady Barbara saw Hornblower dressed in tarpaulins and sou'wester, and she thought, oddly, how well those hideous garments suited him. There were times when he would come sauntering into the cabin, his eyes bright and his cheeks flushed with wind, and she felt her pulses leap in sympathy with his.

She knew she was being foolish. She told herself that this weakness of hers only arose because Hornblower was the one man with any culture or any trace of eligibility on board the *Lydia*, and because life in close contact with him for four continuous months was bound to make her either love him or hate him – and as there was no room for hatred in her system the other thing was inevitable. She told herself, too, that as soon as she returned to civilisation, as soon as she could see Hornblower against that usual background of hers which had faded with the passage of the months almost out of her memory, he would lose his interest and his charm.

On board ship one saw things in a false perspective, she informed herself. Salt beef and salt pork, weevily bread and dried peas, with a glass of lemon juice twice a week; that meant monotony. Trifles assumed an exaggerated importance when leading a life like that. Just as toothache tended to disappear when something occurred to distract the mind, so would this heartache of hers disappear when she had other things to think about. It was all very true; but strangely it made not the least difference to her present feelings.

They had reached the region of westerly trade winds now. Every day they roared harder and harder, and every day the sea rose higher and higher. The *Lydia* was thrashing along magnificently now; there were two or three days when she logged over two hundred and forty nautical miles as her day's run from noon to noon. It was cold, and it rained in torrents, and the main deck was often knee deep in water. There were days when all Lady Barbara could do was to brace herself in her cot while the ship tossed and rolled as though at any moment she would turn completely over, while Hebe (who never succeeded quite in overcoming her seasickness) moaned in her blankets on the deck and her teeth chattered with the cold. No fire could be kept alight; nothing could be cooked, while the groaning of the ship's timbers swelled into a volume of sound comparable with that of an organ in a church.

At the very climax of the voyage, at their farthest south, the freakishness of Cape Horn weather displayed itself, when Lady Barbara awoke one morning to find the ship rising and swooping once more in orderly fashion, and Polwheal knocked at the cabin door with a message from the captain to the effect that this morning Lady Barbara might, if she wished, take advantage of the break in the weather to take the air on deck. She found the sky blue and the air clear though keen enough to make her grateful of the duffle coat which Gerard had lent her. The wind had died away to a mere fresh breeze, before which the *Lydia* was careering gaily along under all sail to the royals, and there was a bright sun shining all around them. It was a joy to walk the deck once more. It was, if anything, an even greater joy to drink hot coffee, steaming hot again, served by a grinning Polwheal to Lady Barbara and the officers on the quarterdeck. There was an excruciating pleasure in filling her lungs with pure air after days of breathing the mephitic vapours of below decks. She caught Hornblower's eyes and they exchanged smiles of delight. In all the rigging the sailors' clothes, spread hastily to dry, were gesticulating as though with joy, waving a thousand glad arms and legs in the sparkling air.

Cape Horn allowed them just that one pleasurable morning; before noon a thin cloud had spread itself over the sun, and the wind was increasing in force again, and to windward there were solid banks of black clouds coming up and overhauling them rapidly.

'Get the royals in, Mr Bush,' growled Hornblower, glowering aft. 'Lady Barbara, I am afraid that you will have to retire to your cabin again.'

The gale fell on them with a shriek when Lady Barbara had hardly reached her cabin; they ran before it all the afternoon, and at evening Lady Barbara could tell by the motion of the ship (so experienced a sailor had she become) that Hornblower had been compelled to heave her to. For thirty-six hours the *Lydia* remained hove to, while the heavens tore themselves to pieces around her, but there was comfort in the knowledge that on her easterly course all her drift to leeward helped her on her way. Lady Barbara found it hard to believe that men had ever succeeded in sailing a ship westward round the Horn. It helped her to agree with Hornblower that before very long, at the latest as soon as a general peace was concluded, the whole world would arise and write in the demand for the cutting of a canal through the Isthmus

of Panama. Meanwhile, there was nothing to do except to wait
for the happy day when they would reach St Helena, and could
enjoy fresh meat again, and vegetables, even – impossibly Utopian
though it might seem – milk and fruit.

CHAPTER XXIII

On that voyage, the change in conditions after rounding the Horn was most dramatic. It seemed to Lady Barbara almost as if one day they were labouring along over grey seas before the south-westerly gales, cold and uncomfortable, with waves running as high as the yard arms, and the next they were enjoying blue skies and gentle breezes from the south-east. They had, in fact, been fortunate, for the last thundering gale from the south-west had carried them well into the region of the southerly trades. They were leaving the Antipodean autumn behind them, and the northern spring was coming down in the track of the sun to meet them. The sea was blue again, as blue as any blue well could be, in its usual marvellous contrast with the white foam. There were flying-fish furrowing the enamelled surface. In a flash, the privations and discomforts of the Horn were forgotten.

It seemed the most natural thing in the world that as night fell Lady Barbara should find herself seated as ever by the taffrail, and just as natural that Hornblower should loom up in the half light beside her and should accept her unvaryingly polite invitation to a seat beside her. It was perfectly natural that the officers should accept this state of affairs as one which had long existed, and that the officer of the watch should confine his walk to the forward part of the quarterdeck. At eight bells, when Gerard came up to relieve Rayner, the latter, with a jerk of his thumb and a cock of his head, called the former's attention to the little dark group by the taffrail. Gerard grinned, his white teeth in his swarthy face gleaming in the starlight.

He had made his trial of the lady's virtue in the long ago, before the captain had noticed her existence. He did not think that Hornblower would succeed where he had failed, and in any case Gerard prided himself on having sufficient sense not to try

to compete with his own captain. Gerard had conquests enough
to think about during the silent night watches, and he was philos-
opher enough to wish his captain good luck while keeping his
back turned squarely to them as they talked quietly, only just out
of earshot of him.

Yet to Hornblower – and to Lady Barbara – things were
not the same here in the Atlantic as they had been in the
Pacific. Hornblower seemed to feel a tension he had not felt
before. Perhaps the rounding of the Horn had forced it home
upon him that even sailing-ship voyages must end sometime,
that even the five thousand odd miles that lay between them
and Portsmouth would not last forever. In the Pacific, appro-
priately enough, he had found peace in Lady Barbara's
company. Here in the Atlantic he was conscious of uneasiness,
as he might if the barometer were falling rapidly in a glassy
calm in West Indian waters.

For some reason – perhaps merely because he had been
thinking of England – the image of Maria had been much
before his eyes of late; Maria, short and tubby, with a tendency
to spots in her complexion, with the black silk parasol which
she affected; or Maria in her flannel nightshift and curl papers
with a loving note sounding hoarsely in her voice; Maria
arguing with a lodging-house keeper, and Maria on board the
ship at Portsmouth, her poor opinion of common sailors evident
in her expression. It was disloyal to think of Maria like that;
rather should he think of her as she was that feverish night in
the Southsea lodgings, her eyes red with weeping, struggling
bravely to keep her lips from trembling while little Horatio
died of the smallpox in her arms and little Maria lay dead in
the next room.

'Ha – h'm,' said Hornblower, harshly, and he stirred uneasily
in his seat.

Lady Barbara looked at his face in the starlight. It bore that
bleak, lonely expression which she had come to dread.

'Can you tell me what is the matter, Captain?' she asked gently.

Hornblower sat silent for some seconds before he shook his head. No, he could not tell her. For that matter he did not know himself; introspective though he was, he had not dared to admit to himself that he had been making comparisons between some-one short and stout and someone tall and slender, between someone with apple cheeks and someone with a classic profile.

Hornblower slept badly that night, and his morning walk which followed was not devoted to the purpose for which it had originally been destined. He could not keep his mind at work upon the problems of stores and water, of how to keep the crew busy and out of mischief, of winds and courses, which he was accustomed to solve at this time so as to appear a man of decision the rest of the day. Part of the time he was too unhappy to think connectedly, and for the rest his mind was busy wrestling with suppositions so monstrous that they appalled him. He was tempted to make advances to Lady Barbara; that, at least, he could admit to himself. He wanted to do so badly. There was an ache in his breast, a most painful yearning as he thought of it.

What was monstrous about his thoughts was the suspicion that possibly Lady Barbara would not repulse him. It seemed incon-ceivable and yet possible, like something in a nightmare. He might even put his hot hand on her cool bosom – a thought which made him writhe in strange anguish. His longing to taste her sweetness was excruciating. He had been nearly a year cooped up in the *Lydia* now, and a year of unnatural living breeds strange fancies. Somewhere just over the gloomy horizon of Hornblower's mind there lurked fancies stranger yet; dark phantoms of rape and murder.

Yet, even while Hornblower thus toyed with madness, his cursed analytical powers were at work upon other pros and cons. Whether he offended Lady Barbara, or whether he seduced her, he was playing with fire. The Wellesley family could blast him at their whim. They could snatch him from his command and leave him to rot forever on half pay; even worse, they could find, somewhere in his actions of the past year, if their animosity were sufficient, grounds for a court martial, and a court martial under Wellesley pressure could strip him of his commission and leave him a pauper dependent on parish relief. That was the worst that could happen – save perhaps for a duel with a result fatal to himself – and the very best was not much better. Supposing, as was just conceivable, the Wellesleys could tolerate the seduction of their sister – supposing that, confronted with a *fait accompli*, they resolved to try to make the best of things. No, that was not conceivable at all. He would have to produce a divorce from Maria, and that would involve an Act of Parliament and the expenditure of five thousand pounds.

To meddle with Lady Barbara would mean risking utter ruin – professional, social and financial. And he knew he could not trust himself where risks were concerned. When he had had the *Lydia* towed into range of the *Natividad* and had fought it out with her, gun to gun, he had run such appalling risks that to this day he felt a little chill down his spine on recalling them. Risk and danger lured him even while he knew he was a fool to expose himself to them, and he knew that no risk would deter him once he had embarked on a course of action. Even at this moment, thinking about it in cold blood, there was something dangerously fascinating in the thought of wiping the eye of the whole Wellesley family and then daring them to do their worst.

And then all these cold-blooded considerations were swept away to nothing again in a white-hot wave of passion as he thought of her, slim and lovely, understanding and sweet. He was trembling with passion, the hot blood running under his skin, and muddled images streamed through his mind in a fantastic panorama. He stood by the rail, staring unseeing over the blue sea with its patches of golden weed, conscious of nothing save the riot in his own body and mind. When his heart had at last slowed down to normal, and he turned to look round over the ship, everything was oddly sharp and clear. He could see the smallest details of the complicated splicing which one of the hands was engaged upon on the forecastle a hundred and twenty feet away. Immediately afterwards he was heartily glad that he had regained his self-control, for Lady Barbara came on deck, smiling as she always did when the sun shone on her face on emerging from the deck cabin, and soon he was in conversation with her.

'I spent last night dreaming dreams,' said Lady Barbara.

'Indeed?' said Hornblower, awkwardly. He, too, had been dreaming.

'Yes,' said Lady Barbara. 'I was dreaming mostly of eggs. Fried eggs, and buttered eggs. And slices of white bread spread thick with butter. And *café au lait* with plenty of cream. And cabbage – plain boiled cabbage. My dreams were not extravagant enough to run to a puree of spinach, but I almost attained to a dish of young carrots. And behold, this morning Hebe brings me my black coffee and my weevily maize bread, and Polwheal sends in to ask me if I will be pleased to take beef or pork for my dinner. Today I think I start on the seventh brother of the pig whose chops I first tasted at Panama. I know his breed by now.'

Lady Barbara could still laugh and show her white teeth in her brown face, as she made this speech, and her laugh whisked away Hornblower's passion for a space. He was in sympathy with her – months of ship's fare set everyone literally dreaming of fresh food – but her fine naturalness acted upon Hornblower's state of mind like an open window on a stuffy room. It was that talk about food which staved off the crisis for a few more days – golden days, during which the *Lydia* kept the south-east trades on her beam and reached steadily across the south Atlantic for St Helena.

The wind did not fail her until the very evening when the lookout at the masthead, the setting of the sun in a golden glory having enabled him to gaze ahead once more, caught sight of the tip of the mountaintop just as the light was fading from the sky, and his cry of 'Land ho!' told Hornblower that once more he had made a perfect landfall. All day long the wind had been dying away, and with the setting of the sun it dwindled to nothing, tantalisingly, just when a few more hours of it would have carried the *Lydia* to the island. From the deck there was still no sign of land, and as Gerard pointed out to Lady Barbara, she would have to take its proximity on trust until the wind condescended to blow again. Her disappointment at this postponement of her promised buttered eggs was so appealing that Crystal hastened forward and stuck his open clasp-knife in the mainmast. That was a sure way of raising a wind, he said – and if by any mishap it should fail on this occasion he would set all the ship's boys whistling in unison and chance the tempest such imprudence might summon from the deep.

It may have been the mere fact of this respite working on Hornblower's subconscious mind which precipitated the crisis; for undoubtedly Hornblower had a lurking fear that the call at St Helena might well bring about some undesired alteration in affairs on board the *Lydia*. On the other hand, the thing was bound to happen, and perhaps coincidence merely allotted that evening for it. It was coincidence that Hornblower should come into the main cabin in the half light at a moment when he thought Lady Barbara was on deck, and it was coincidence that his hand should brush against her bare arm as they stood cramped between the table and the locker and he apologised for his intrusion. She was in his arms then, and they kissed, and kissed again. She put one hand behind his shoulder and touched the back of his neck, and they were giddy with passion. Then a roll of the ship forced him to let her go, and she sank down upon the locker, and she smiled at him as she sat so that he came down on his knees beside her, his head on her breast, and she stroked his curls, and they kissed again as if they would never tire. She spoke to him with the endearments which her nurse had used to her when she was a child – she had never learned yet to use endearments.

'My dear,' she whispered. 'My sweet. My poppet.'

It was hard to find words that would tell him of her love for him. 'Your hands are beautiful,' she said, spreading one of them on her own palm, and playing with the long slender fingers. 'I have loved them ever since Panama.'

Hornblower had always thought his hands bony and ugly, and the left one bore the ingrained powder stain he had acquired at the boarding of the *Castilla*. He looked at her to see if she were teasing him, and when he saw that she was not he could only kiss her again – her lips were so ready for his kisses. It was like a miracle that she should want to be kissed. Passion carried them away once more.

Hebe's entrance made them part; at least it made Hornblower spring up, to sit bolt upright and self-conscious, while Hebe grinned at them with sly eyes. To Hornblower, it was a dreadful thing for a captain to be caught toying with a woman on board his ship actually in commission. It was contrary to the Articles of War – worse, it was undignified, subversive of discipline, dangerous. Lady Barbara remained quite unruffled.

'Go away, Hebe,' she said, calmly. 'I shall not need you yet.'

And she turned back to Hornblower, but the spell was broken. He had seen himself in a new light, grovelling furtively on a couch with a passenger. He was blushing hotly, angry with himself, and already wondering how much the officer of the watch and the man at the wheel had heard of their murmurings through the open skylight.

'What are we to do?' he asked feebly.

'Do?' she replied. 'We are lovers, and the world is ours. We do as we will.'

'But—,' he said, and again 'but—'

He wanted to explain to her in half a dozen words the complications he could see hedging him in. There was a cold fit on him; he wanted to tell her of how he dreaded the ill-concealed amusement of Gerard, the utterly tactless tactfulness of Bush, and how the captain of a ship was not nearly as much his own master as she apparently thought, but it was hopeless. He could only stammer, and his hands flapped feebly, and his face was averted. He had forgotten all these practical details in those mad dreams of his. She put her hand on his chin and made him turn to her.

'Dear,' she asked. 'What is troubling you? Tell me, dear.'

'I am a married man,' he said, taking the coward's way out.

'I know that. Are you going to allow that to interfere with – us?'

'Besides—' he said, and his hands flapped again in the hopeless effort to express all the doubts which consumed him.

She condescended to sink her pride a little further.

'Hebe is safe,' she said, softly. 'She worships me. Nor would she dare to be indiscreet.'

She saw the look in his face, and rose abruptly. Her blood and lineage were outraged at this. However veiled her offer had been, it had been refused. She was in a cold rage now.

'Please have the kindness, Captain,' she said, 'to open that door for me.'

She swept out of the cabin with all the dignity of an earl's daughter, and if she wept when in the privacy of her own cabin, Hornblower knew nothing of it. He was pacing the deck above, up and down, up and down, endlessly. This was the end of his fine dreams. This was how he showed himself a man to whom danger and risk only made a plan more attractive. He was a fine lady-killer, a devil of a buck. He cursed himself in his shame, he jeered at himself as a man who could face the wrath of the Wellesleys in imagination and who flinched from the amusement of Gerard in practice.

It all might have come right in the end. If the calm had persisted for two or three days, so that Lady Barbara could have forgotten her wrath and Hornblower his doubts, more might have happened. There might have been an echoing scandal in high life. But as it was, at midnight a little wind began to blow – perhaps it was Crystal's clasp-knife which had summoned it – and Gerard came to him for orders. Again,

he could not flout public opinion. He could not face the thought
of the suspicions which would arise and the secret questions
which would be asked if he gave orders for the ship to be put
about and to head away from St Helena at a time when the
wind held fair.

CHAPTER XXIV

'There's the devil of a lot of shipping there,' said Bush, his glass to his eye, as they opened up the roadstead in the dawn. 'The devil of a lot. Men o' war, sir. No, Indiamen. Men o' war *and* Indiamen, sir. There's a three-decker! It's the old *Temeraire*, sir, or I'm a Dutchman, with a rear-admiral's flag. Must be the rendezvous for the homeward-bound convoy, sir.'

'Pass the word for Mr Marsh,' said Hornblower.

There would be salutes to be fired, calls to be paid – he was caught up in the irresistible current of naval routine, and he would be too busy now for hours to have a word with Lady Barbara, even if she condescended to allow him one. He did not know whether to be glad or sorry.

The *Lydia* made her number, and the sound of the salutes began to roll slowly round the bay. Hornblower was in his shabby full dress – the faded blue coat with the brassy epaulettes, the worn white breeches, the silk stockings with the innumerable ladders which Polwheal had cobbled roughly together. The port officer came up the side to receive his certificate of the absence of infectious disease on board. A moment later the anchor roared out overside, then Hornblower called for the cutter to take him over to the Admiral. He was actually going over the side when Lady Barbara came on deck – he saw her, just for a second, gazing with pleasure up the green mountain slopes, and looking with surprise at the massed shipping inshore. He longed to stop and speak to her, but once more the dignity expected of a captain checked him. Nor could he take her with him – no captain starting on an official round of calls could go round in his boat with a woman in the sternsheets beside him, not even when subsequent explanation would reveal her to be a Wellesley.

The cutter pulled steadily over to the *Temeraire*.

'*Lydia*,' shouted the coxswain in reply to the hail from her deck, and he held up four fingers which indicated the presence in the boat of a captain as a warning for them to prepare the correct ceremonial.

Sir James Saumarez received Hornblower in the quarter gallery of his flagship. He was tall and spare, of youthful appearance until he took off his hat and revealed his snow-white hair. He listened courteously to Hornblower's brief explanation of his presence; after forty years at sea and sixteen years of continuous warfare he could guess at the wild adventures which remained undescribed in Hornblower's verbal report. There was a gleam of approval in his fierce blue eyes when he heard that the *Lydia* had sunk a fifty-gun two-decker in a ship-to-ship duel.

'You can accompany me and the convoy,' he said, at the end. 'I have no more than two ships of the line and not a single frigate to escort the whole East Indian convoy. One would have thought that the Government would have learnt the need of frigates since the war started in 'ninety-three, don't you think? I will send you written orders this morning. And now, sir, perhaps you will give me the pleasure of your company at the breakfast party at which I am about to be host?'

Hornblower pointed out that it was his duty to call upon the governor.

'His Excellency is breakfasting with me,' said the Admiral.

Hornblower knew that it was ill to continue to raise a series of objections to a suggestion by an Admiral, but he had to raise a fresh one.

'There is a lady on board the *Lydia*, sir,' he said, and when the Admiral's eyebrows went up he hurriedly began to explain Lady Barbara's presence to him.

The Admiral whistled.

'A Wellesley!' he said. 'And you brought her round the Horn? Here, we must tell Lady Manningtree of this.'

He led the way unceremoniously into the lofty Admiral's cabin. There was a long table with a snowy cloth, glittering with crystal

and silver, and by the table there stood chatting a little group of
men and women, beautifully dressed. The Admiral made hurried
introductions – His Excellency the Governor, and Her Excellency;
the Earl and Countess of Manningtree, Sir Charles and Lady
Wheeler.

Lady Manningtree was a short and dumpy woman with good
humour in every line of her face. She showed no sign of the
dignity and reserve which might be expected of the wife of an
ex-governor-general returning from his term of office.

'Captain Hornblower has brought Lady Barbara Wellesley
with him from Darien,' said Sir James, and plunged into rapid
explanation. Lady Manningtree listened in perfect horror.

'And you have left her there? On that little ship?' she said.
'The poor lamb! She must not stay there another moment! I shall
go and bring her away this very instant! Sir James, you must
excuse me. I will not have a moment's peace until she is comfortably in the cabin next to mine on board the *Hanbury Castle*. Sir
James, would you be so good as to order a boat for me?'

She left in a whirl of apologies and explanations, a fluttering
of petticoats and a perfect torrent of objurgations, mainly directed
at Hornblower.

'When women take charge,' said Sir James philosophically,
after she had departed, 'it is best for the men to stand from under.
Will you sit here, Captain?'

Curiously, Hornblower could eat almost nothing of that delicious breakfast. There were heavenly mutton cutlets. There was
coffee with fresh milk. There was new wheaten bread. There
was butter, there were fruits, there were vegetables, all the things
Hornblower had dreamed about when his thoughts had not been
occupied with Lady Barbara, and now he could only eat a
mouthful here and there. Fortunately his lack of appetite went
unnoticed because he was kept so busy answering the questions
which were rained on him, about Lady Barbara, about his adventures in the Pacific, about his passage round the Horn, and then
back to Lady Barbara again.

'Her brother is doing great things in Spain,' said Sir James. 'Not the eldest one, the Marquis, but Arthur – the one who won the Battle of Assaye. He came well out of that court of inquiry after Vimeiro. Now he has bundled Soult out of Portugal, and when I left Lisbon he was in full march on Madrid. Since Moore was killed he is the most promising soldier in the army.'

'Humph,' said Lady Wheeler. The name of Wellesley was still anathema to a certain section of Anglo-Indians. 'This Lady Barbara is a good deal younger than he is, I fancy? I remember her as quite a child in Madras.'

Eyes were turned towards Hornblower, but Lord Manningtree in the kindness of his heart spared him the embarrassment of having to explain Lady Barbara's age.

'She's no child,' he said, bluffly. 'She's a very talented young woman. Declined a dozen good offers in India, too, and God knows how many since then.'

'Humph,' said Lady Wheeler again.

The breakfast began to seem interminable to Hornblower, and he was glad when the party showed signs of breaking up. The Governor seized the opportunity to discuss with him the matter of the stores for which the *Lydia* would have to indent – naval routine still claimed him for her own. There was urgent need for him to return to his ship; he made his excuses to Sir James and said goodbye to the rest of the company.

The Admiral's barge was still hooked on to the *Lydia*'s chains when he returned to her; her crew were dressed in crimson coats with gold-laced hats. Hornblower had known frigate captains who dressed their gig's crews in fancy costumes in this fashion, too, but they were wealthy men who had been fortunate in the matter of prize money, not penniless fellows like himself. He went on board; Lady Barbara's baggage was piled on the gangway waiting to be swung down into the barge. Down in the main cabin could be heard a continuous chatter of female voices. Lady Manningtree and Lady Barbara were sitting there deep in conversation; obviously there had been so much to say that they could not wait until they had reached the *Hanbury Castle*. One topic had led to another so enthralling that they had forgotten the barge, forgotten the waiting baggage, forgotten even about breakfast.

Apparently Lady Barbara had taken the opportunity, when her baggage had been brought up from the storeroom, to unpack some new clothes. She was wearing a new gown which Hornblower had not seen before, and a new turban and veil. She was very obviously the great lady now. To Hornblower's startled mind she seemed as she stood up to be six inches taller than when he saw her last. And clearly Hornblower's arrival, breaking the thread of their conversation, constituted for them a signal for their departure.

'Lady Barbara has been telling me all about your voyage,' said Lady Manningtree, buttoning her gloves. 'I think you deserve a world of thanks for the care you have taken of her.'

The kind-hearted old lady was one of those people who can never think evil. She looked round the tiny ugly cabin.

'Nevertheless,' she went on, 'I think that it is high time that she enjoyed a little more comfort than you can offer her here.'

Hornblower managed to gulp out a few words regarding the superior arrangements for passengers on board a luxurious Indiaman.

'I don't mean to imply that it is your fault, Captain,' protested Lady Manningtree, hastily. 'I'm sure your ship is a very beautiful ship. A frigate, isn't it? But frigates were never made to carry females, and that's all one can say. And now we must say goodbye, Captain. I hope we may have the pleasure of receiving you on the *Hanbury Castle* later. There will be sure to be opportunities during this very tedious voyage home. Goodbye, Captain.'

Hornblower bowed and allowed her to pass before him. Lady Barbara followed.

'Goodbye,' she said. Hornblower bowed again as she went down in a curtsy. He was looking straight at her, but somehow he could see no detail of her face – only a white blur.

'Thank you for all your kindness,' said Lady Barbara.

The barge left the ship's side, and rowed steadily away. She was all blurred, too, a vague patch of red and gold. Hornblower found Bush beside him.

'The victualling officer's signalling, sir,' he said.

Hornblower's duties were clamouring for his attention. As he turned away from the ship's side to plunge into them he found himself, idiotically, remembering that in two months' time or so he would be seeing Maria again. He felt vaguely glad about that before it passed out of his mind again. He felt he would be happy with Maria. Overhead the sun was shining brightly, and before him rose the steep green slopes of St Helena.